AVENGING AVERY

What Reviewers Say About
Sheri Lewis Wohl's Work

Drawing Down the Mist

"Vampires loving humans. Vampires hating vampires. Vampires killing humans. Vampires killing vampires. Good vampires. Evil vampires. Internet-savvy vampires. Lovers turning enemies. Nurturing revenge for a century. Kindness. Cruelty. Love. Action. Fights. Insta-love. This one has everything for a true drama."
—*reviewer@large*

Cause of Death

"I really liked these characters, all of them, and wouldn't say no to a sequel, or more."—*Jude in the Stars*

"*CSI* meets *Ghost Whisperer*. ...The pace was brilliantly done, the suspense was just enough, and I'm not ashamed to admit that I had no idea who the serial killer was until almost the end."
—*Words and Worlds*

"*Cause of Death* by Sheri Lewis Wohl is one creepy and well-written murder mystery. It is one of the best psychological thrillers I've read in a while."—*Rainbow Reflections*

"[A] light paranormal romance with a psycho-killer and some great dogs."—*C-Spot Reviews*

"There's a ton of stuff in here that I enjoy very much, such as the light paranormal aspect of the book, and the relationship between our two leads is very nice if a bit of a slow burn. The case was engaging enough that I didn't really set this title down once I started it."—Colleen Corgel, Librarian, Queens Public Library

"Totally disturbing, and very, very awesome. ...The characters were amazing. The supernatural tint was never overdone, and even the stuff from the killers point of view, while disturbing, was awesomely done as well. It was a great book and a fun (and intense) read."—Danielle Kimerer, Librarian (Nevins Memorial Library, Massachusetts)

"This thriller has spooky undertones that make it an intense page turner. You won't be able to put this book down."—*Istoria Lit*

The Talebearer

"As a crime story, it is a good read that had me turning pages quickly. ...The book is well written and the characters are well-developed."—*Reviews by Amos Lassen*

She Wolf

"I really enjoyed this book—I couldn't put it down once I started it. The author's style of writing was very good and engaging. All characters, including the supporting characters, were multi-layered and interesting."—Melina Bickard, Librarian, Waterloo Library (UK)

Twisted Screams

"[A] cast of well developed characters leads you through a maze of complex emotions."—*Lunar Rainbow Reviewz*

Twisted Echoes

"A very unusual blend of lesbian romance and horror. …[W]oven throughout this modern romance is a neatly plotted horror story from the past, which bleeds ever increasingly into the present of the two main characters. Lorna and Renee are well matched, and face ever-increasing danger from spirits from the past. An unusual story that gets tenser and more interesting as it progresses."—Pippa Wischer, Manager at Berkelouw Books, Armadale

Vermilion Justice

"[T]he characters are so dynamic and well-written that this becomes more than just another vampire story. It's probably impossible to read this book and not come across a character who reminds you of someone you actually know. Wohl takes something as fictional as vampires and makes them feel real. Highly recommended."—*GLBT Reviews: The ALA's GLBT Round Table*

By the Author

Crimson Vengeance

Burgundy Betrayal

Scarlet Revenge

Vermilion Justice

Twisted Echoes

Twisted Whispers

Twisted Screams

Necromantia

She Wolf

Walking Through Shadows

Drawing Down the Mist

The Talebearer

Cause of Death

Avenging Avery

AVENGING AVERY

by
Sheri Lewis Wohl

2020

ISBN 13: 978-1-63555-622-3

This Trade Paperback Original Is Published By
Bold Strokes Books, Inc.
P.O. Box 249
Valley Falls, NY 12185

First Edition: November 2020

CREDITS
Editor: Shelley Thrasher
Production Design: Susan Ramundo
Cover Design By Tammy Seidick

Dedication

To all the librarians. Without your patience and guidance, I might not have grown from the inquisitive young girl reading every book I could get my hands on into the writer crafting stories of the strange and unusual that allow my imagination to soar. I thank you all.

That the wicked is reserved
to the day of destruction?
they shall be brought forth
to the day of wrath.

Job 21:30
The Holy Bible
King James Version

PROLOGUE

Poland
November 10, 1779

She stood in the shadows, far behind the others, and pressed her lips together to keep from screaming. Her hood draped over her head, the darkness obscuring her features and the tears that slid down her cheeks. She had not asked for this life, nor had she rejected its offer when it came. The weight of her reality made it hard to keep her shoulders straight.

He took her hand, not noticing her hesitation because his eyes were intent on the activities in the center of the great hall. As her gaze fell upon his face, she could see how it enthralled him, while it twisted her stomach. "Is it not wonderful?" he asked.

"Is it?" Her words were barely audible. With her free hand she wiped away the tears, not wanting him or anyone else to see them. She could not show fear or any emotion. Though her time here thus far had been short, she had seen enough to know what happened to those who displayed anything other than delight.

"It is." His tone held awe and wonder. "All your earthly ties have been severed. This, my darling, is freedom like you have never known." He pulled her hand to his lips and kissed it. She tried not to yank it away.

Truth flowed through her even though she willed herself to stay silent. How she wanted to scream in protest as loud as she could but dared not. Not on this night. "I never asked for freedom." Her vow to keep her silence impossible.

He kissed her hand again. "You did not need to. They know your deepest desires. They know what each of us needs, and that, my love, is why we stand here tonight. Only the worthy are invited to the inner halls, and you have earned the right to be here. You are precious, and that is why I had to bring you into the family. They love you as much as I."

"This is not a family." That one truth she would not hold close. It must be spoken.

His laughter floated softly on the night air as he leaned close, his breath hot on her ear. "Oh, my darling, it is the finest family, and you will never again want for anything. Here you will find your new place in the world order, and here you and I will be together for eternity."

Energy pulsed throughout the great room with its tall walls covered in fine tapestries, the marble floors a beauty rarely seen, a massive fire snapping and crackling in the fireplace so large it could hold several bodies. The first time she'd stepped inside this room she had been like a small child seeing something glorious for the first time. Her excitement at the invitation issued had made her heart beat faster than she could ever remember. It had presented the kind of adventure she had longed for her whole life and never believed would happen for her. She had not seen it then for what it was: a chamber of death masked in a façade of beauty.

On that night, she had kneeled before the one known as Eve and accepted the offer made to her. By taking her vow of obedience and loyalty, she had become one of the elite in the Redcap Society. Though she believed herself to be a learned woman, in that moment, she had not fully understood the irrevocable decision she had just made. For five oblivious days she embraced happiness and the excitement of a new life. Never had she felt so strong and vibrant, so free of the constraints of the life and time she had been born into. Every one of those five days, she believed the choice to embrace darkness a perfect escape from the life otherwise open to her.

Until tonight. Now she stood powerless against the legions of a society into which she had willingly accepted membership. This atrocity unfolding before her eyes happened, she understood, to test those vows she repeated while kneeling at Eve's gold-embellished slippers. Like taking the oath of marriage, she had agreed to love, honor, and cherish the elders of the Redcap Society for all eternity. In the moments when those words crossed her lips, she had not understood the depths to which her vows would be called into practice. She did now.

He squeezed her hand. "It is done. You are free from all earthly bounds. One of the chosen ones, now and forever. Welcome home, my darling." He kissed the top of her head without pushing back her hood, and instead of the joy he surely expected her to experience, coldness enveloped her at his touch.

The smell of blood wafted through the air, both horrifying and enthralling. She hated the latter. The reality of the existence she had unwittingly embraced made it a necessity. Without it, she would die. Even so, and despite the enticing scent, she cringed inwardly at the thought of even a drop of it crossing her lips.

Cheers erupted as the ceremony concluded, and the frenzy that commenced made her want to retch. She did not move even as he released her hand and joined the vibrating mass. While they fed upon the three bodies sprawled in the center of the stone floor with the intricate design that, just yesterday, she had considered beautiful, she stood in silence and watched. Only now did she understand where the slight shades of color in the stone had come from, stains that could never fully be cleansed.

When the bodies of her father, mother, and brother, drained of blood, were tossed one by one into the blazing fire, she didn't turn away. She didn't turn away when the others left the room laughing and singing, urging her to join their celebration.

After the remains of her family were reduced to ash, she stood alone in the great room, where the air smelled of burning hair and charred flesh, and where the smeared blood added to the stains on the floor. Her gaze stayed on the fire until the embers died away, and only then, did she turn away. When she at last walked from the room, she silently made another vow.

CHAPTER ONE

Present Day

Jeni Denton slipped on her jacket and pulled at the hem like doing so would magically give it a perfect fit. The most important goal in slipping it on had already been achieved as it covered the shoulder holster and the Glock 19 she slid into it. Both the jacket and the holster felt loose, not that she should be shocked, and that's what made her keep tugging. How much weight had she lost in the last year? Grief could do that to a person. She'd seen it happen to others, and her only surprise was that it took so long to hit her.

She walked around the little house this morning and couldn't help thinking how much Avery would have liked the place. If she'd told Jeni once, she'd told her twenty times, how she wanted to move away from the city and come to someplace with the same vibe as Clayton. A tiny community halfway between Suncrest and Chewelah, it became her new home when she signed on as a deputy sheriff in the Stevens County Sheriff's Department. The sheriff's department was in desperate need of experienced deputies, and her drive to get out of the city brought her here. A little too little, a little too late for Avery, but in a way, this move made her feel closer to her departed wife. She just wished Avery could be here too.

To prepare for the move from temperate Portland to Stevens County, Washington, where the climate ranged from scorching hot in the summers to piles of snow in the winters, she'd traded in her

BMW sedan for a four-door SUV. That had been a sad day because she and Avery had purchased that BMW together. Turning over the keys felt like the last of Avery had been wiped from her life. After she'd finished crying, the realization that nothing could ever remove Avery entirely hit her. She'd be in her heart forever. That's just the way love worked.

Besides, Jeni had made this move because of Avery, not to mention a whole world of shit she'd had no idea even existed before she lost the love of her life. For every action, a choice existed, or so she'd thought. She didn't believe that anymore. The change of job, the move to another state had all happened because she didn't have a choice. Not if she wanted to put some distance between herself and the creatures responsible for Avery's death anyway.

For a few seconds, she leaned her head back and closed her eyes. While she might miss the sporty BMW, this SUV possessed a pretty nice pep. She enjoyed driving it. Pretty sweet that it also had a whole lot more room than her old car. Made her consider the idea of getting a dog. Plenty of room for a canine companion. Perhaps another day. Right now, time to get into the groove of her new life. She opened her eyes and pulled out of her driveway.

Her new office, located in a corner of a county-owned building just off Highway 395, appeared, on the surface, to be a huge slide down from where she'd come from. Her office in Portland had been more than twice the size, with all the latest and greatest in tech. She'd been well-respected and on the move up the proverbial ladder. In all probability, she could have made it all the way to the top. She wasn't bragging. Facts were facts, and she excelled at her chosen profession. Just the same, she'd walked away from it all with no desire to go back.

"Kind of fancy for this place, don't ya think?"

Jeni shook her head and smiled. She'd liked Trent Whitmire from the first hello. Big, burly, and sharp, he welcomed her into the fold the moment they were introduced. Given that she came from a large, urban police force, she'd fully expected a cold shoulder from the more established members of the relatively small sheriff's office. To her surprise and immense relief, no one seemed to care that she'd been part of a radically different force that had been subject to far more people and opportunities. She'd even trained at Quantico at one point.

That didn't mean they weren't curious. Though everyone she'd met so far had been kind and welcoming, they also wanted to know why she'd made the move and why she chose the small force here over a federal job her advanced training could afford her. A couple of the younger deputies told her they'd considered a move in the opposite direction of hers. She had a simple standard answer at the ready, even if it left out the most pressing reason for her move. The explanation she gave everyone, and the one they all accepted at face value, was her need for a radical change after the death of her wife. No need to mention she'd lost her wife a decade ago or that her knowledge when it came to unexplained deaths exceeded the traditional training provided to law enforcement.

To come here to a largely rural county that loved conservative politics and gun rights represented a gamble. She didn't know how they'd react to her. Portland embraced its liberal roots, and she had fit right in. Up until she'd lost Avery, she'd believed it the perfect place to live. The thought of leaving never occurred to her. That all changed one rainy night in April. What should have been a normal spring rainstorm turned into a life-changing horror.

Though she leaned liberal, she hadn't hesitated to move here. When it came to making a complete change, this place offered it all. And when she'd mentioned her wife, only a couple had done a double take. If they took issue with her marital status, they hid it well. After the initial flinch, they all moved forward and welcomed her into the fold. She appreciated their acceptance because she had a heavy job in front of her, and she wasn't talking about her job as deputy sheriff. At least here peace and quiet were more common, which would help her a great deal in the days ahead.

She shrugged. "Until my uniforms come in, you're stuck with this outfit, and besides, I make it look good." She spread her arms wide. The movement pulled open her jacket, revealing the gun and holster beneath.

He pursed his lips and then said, "I like that setup. Routine PPD equipment?"

Portland Police Department standard issue? She shook her head. "No. It's all mine. Just like the way it fits."

"Yeah. Nice look too. Couldn't tell you had it on under that jacket when you walked in." He paused for a second as his eyes narrowed. "Dude, you're gonna stand out around here. That isn't exactly what we call plainclothes in this part of the world. We like ours a little more on the ordinary side."

"Come on. I don't believe it." A jacket over a light-blue shirt and khaki pants didn't exactly equate to dressing up. While she'd seen plenty of pickup trucks and ball caps, her opinion thus far came in as rural but not hillbilly. Many of the folks she'd met since coming here a couple weeks ago had been positive in most ways. She arrived with no illusions everyone would be welcoming, though that could be said about any place. She'd take what she could get and so far, so good.

"Let's just say we do casual in this county really well. A lot of the urban types down in the south county dress up because it's so close to Spokane. Most of those folks work in the city. The rest of the county is far more laid-back. Not much khaki, if you get my drift. A nice pair of Carhartts—now that's a different story."

With some luck her uniforms would show up today or tomorrow. Her goal wasn't to stand out. Rather, she wanted to blend in and didn't own a single pair of Carhartts. At least it would play to her advantage that one other deputy sheriff was a woman. It helped to not be the only one out in the field, an anomaly that made people stop and stare. Then again, she came on board as the only female detective. They'd hired her because they were in desperate need of help and because she came with a ton of experience that made her ready to hit the ground running, as the old saying went. It would take years for someone to obtain the kind of training and on-the-job skills she brought with her.

"I can do laid-back, and this, for the record, is not dressed up." It sounded weak even to her.

Trent laughed and then stood. "Yup. I believe you can, but my fine new partner, trust me when I say you're going to have to dress it down even more to hit casual around here. Now come on. We gotta roll. We got a body up in Hunters."

"Hunters?"

He nodded toward the door. "It won't take you long to get the navigation down. Loon Lake, Clayton, Suncrest, Williams Valley—they'll all be old hat in a couple of weeks. But until then, I'll drive."

Isa awakened when the frenzied chatter coming across her scanner grew loud and tense. She'd known that sooner or later this exact message would come across. They would come because, after all this time, she knew exactly how they worked and what their patterns were. Predictable.

More than that, she'd drawn them here, or rather drawn him here. They'd made it easy enough, although the whole thing had taken far longer than she'd anticipated. Early on she'd believed those who put this whole thing into motion would have been turned into dust centuries ago. Now she understood how full of herself she'd been back when it all began. Kind of like a teenager who thought herself invincible. Isa had felt the same way. Powerful, beautiful, and obscenely rich, she'd been in an enviable position. They had done her wrong and payment was now due. In her naïveté, she'd believed that would be enough to achieve her righteous revenge.

Not even close. Her one good move in the early days had been to stay put and remain silent, even though at times the struggle became almost too much to bear. She'd managed to stay the course and used those years to learn. The biggest lesson: many were older, smarter, and richer. While her family stood in the company of an elite few as one of the wealthiest in the country, she had learned of the hidden ones who made her family look like paupers. The power and influence of her family paled in comparison to those who'd lived for centuries amassing wealth and knowledge. It didn't deter her and instead morphed into a game of wits. Now the chess match moved closer to the moment when she would declare checkmate. Many of the old ones had already fallen, though not by her hand. That was fine. She didn't care how they ended their days on earth, only that they did. To hold the last and most important one responsible represented her endgame. She'd prepared for this last confrontation for a full decade, and she was ready. She smiled and lay back down. The morning was young and they would be working the scene for hours. Her time would come later.

Hours later, Isa looked out the window, her fingers interlaced and resting on her midsection. The morning sun was buttery and hours away until it would set. Strong enough to move in daylight, she preferred not to. Night had been her companion for so long, she found comfort in the long shadows and cool air. Darkness was always the best time to do her work. Patience didn't hurt either. To see this end before the sun rose again would be nice. Wishful thinking, for it would take far longer. Nothing with him was ever quick or easy, and while she'd been able to draw him here, no doubt he would come with a force behind him. Unfortunate for those who had thrown in with him because they would go down at his side. Fealty had its price.

She turned away from the window and dressed, as she always did, in full black. Her kinship with the darkness went beyond the physical. It had become emotional as well, and the choice of clothing gave her even more commonality with the environment. She became the shadow they feared, as well they should. At her defection, the elders had laughed, believing her to be nothing more than a minor annoyance they would soon destroy. She hadn't been the first to rebel, and they knew she wouldn't be the last. Their plan had been simple: stop her, just as they stopped every other rogue vampire, inside and outside of the Redcap Society. Turn her to dust and share a toast as the wind picked up and scattered her remains.

"So how did that go for you?" she whispered to no one. Karma sure could be a bitch. All but one who'd sat at the table and discussed her demise had instead been turned to the dust they'd envisioned for her.

Soon it would be finished, at least for her. She supposed in her quest for justice, she had made enemies of those who had become true believers of the elders who'd sat around the table like gods. They were the followers, who as the humans liked to say, drank the Kool-Aid. The ones who would try to do to her what had happened to the old ones. They didn't realize that, unlike the elders, she had no real investment in her ultimate survival. Upon the completion of her quest, she would no longer care if she carried on.

She had friends—those who knew and understood who she'd been and the critical importance of the journey she'd embarked upon. They were few, though mighty in both power and conviction: a necessity both for her safety and theirs. Too many she cared about died because of her, and she didn't wish to be responsible for the loss of even one more. She walked a solitary path, and it could be no different.

She ignored her longing for the touch of another. After her family had been taken from her, she never dared to love again for fear the floors would again run red. Her soul couldn't take the weight of that responsibility. Instead, she'd found peace in solitude broken only by occasional, and brief, companionship. When the end came for her, a very few would mourn only briefly, and that gave her a strange sort of peace. She held onto those thoughts as she paced the house. She waited until finally the sun gave up its hold on the day. Only then did she step outside to begin her work.

Here in a geographically large county that was small in terms of services, she waited for the darkness that would provide cover for her first stop. Government offices in this place didn't function 24/7, as they did in many of the larger metropolitan areas. The medical examiner's office routinely vacated shortly after five, so by the time she got inside a little after seven, no one remained. Upon her relocation here, she did her homework and knew the location and angle of each surveillance camera. While a camera might capture her movement, her speed would cause her image to blur, and they would never be able to make out her face. Again, as the humans liked to say, this wasn't her first rodeo. That thought made her smile. In this county, it seemed most appropriate. She saw horses, cows, and livestock everywhere. She'd put money on rodeos being a popular attraction.

Inside, she found what she came for rather quickly. The woman's toe tag identified her as *Rose Paxton, age 28*, and, from the condition of her body, not yet subjected to an autopsy. Isa didn't require an autopsy to observe what she needed to see because the once-lovely face sent a clear message. They were going for the young ones, and that told her a couple of things. They were targeting recruits, and they hadn't selected her for a meal, although something had gone wrong or she wouldn't be here now.

Isa smoothed back the fine, dark hair from her cold forehead. Her age and good looks had been to her detriment. A deciding factor in bringing any potential candidate into the blood always came down to youth, beauty, and one other important trait: wealth. If Isa did a little more research, she would put odds on discovering that Rose came from a well-to-do family. The Redcaps had their standards, after all, and she should know. Once upon a time she'd been just such a recruit: young, beautiful, and her family's wealth second only to that of the monarchy.

"I'm so sorry," she said to the immobile body. No one knew why it happened, but not everyone could be turned. Though the Redcaps had spent centuries trying to discover why some were immune, the secret stayed intact. Unlimited wealth and time could not unlock the mystery. As she gazed down at the still face, Isa felt, as she always did in a situation like this, that death a far better alternative than being brought over. "Rest in peace, pretty one."

She could leave, and undoubtedly tomorrow the body would be here cold and still, just as it was right now. Taking chances wasn't a strategy she rolled with. While the folk legends about vampires were full of fantasy, some parts were based on truth—like a stake in the heart. From the bag slung over her shoulder, she pulled out a small stake and, with one powerful thrust, shoved it into Rose's. With an equally strong pull, she brought it back out, wiped it off, and tucked it back into her bag. In the morning, the medical examiner would make note of the puncture inflicted post-mortem, and investigators would spend hours trying to determine how and why. They would never find their answers.

George came into the house and threw his coat to a young woman, whose name he couldn't recall. Mary? Mina? Matty? He didn't care. One in the many who served him over the years, they were of little significance beyond what they could do for him during their term of service. A steady parade throughout the ages, eventually they all began to look alike, and he bored of them quickly. Just as quickly he got rid of them. A new and eager convert waited around the corner. Always beautiful, always young. As a human he didn't settle, and he certainly did not as an immortal.

His mood remained jovial as he walked through the house and toward the deck. Thus far, it had been a good night. In fact, it had been a good couple of nights. Last night, in particular. Josef's judgment in calling him here had been right on target. His top aide could read a situation better than anyone he'd met. A useful skill to have in the one he allowed inside his inner circle. The preparations had all been made for his arrival and accomplished to his very particular specifications. The house, with its impressive size and luxury appointments, met with his approval. More kudos to Josef for always anticipating his wants and needs. He particularly liked the master suite with the dual-headed shower, jetted tub, and king-sized bed though the massive windows in the great room with a spectacular view were a close second. Like the turrets of the castles he inhabited for centuries, they allowed him to gaze from on high down upon the plebian masses. Very fitting.

In this little blip-on-the-map place, he could actually grasp why she'd relocated here, though most others would not be able to see it. In many ways it reminded him of home, with its rolling hills, pastures and fields, and regal mountains in the distance. No doubt she saw it the same way he did and found the lure of a little piece of the past too hard to pass up.

At times he missed the past. No individual rights. No complaints. Just unquestioned obedience. The lesser did what they were told. Period. Not so in this era. Even the vampire young were more difficult to control in recent decades. Despite his undisputed dominance within the Redcap Society, her actions over the last ten years had effectively weakened it, which allowed for the discontented to garner more of a voice. Putting out fires had taken far too much of his time. Resistance pained him but, despite her best efforts, didn't diminish the control he'd wrestled from the elders. Any celebration she might indulge in would be most premature.

One of the perks of a long life was the ability to not only study the strategies of those who successfully grabbed power away from incumbents, but also to meet them. Learning from them served him well, and today he alone stood at the helm of the society and ruled without equal. In the beginning, he had been as grateful as anyone else invited to join the inner circle. At the hands of the masters, he learned everything about the vampire world and, in turn, had become a master himself. The only difference between him and those who'd mentored him was that he had ascended to a height without equal. His wealth grew to staggering levels, his influence unparalleled. If not for her, perfection would be his.

His fury with her went beyond her disruption of his carefully crafted order and the Redcap Society he molded to his needs and wants. Her betrayal became impossible to overlook. He had loved her, trusted her, and she turned on him. No one did that to him and lived. Yet she'd managed to survive for over a decade, eluding him and undermining his reputation at every turn. No wonder an element of his underlings were empowered to question his authority. If she could do it without being held accountable, then so could they. He suspected that repercussion had been part of her plan all along.

He stood on the deck where a sofa and three padded chairs formed what the humans described as a conversation grouping and gazed out into the night. Down five steps, moonlight sparkled on the water of a pool bordered by lounge chairs. Green grass stretched for several acres, and beyond, thick trees gave the oasis a natural privacy. Yes, Josef did well when he found this one. A lovely place to relax and enjoy, well, just being him. He turned and walked back to the double glass doors, stepping inside. Relaxation would have to wait for just a little longer.

Soon, he would put an end to her treachery, one way or the other, and once more restore the unquestioned respect and obedience her actions had stolen from him. The game of cat and mouse they'd been playing for a decade would be over. His adventure last night signaled the beginning of the end. She could be put in her place, and the Redcap Society, under his rule, would continue to grow larger and more powerful than it had ever been. All would bow to him, vampire and human alike. A new world order awaited just beyond the horizon, and he could see it all in his mind's eye. The vision caused him to smile. He needed only one thing to make it perfect: Isa.

CHAPTER TWO

Jeni couldn't shake off the day, and she tried. Her first official workday, no less, and it left her unsettled in a way she hadn't experienced for a very long time. Here she thought she'd relocated to a nice, quiet little county where she'd have plenty of time to do what she'd come here for without undue stress. So much of her life over the last decade had been devoted to finding the one responsible for destroying her world. She'd lived it, breathed it, and it had almost taken her down. Coming here had been a step back, a breather, for lack of a better description. Since she'd lost Avery she'd been on a mission, and that obsession took its toll on her body and her soul. It didn't mean she'd given up on finding the one responsible. On the contrary, it remained on her mind all the time, and she continued to search. When she found him—or her—she'd kill without hesitation and look them right in the eye when she did it. In the meantime, she needed a little rest. This seemed a perfect place to recharge, even though she'd come here aware *their* presence was everywhere, a byproduct of her education of the last decade.

The old, lovely house she'd found only a few miles from the satellite station where she'd been assigned, beckoned her from the moment she put her car in park. The previous owners had gutted the inside of the early twentieth-century farmhouse and made it beautiful and twenty-first-century livable. She stood now on the massive back deck with a cup of coffee in hand and stared out across the acres of green fields. In the morning, deer raced across that same field, their movements so graceful they seemed to be flying. Watching them made her smile each time, and a funny kind of tranquility would settle over her. The moment she'd moved in here, the word home played over and over in her mind.

Analyzing her feelings didn't factor in tonight. Not that they held any significance anyway. The woman they'd found murdered this morning did matter. How she'd been murdered mattered even more. The possibility of it happening anywhere she moved was a reality she couldn't escape. Still, it was the last thing she expected to come across on her first day on the job.

What had happened today changed everything. She'd believed the idea to come here had been all about letting go and finally moving on with whatever would pass for a normal life. Now she believed it had more to do with destiny. She'd been brought here for a much bigger reason, and a charge of righteous energy pulsed through her at the dawning truth. She should be upset that it appeared to be starting all over again. She wasn't.

Avery would disapprove of what she planned to do next, and she understood why it would bother her so much. In their marriage, Avery had always been the calm and forgiving one, the woman who trusted far too many, far too easily. She'd tried to warn her against it and had hoped that some of her cop-trained instincts might rub off at least a little on her wife. For a while, she'd believed they had and that Avery had become more discerning about those she let close. In the end, Avery's trusting ways had never changed, and they had come at a price no one should have to pay.

Jeni ran a hand over her face and sighed. Not the time to go there. She would be beating her head against a brick wall, and she just couldn't do that again. She dropped her hands away from her face, and once more she focused on the serene landscape that spread out like it had been groomed for a big-budget movie. It hadn't been wrong to make this move, though she hadn't expected the evidence of a fortuitous decision in the face of a murdered woman to confront her either. Yet there it was. In her altered reality, she couldn't turn a blind eye to it.

Trent had done his work as an officer investigating a suspicious death, and his professionalism impressed her. Despite hailing from a rural county, his skills were metropolitan sharp. Their partnership got off to an encouraging start this morning, and that came like the bright light to an otherwise gloomy situation.

Simultaneously she'd done her own investigation. The difference between her work and Trent's had nothing to do with their diverse law-enforcement experience and everything to do with her personal experience with a world that hid in the shadows. He'd seen an unfortunate murder victim and set about finding the man or woman responsible. Although her investigation had also been predicated on finding the responsible party, she saw something different because she possessed one truth Trent did not: a vampire had murdered this woman.

Isa didn't care for what she needed to do. Nor would she hesitate to do it anyway. A long time ago she'd learned not to let the nature of a task dictate her actions. To do that would open her up for mistakes and expose her to those who could end her life in a second. She might not have asked for this life, but it belonged to her, and she'd made peace with it as best she could. Nonetheless, she lived it on her own terms. The elders of the Redcap Society never liked that reality. No, indeed, they had not. Now they were gone, and he stood alone on the raised dais. The fire had always been in him, though she hadn't understood its power in the beginning. Neither had the elders. They had wanted to make the rules and, in their quest to be all, missed the warning signs, as had she. In her defense, she'd been young, foolish, and entitled. The elders really had no defense beyond their incredible arrogance.

His rules were now the law of the darkness. She escaped before he could fully assert his dominance, and that played in her favor. In this century it reminded her of an often-used term: micro-manager, which aptly described the leader of the Redcap Society. Every move, every breath, every action required his stamp of approval. Her defection would have given him a fatal stroke had he been human.

Despite his iron grip on the vampire community, she'd stopped playing the game not long after he'd turned her. Not that she'd ever allowed George, or any of them, to know she possessed her own code. Her father had been big on the concept of honor, which, in her book, never went out of style. She embraced honor even as she had become a killer, and not grasping that basic trait about her became a fatal mistake for more than one.

Some might say that describing herself as a killer represented an oxymoron of sorts. Her personal code mandated that she didn't kill the living. No, rather, she dispatched the already dead to their final destination, the one denied them the first time they died. She didn't take human lives. Not anymore.

But enough of remembering. She didn't care to dwell on the past, particularly those early times before she found her strength. Besides, after she finished here, the past would be behind her once and for all. Peace would be hers, and she would never need to check behind her again.

Now she stood staring at the spot where the body of the woman in the morgue had been found. The yellow tape no longer marked the area, and only trampled grass and broken undergrowth remained to tell humans a tale of what happened here. Soon even that would be gone as nature reasserted its command over the damage inflicted by people. In a couple of hours runners, walkers, or the curious would trek over the ground, never realizing a life had faded into darkness here. Her acute senses were a different story. Even in the moonlight she could easily make out the slightest depressions in the landscape. The foot patterns of the many who had walked over this land in hours just past, observing and documenting something they had no capacity to comprehend, were still visible to her keen eyes.

More than sight created a full picture for her. The smell brought another layer of detail and, with it, a great deal of information not attainable for humans. It washed over her as if a windstorm blew through, even though in reality the slight breeze barely disturbed the tall grass. Ripples of sensation ran down her back as the scent of blood reached her. She closed her eyes and inhaled deeply, reaching deep for inner calm. It happened every time human blood spilled, and by now she should be used to it. That she wasn't actually pleased her. It told her she hadn't lost all traces of her humanity. George tried for centuries to wipe that away, and the fact he'd failed gave her much satisfaction.

She opened her eyes and kneeled on the ground to touch the soil. Cool dampness made her fingertips tingle, and all around her the world began to fade as if a filmy white curtain had been dropped.

"I don't know who you're talking about." She stood in the grassy field shaking, the woman whose body now lay in a morgue with a hole in her heart the size of a small wooden stake.

"Oh, but I believe you do." The voice of the man, small in stature by today's standards, though big on presence, responded to her, sounding cold and even. "Everyone notices her regardless of the name she uses. I knew her as Isa, though it's hard to know what name she might be going by in your little berg."

"Isa?"

A smile as cold as his words crossed his face. "Ah, well, this is a pleasant surprise. She isn't hiding this time. Brave."

"I didn't say I know an Isa."

"You did not have to, my dear. It is all over your face."

"I don't..."

"But you have heard her name, and that is why I'm here."

"You're wrong. I don't know anybody with that name."

"Yes, you do."

"No," she cried out. "I don't. You're wrong."

"I was wrong once, my dear, only once, and that was very long ago." He smiled, and this time his fangs were on display. She screamed.

Isa pulled her hand away from the ground. She didn't need to see any more. She didn't want to witness how that confrontation had ended because it always ended the same way when George ran the show. A powerful and wealthy man before he had been turned, immortality amplified what he'd been born with. The Redcap Society fed the narcissism that came naturally to him, and his own sense of self-importance exceeded anything she'd seen with another living being before or since. She blamed herself for some of it, for she had unwittingly provided him with a coup d'état. That unintentional result of her vendetta had been a mistake on her part. She should have made George her first target, and she would live with that regret until her last breath.

In her human days, she'd fallen under George's spell, and it had been hard to break free even as she silently harbored the truth. What had one of her friends, a licensed psychologist, told her? George was more than a simple narcissist; he also had a borderline personality disorder, and the combination made him very dangerous. In her defense, until this century she'd had no idea that BPD even existed. She simply chalked up George's pattern of manipulation to the ever-functional characterization: crazy.

BPD or crazy did not come into consideration now because they were irrelevant. The end game would be played to conclusion in this out-of-the-way place with mountains, forests, and clear, cool water. Where the people were friendly, helpful, and unaware of what existed in their midst. Her head tipped back, Isa closed her eyes and took a deep breath. Guilt tapped at her soul over the young woman who'd been brought here. If Isa had been more alert, perhaps she could have saved her.

A calculated risk to use her real name, and she had done it intentionally to draw the Redcaps here. To draw George here. Great that it worked. Sad that already blood stained the ground. Some might call this death a casualty of war. She wasn't one of them. Still, she had accomplished a long-awaited goal, and the final battle had already begun. The only certainty in this was that she would prevail. At the same time, she truly hoped to keep the civilian casualties to a minimum. So far, the score on that one sucked. George: 1. Isa: 0.

❖

The house Josef procured for him, while not in the league of any of his other homes, was nonetheless quite acceptable. While the previous owners had been unwilling to relinquish their property in a civilized manner, their reluctance hadn't presented an insurmountable problem. In fact, it worked out to their advantage. By the time he had driven down the long, well-tended driveway on the day of his arrival, he'd been famished and anxious to find nourishment. One look at the protesting homeowners and two problems were solved at once. The house became his to do with as he pleased, and as he settled into the master suite, he sated himself with Mr. and Mrs. Reluctant. The bodies resting in the basement furnace room now would undoubtedly be discovered at some point, but by the time that happened, Isa would be his, and they would be long gone from the lovely little community.

He stretched out in the king bed with a lovely woman on either side of him. Given the short time he had been here, this small town had proved fruitful in terms of young, willing women. He preferred variety, and Josef delivered. One had short red hair and a runner's body. The other, a dark-haired lovely with beautiful curves. Neither had objected when he availed himself of sustenance from their smooth necks. Alas, he had gotten carried away with Red, who now lay still and cold. He touched Curvy's cheek. If things went as he hoped, she would be joining his chosen few by the next nightfall. He smiled and rolled out of bed. Sex, blood, and a convert, the vampire hat trick.

"Josef." He didn't raise his voice, yet Josef appeared quickly.

"Sir George."

One would think that after several centuries of hearing the formal title it would grow old. One would be wrong. He never tired of the declaration of his nobility for all to receive. It saddened him only that he had been the last of his line, with no heirs to carry his name into the succeeding generations. For all the world, though his line had died out with his supposed death, he had yet been young and unmarried. Given his shadowy existence since that day, he had no practical way of showing the world that he, in fact, still existed. The only comfort he got came from hearing his nobility articulated by those of his inner circle. Someday, when his plans all blossomed, his name would once again be spoken for all to hear, living and undead.

Tying the belt of his robe, he inclined his head toward the bed. "One of our guests must be disposed of. Clean it up."

Josef nodded in the direction of the body. "I will take care of it."

His earlier scouting trip had given him an excellent plan for the coming night. His work from the previous night with the lovely young country girl had caused just the appropriate amount of chaos and would be sure to garner her attention. Another perfect move on his part.

George turned away, his thoughts no longer on the mess in his bedroom but on the adventures the night would present. Josef would take care of it as he always did. He took great pride in being a cleaner of the most excellent variety. Strangely enough, Josef had been a rail-thin porter of a wealthy miser when he had run across him in nineteenth-century Russia. His threadbare coat provided little protection against the bitter Russian winter, and while his benefactor wore a fur hat on his head, Josef's hat, a wool scrap, spoke volumes about where he stood with his employer. Even attired in such wretched garments, George had been able to see the beauty of the man beneath. He'd wanted him and he'd secured him. Really, it hadn't taken much to recruit him, first as a servant and then as a trusted underling in the Redcap Society. Josef had proved himself a thousand times over. Unlike Isa, Josef could be trusted.

CHAPTER THREE

Jeni couldn't sit around any longer. Feeling caged and uneasy, she just wanted to move. Instead of doing nothing, she could at least get out for a while. Fresh air and movement would help her think this whole thing through. No better place to do it than at the scene of the crime, trite as that sounded. Weird as it might be, she'd become a master at reconstructing events when she had the opportunity to be at a scene without anyone else around. Some might call her ability supernatural. She preferred to think of it as having an insight into human nature. She didn't care to dwell on the fact that the human nature she locked into came in the form of evil walking the earth.

In the driveway she debated on taking her rig or going with the marked Sheriff's Department SUV a deputy from Colville delivered earlier. It would be nice to take the drive incognito. It would also be nice to have all the tools of her trade with her. Tools of the trade won the debate. In particular, she wanted the radio. If something else happened, and she suspected eventually it would, she wanted that knowledge ASAP.

Now she stood stone still as she stared straight ahead into the night illuminated by a bright golden moon. A light breeze blew her hair against her face while she tried to make sense of this situation. No way anyone else should be here. The crews had cleared out hours ago, and for anyone who could see it now, nothing evil happened in this lush field where the deer tramped down trails and the wind made the wild grass sway. Unlike Jeni, she didn't hold a flashlight. So why did a woman stand right on the spot where the body had been dropped lifeless and drained earlier, staring down at the ground as if she could see it all? What in the actual fuck?

"Who are you and what are you doing?" She stuck the flashlight in her pocket, pulled her gun, and pointed it at the woman's back as she walked close enough to see her long, dark hair. The moon's light was enough to make out the color, not enough to see if the woman might be armed.

Her cop voice didn't prompt the woman to turn and face her. That lack of reaction made this encounter unusual. People typically responded in a different way when she barked at them. Instead, this woman turned slowly, without any sense of urgency or surprise that another person approached a murder site. When she finally faced Jeni, her finger tightened on the trigger while her pulse took off racing. Fuck. Fuck. Fuck.

"I'm here for the same reason you are."

"No. I doubt that." Bile rose in Jeni's throat, and it took a lot of effort not to pull the trigger. She didn't because, even if she emptied the clip, it wouldn't do any good. The fact that she still pointed the gun at the woman's chest was ridiculous. A false sense of control, yet she didn't lower it. Control, even if it was an illusion, was better than nothing.

"Oh, I very much am."

Hearing the woman's insolent tone, fury raced through her like a fire fed by five gallons of gasoline. She didn't fully appreciate who she faced. "You're one of them, and I know exactly what you are."

She tilted her head and studied Jeni. The intense gaze made her uncomfortable, for good reason. In other circumstances, the woman looking at her now might be described as beautiful, with her long, black hair, dark eyes, and smooth skin. She didn't appear to be more than twenty-five, though the knowledge Jeni amassed over the last ten years told her that the façade hid a frightening truth.

"I believe you do." She hated the cool, unhurried tone.

"Damn right I do. What are you doing here? Why did you kill that woman?" How she wished she'd brought her other gun loaded with the special bullets. The cost of the oversight could very well be her life. Why had she thought coming here would be any different? These monsters were everywhere, almost like they were following her. Taking Avery hadn't been enough. They wanted to make her life a living nightmare as well.

"I killed no one." The calm way she spoke made Jeni even more agitated. Bitch didn't realize the extent of Jeni's insider knowledge.

"I know what I saw. I know what you did. That woman died at the hands of a vampire."

She gave Jeni a slight nod. "Ah. You do know of us."

She wanted to pull the trigger in the worst way, even as ineffectual as that might be. "More than you can imagine."

"Then lower your gun. It will do nothing, and I won't hurt you. You have my word." She put a delicate hand over her chest.

Whether she spoke the truth remained to be seen. At the same time, Jeni suddenly saw the foolishness of her position. Vampires didn't die from a bullet wound. While it might slow them down, it wouldn't end their existence. At least with traditional bullets. The special variety she kept loaded in another gun back at her house was a different story. She lowered her arm and slipped the gun back into the holster, her hand trembling. Stupid to keep holding it out there like it could actually threaten this monster.

"Why did you kill her?" At least if she were to die here, she wanted the truth before she did.

Again, the woman shook her head. "I swear that I didn't."

"Right..."

"I know who did."

"Are you telling me you're not the only one here?" The thought both made her sick and thrilled her. When she'd relocated here, she'd told herself it was all about moving on. To get past what had happened to Avery and begin living again. A good lie that she'd believed until right this second.

Truth slapped her as hard as running face-first into a brick wall. She hadn't moved on, and she hadn't stopped tracking the monsters who'd taken Avery away from her. The hunt had only stalled, not stopped. In her mind, she wanted to wipe vampires out of existence, and while her goal might be unrealistic, it gave her purpose and drive. Everyone had their own way of dealing with loss and grief.

She itched to run home and grab the weapons made for just this kind of encounter. She didn't move. Curiosity pushed aside her anger and kept her face-to-face with a creature she very much wanted to destroy. In a weird way, she found herself intrigued. Her previous encounters with vampires had gone in a decidedly different direction: shoot first, ask questions later. This time, she wanted answers.

The woman tilted her head and stared. "I am most assuredly not."

Well, that sucked. She hadn't come in search of vampires, which was not to say she hadn't arrived at her new home prepared nonetheless. It was a little like being a cop and always carrying her gun. Vampire hunting and law enforcement were a lot alike, just different bullets. "You know who they are?"

She nodded, and the silky hair swayed into her fair skin. "One in particular. I have been stalking him quite a long time."

"Why is he here, of all places?"

She smiled and brushed the hair off her face. The dark eyes grew hard. "Because of me."

❖

That the woman with the gun knew Isa's secret came as a shock. She'd come to this place expecting to move quickly and in anonymity. Lure George here, kill him, and leave. No one would be the wiser, and the human casualties would be kept to a minimum. The plan didn't include humans stepping into her war.

In the larger cities, a small percentage of the population always knew of the reality of vampires. Some were allies, while others were survivors or those close to victims who sought justice. Working under the radar always became more difficult when humans were aware of their existence. When she moved to the lovely house with the tall trees and wildflowers, she expected to be able to work in anonymity.

After only a short time here, several mysterious and unsolved murders hinted that her presence had been noticed. While she hadn't been surprised that a victim had been found today, the presence of this human did. Both intriguing and complicating. Much easier to do what she needed to without a nosy human. Running into one in the middle of nowhere who knew about vampires—well, that fascinated her.

"Explain." The woman's barely contained fury didn't escape her. One piece of information offered: not an ally. A justice seeker? Perhaps, but something about this woman was somehow different from those she had encountered in the past. The aura of tragedy surrounding most of those intent on justice didn't appear to envelop this one, or at least it wasn't immediately apparent. Interesting.

At the same time, she didn't want or need to get into particulars with any stranger, interesting or not. The coming battle belonged to only her. She would do her best to minimize casualties. Unfortunately, much would be out of her control, like the death of an innocent woman on this ground. So, in this case, the less information shared, the better. At least for the moment. Maybe this woman could be coaxed to her side if the need arose later, not that she expected to require any help. She had learned to expect the unexpected. And, if she did need assistance, why not an attractive woman who handled a gun like a pro?

"Yes," she said as she squared her shoulders. That her gaze never wavered from Isa's face impressed her. A little truth couldn't hurt…she hoped. "I am what you say I am. I didn't come here to harm anyone, including the dead woman. Another took her life, and I will hold him responsible."

"Right, and you're the vampire sheriff. Is that the crap you're trying to feed me? How stupid do you think I am?"

Another piece of information offered, albeit unintentionally. Definitely someone with a history and, though curious right now, she didn't have the time or the inclination to figure out what it might be. Ending the war she started remained her sole focus. It had to be. Diverting her focus could prove disastrous.

She shook her head. "No such beast. I came here to right a wrong, and I will. Mine and the woman who lost her life on this ground. The one responsible will pay with his own blood, and that is a promise." She planned to make good on it too. Time was up for George and his minions.

"Spare me. I know your kind, and if I could, I'd end your life right here, right now."

Interesting that she showed no fear of Isa, in all likelihood aware that if she wanted, she could snap her neck in the space of two seconds. She could drain her dry of blood and drop her body on the same spot where the woman in the morgue had been left. This woman who challenged Isa so fiercely had to appreciate how precarious her position with her, with any vampire, would be under these circumstances, yet not a hint of fear showed in her face or came across in her words. Stupid and admirable at the same time.

"Save your bravado for another. You're going to need it."

In the instant the last word crossed her lips, Isa moved so fast, no human could possibly follow. Exactly her intent. It took her only seconds to reach the gravel area where a still-warm vehicle was parked, and as she touched it, much became clear. Besides being a human with knowledge of the parallel world of vampires, she was a cop, which might complicate things. If things went as she believed they were destined to, this would all be over and done with before the cop could even begin to dig deep, so probably nothing to get too worried about.

❖

The night grew deep and dark, the air taking on a delightful chill. George preferred cool over the heat of many of the places he had lived in during his long years. In his successful journey to ultimate power, he had been forced to make a number of unpleasant places his temporary home. All part of the process. Just one of the lessons he'd learned from the man whose name he still carried. His father had been an excellent teacher—harsh though quite effective. He still bore the scars on his back and buttocks where whips had met his flesh, his punishment for failing to meet the standards of his sire.

How he had hated him at the time. That wasn't quite accurate. He had hated him at the time, and still did all these centuries later. In fact, his hatred might even have grown in the intervening years. His investigation of the world had shown him that, even in the century of his birth, not all fathers carried the cruelty that his own did. His father, a cold man, had possessed it to the depths of his soul. Beating his son until his skin split and bled thrilled him, and George would always remember how he reveled in the fact that he could pass his actions off as necessary to make his progeny a better man.

In the end, said progeny turned around to teach his esteemed father a lesson of his own. It hadn't been a quick one either. As they liked to say in this century, payback was a bitch. The memory made him smile as he stood on the deck and stared into the night, even as the scars on his back twitched as if to remind him that once upon a time he had been a victim. He didn't care to dwell on thoughts of his father or that impotent time in his life. He turned instead to thoughts of the gentler sex.

What was she doing this night? She had to know he would come once he became aware she'd relocated here. She would expect him just as she would know how deliberately he'd cast his own bait in this out-of-the-way place. Actually, though Josef was responsible for scouting the area, it seemed perfect to him. In many ways it reminded him of where it had all started. To make the circle complete, it might have been better to take the final battle all the way back home. But that was too obvious, and she never went for the obvious. Strategy had brought him here. Confidence prepared him for ultimate success.

With its widespread geography and smaller law-enforcement presence, this location offered unparalleled freedom, and he appreciated it. When he finished, however, he would most certainly leave, for despite its beauty, its sparse population, and rural identity, it didn't suit his needs in the broader picture. He required larger cities—larger herds to hunt—and the energy of significant human numbers to keep his interest piqued. Think New York City, Los Angeles, Seattle, London, or Paris. Now, those were cities that spoke to his spirit and his hunger, places where he would soon rule more than just the vampires.

As he inhaled the fresh, unpolluted air, he swore he could catch her scent. One never forgot the smell and the touch of their first love. She had been that for him. First and last. Even before he'd been turned, he had been content to bed who he wanted and then toss them away. After his initiation into darkness, his appetites grew, and he indulged himself without consequence or conscience. When he'd met her, it had come as a shock to discover he could open his heart to another. She captured a piece of him that no other, before or since, had been able to, and for that fury became a constant companion. She'd made him love her, and then she'd turned on him. His trust in her had been absolute, and she'd lied to him while staring straight into his eyes. Not so much as a blink gave her away and his fall was complete. His fingers twitched, and his regret assailed him as it occasionally did when he allowed himself moments of reflection. He held onto the anger like the dying man he would never be because he preferred anger to pain.

Breathing in the clear, fresh air, he lifted his chin, narrowed his eyes, and clenched his hands into fists. His determination hardened, and his shoulders squared. Into the night he whispered, "I'm coming for you, my darling."

CHAPTER FOUR

Now that just pissed her the fuck off. God-damn fucking vampires. Freaking monsters! The fact that Jeni didn't stomp her feet and throw a massive screaming tantrum demonstrated her supreme self-control and professionalism. What good would it have done anyway? That full-of-herself vampire quite literally left Jeni standing in the dust. She'd have been throwing her tantrum for exactly one person: herself. Not worth the effort.

Her anger cooled as she stood staring into the night and taking in long, deep breaths of fresh air. The yoga she'd started after losing Avery came in handy in more ways than one. The breathing exercises her yogi insisted upon had proved to be the savior she needed to get through each day, particularly during that first couple of years. Now she called on that same technique to help her find her center once more. She focused on her breath and let everything else go. Good energy in. Bad energy out. After the fifth one, her shoulders relaxed, and the tirade of foul language faded.

She continued the long, measured breaths and thought through the surprise encounter with the vampire. Awareness gave her strength she would need. While her move to the sheriff's office had been a valid attempt to simplify her life, tonight proved that simple wasn't in the cards. A normal person would be pissed off by the unfairness of it all. Instead, energy flowed through her and once more charged her with purpose. Anyone who dedicated their life to public service already embodied purpose. This war against vampires went beyond just helping one's family, friends, and neighbors. This kind of purpose went global.

Hands in her pockets, she stared down at the flattened grass. She found comfort in the idea that what this vampire didn't know would definitely hurt her. Undoubtedly, she thought Jeni to be a run-of-the-mill cop, which was a perfect assumption and quite handy. Jeni might have come here to take her own life down a notch. That didn't mean she hadn't come locked and loaded…just in case.

In a way it amazed her the vampire hadn't dropped her where she'd stood. From what she'd seen in the others encountered, she learned that very few humans were left standing once they understood the nature of the children of darkness. Even more so if they were members of the blood cult she'd uncovered in her quest for vengeance. The Redcap Society. The name alone had the power to make her fury ratchet back up. The society had been around for centuries and, from everything she'd gathered, evolved into the governing body of the creatures of the night. Seemed odd that the undead would need governing, yet everything she'd found pointed to that truth. The society did more than simply create laws. Its members were wealthy, influential, and well-placed. Untouchable. Entrée into the society didn't come easily or cheaply, but the benefits were worth the climb.

The Redcap Society also kept control by flexing its muscle against both the human population and its own. Those who chose not to comply found eternity stripped from them. No one, human or vampire, had ever been able to stand up against the elite. It made her want to wipe out every single one of them and had given it the old college try before she left Portland. If she did say so, she'd made a pretty impressive dent in the vampires around the Pacific Northwest. Not an unimpressive feat for a human.

The one who'd left her standing here fuming would find out that she would and could take a stand against those who made the night their home. That vampire, beautiful as she might be, had made a critical error in coming to her town. It would be her last mistake. Yes, she'd moved here to start over. She also understood better than most that sometimes things didn't work out as planned. She hadn't come to continue the fight. Nonetheless, it had come to her, and backing down wasn't in her nature. That thought buoyed her spirits and made her stride long and confident as she turned and walked back to her car.

Her confidence remained high as she drove the dark country roads to reach her new home. In all honesty, she'd like to be more proactive and get right to the hunt. Experience told her not to. There was important work to do before she could launch into full-on battle mode. Those with long lives amassed incredible amounts of intelligence in their years, and frankly, if they didn't, they wouldn't have been able to survive century after century. Yes, the society afforded the elite many things, including protection. It came at a price and with a whole lot of strings attached. The Redcap Society only targeted the best and the brightest. That, in her opinion, made the organization dangerously strong, and it also opened it up to weakness.

She liked to exploit its main weakness: the best and the brightest didn't always play nice together. She'd toyed with the egos of those who'd crossed her path, and it hadn't ended well for them, even as her success had brought her into enhanced danger. The survivors of her vendetta didn't take well to her meddling, another reason she'd decided to come here. Time for a break from always checking over her shoulder. She thought she'd have a longer break. Wouldn't be the last time her best-laid plans went sideways.

First things first. It would be in her best interest to take some time to get the lay of the land, so to speak. The surprise encounter didn't need to be repeated. Sleep wasn't likely to happen, and she was okay with that. Wouldn't be her first all-nighter, and even after this battle ended, it wouldn't be her last. Nature of the beast when a person chose a career in law enforcement...or vampire hunting. Throw in a renewed personal vendetta, and it became more than a mission. It became a way of life. She would have plenty of time for sleep when the dust settled.

Of course, she'd already stocked the pertinent supplies for any sleepless nights that might come her way. She had a system, though what worked for her would undoubtedly make a good nutritionist cringe—full-sugar cola, along with Skittles and a pack of those chocolate cupcakes made to withstand the apocalypse. A sugar and caffeine junkie's ambrosia.

Once back at her house, she grabbed a two-liter bottle of cola from the refrigerator, pulled out a brand-new bag of Skittles, and tore open the cellophane wrapper on the dual pack of cupcakes, taking a moment to inhale the sweet scent of chocolate. At the table, surrounded by her power snacks, she booted up her laptop.

Before she put her hands on the keyboard, she took a sip of the cola. A wave of delight flowed through her as it slid down her throat, cold and sweet. As bad as soda might be, it was exactly what she needed to kick-start her mission. She began to type. "Come on, baby. Talk to me." The search didn't take long. "Bingo."

Isa knew she'd pissed off the pretty cop. Not surprising, given that real talent she possessed for upsetting people. Keeping law enforcement off kilter had developed into a highly refined skill that proved to be quite useful. Her universal observation was that those who carried a badge had what felt like a hard-wired tendency to meddle in matters they shouldn't. In the brief time she'd faced off with this one, she could tell that, left unchecked, this woman would turn out to be a pain in the ass. She just didn't have time to deal with that right now. Neither could she ignore her. Just because she didn't want her to meddle didn't mean she wouldn't.

Outside in the darkness, she stood watching said cop through the curtain-less kitchen window. Surprising for one in law enforcement to allow herself to be so exposed. Made Isa's job easier and it took only a minute for her initial impression to be reinforced. Definitely pain-in-the-ass material. Most would be in bed this time of night. From the looks of things, this woman didn't intend to move to the bedroom anytime soon.

Isa squinted and stared harder. What the hell? With her better-than-human eyesight, she could make out candy, cake, and soda. Good Lord. How could she keep such a toned and athletic body and eat that kind of garbage? Even if Isa wanted to consume human food, those kinds of things would be about the last she would choose. In this century, with so much wonderful, fresh food readily available, it amazed her how people reached for the type of junk spread out on the table around the deputy. So awful, it was almost criminal.

Let it go. What the woman put in her body didn't merit additional thought because her only role in what would come to pass would be as a bystander. Unless, of course, she got in Isa's way. And if she did? One term came to mind: collateral damage.

Too much time and energy required to let anyone, regardless of how attractive, clutter her path. Besides, she didn't need some human with a competing agenda to complicate things. She would have to back the hell off and let Isa take care of this. A smart woman would get that, and if she didn't turn out to be a smart woman, Isa could deal with that too. It wouldn't be the first time someone with basically good intentions got in her way.

A bigger question was how this woman had become one of the knowledgeable. Something must have happened in her life to put in her the vampire orbit, and for the vast majority, that typically resulted in the same predictable end. That she survived was no small feat. Hell, the fact that Isa had survived after her all-out assault was an equally impressive feat, and she wasn't even human. Curiosity made her want to find out the story behind the woman, just not right now. Too much to prepare for at the moment to concern herself with some human's backstory. Besides, she had her own past to deal with, and the urgency of that burden pushed all other thoughts out of her mind.

For another thirty minutes, she stood in the shadows and watched the deputy through the window, even though her best move would be to leave here and gather more intel on George. She pushed the best move to the background and stayed. Jeni was visible in the kitchen light, and Isa shook her head at the woman's blatant exposure, something unheard of in this day and age anywhere except for a trusting place like this. Of the law enforcement she'd become acquainted with through the years, not one of them would leave a window uncovered so that anyone could see inside.

She finally turned her gaze away from the house and toward the heavens. A light breeze blew clear and fresh, the night sky dark and filled with stars. It brought back memories of home. In her youth, it too had been beautiful and unspoiled, the air fresh and the sky a beautiful canopy filled with twinkling stars. For a moment, she no longer saw the here and now.

Isa held his hand and pretended. He believed her because they all did. No one in her circle understood the true nature of her heart. Not now. Not ever. They didn't try, and even if they did, it would be impossible for them to believe. No matter the circumstances, life would fail to give her what she wished for, and she understood that more than anyone. She had made peace with it, and she told herself that each night as she stared out into the darkness. The lie gave her comfort, and she could ask for no more.

He leaned in and kissed her cheek, for he did so like to press convention. The gesture would certainly displease her father. No arrangement had yet been made, though all expected an agreement soon between the young, handsome noble and her family. It made her a little sick to think about it, even though she knew with certainty it would come to pass. It would be best for all of them. Her money. His title. Two beautiful people who would surely produce equally beautiful children to carry their blood forward into the ages. It was simply the way things were done. It was expected.

"I love you." His lips brushed her ear. Any of the women who were her friends would swoon to hear those three words from him. They all considered her the luckiest young woman in the country. He was the one all the mothers tried to snare for their own daughters. For some time she had been aware that his affection belonged to her. It reflected in his eyes and in the butterfly touch of his fingers as they brushed her cheek. He didn't care that he flaunted convention. He didn't care who knew of his interest in her.

He had descended upon their village, and every mother had taken notice, readied every unmarried daughter for the auction. Dressmakers worked night and day to sew the gowns. Parties were planned. Invitations were issued. She tried her best to stand in the shadows. It hadn't worked out. In fact, he had seemed to be more taken with her because of her reticence. Shortly after his arrival, his focus narrowed to her alone.

Tears pricked at the back of her eyes. His declaration of love had been honest, somewhat. All his outward displays of affection presented a perfect picture of devotion, yet despite all the signs to the contrary, she harbored distrust. What did it really signify: love or possession? Did he cherish her? Or did he simply wish to own her? Her soul whispered the answer she wouldn't speak aloud.

Just as she knew that she would never love him, her gaze settled on another who stood smiling on the other side of the room. Like her, Alda's mother had dressed her up in her finest dress and piled her shiny black hair on her head like a crown. She looked beautiful, more beautiful than any other woman in the room. If he couldn't see her loveliness, then he was blind. She willed her tears not to fall.

Her back straightened and her shoulders squared, instead of giving in to emotion, she stood tall. She understood her place and what destiny lay in the future for her. What she dreamed of would never come to pass because it could not. The love she longed for, impossible. She turned her eyes away from the unreachable beauty and back to the one who still held her hand in his. His eyes were upon her, and in them she saw something that went beyond love. Something she hadn't caught before, and it sent chills through her body.

Obsession.

Isa shook her head to banish the past she hated to revisit yet went to again and again. In those days dreams buoyed her, the kind only the innocent and naive can possess. None of them had come true. Not even close. She had different dreams now, and, unlike the unobtainable ones of her youth, they would come to pass.

Finally, as the moon rose high in the sky, Isa took one last through the kitchen window where the woman still sat hunched over her laptop, then turned and walked away. The breeze blew tendrils of hair into her face, and she brushed them away. No reason to stay and continue the stakeout. It seemed clear the woman would be absorbed by her computer and whatever mission she seemed compelled to follow. Besides, she had her own work to do, based upon her particular style of research that didn't require junk food or modern technology.

❖

George wasn't happy. At last he found himself in the position to face her down one final time, and now this? An urgent call from a loyalist in Boise reporting an attempted takeover of his property there. When did getting good people, vampire or human, become such a chore? It had become clear when he took over the leadership of the society why the previous elders had placed such a premium on recruiting only the most intelligent and strongest. What motivated them also made them a pain, and that complicated things a great deal. They constantly pushed for bigger and better roles in the leadership. A bit of himself manifested in them, and while he understood the drive, he also knew it would be a mistake to ignore their ambition. He could not and would not tolerate even a hint of insubordination. They needed to know their place in the hierarchy, and he never hesitated to remind them of it.

Precisely why he needed to leave immediately. He settled into the passenger seat of the luxury SUV for the relatively short drive. The small community he found himself in now had one important feature, an airport, which was where his private plane sat fueled and waiting. One with his means didn't travel commercial, and he didn't care for cars, despite owning more than a dozen high-end vehicles. Unless forced to because he had no other options, he moved from place to place by plane.

At least tonight's trip would be a quick one, both in terms of getting to the airport and the flight itself. A few hours and they would touch down in Boise, where one of his senior staff prepared what would be an efficient coup. The foolish little vampire with dreams of glory didn't have a clue how far his reach extended. No one in the vampire community, neither within the society nor outside, could make a move without him being fully apprised of it. He had his own form of magic, which propelled him into the all-encompassing power he possessed.

It might take him a few days to clean up the mess created by the miscreant, and that didn't bother him. No clock ticked in the background, making speed imperative. He would be back here in plenty of time to triumph over the final battle with beautiful little Isa. The journey to confront her had been years in the making, and thus a delay of a couple of days or even a week meant nothing. Soon they would stand toe to toe and eye to eye.

Always a smart woman, she possessed an intelligence he'd fallen for way back when. Given the years since he first gave her his love, she would have grown even smarter since last they met. Women in general had come so far since their long-ago first meeting, and he found the new breed both interesting and challenging. Her talent for adapting to the times and culture of her surroundings always intrigued him. That would make the coming day of reckoning even more satisfying.

His driver pulled the SUV onto the tarmac. George said nothing as he watched out the window. Josef stood at the base of the steps waiting for him to ascend first. He almost shook his head. The man watched too many movies. Like a popular character in a series of vampire movies, Josef appeared to be emulating the fictional protagonist by wearing leather pants, a skin-tight shirt, and a long leather coat, all in black. The only thing missing was wrap-around sunglasses.

Shaking his head, he got out of the car and walked to the plane steps. Zion, another loyal member of his staff, brought the bag George perpetually carried in his hand. Some things were never left behind, just in case. He turned to Zion. "You stay here."

Disbelief crossed his model-handsome face and then disappeared as quickly as it had appeared. Zion knew when to question and when to do as he was told without further comment. The latter applied here. "What would you like me to do?"

Good boy. "Follow her. Keep me apprised of her activities. Keep everyone else in line. We don't need to draw unwanted attention to our presence here."

"The staff has to eat."

"Yes, they do, but keep it tidy and quiet. Out of the way and no one high profile. I will not tolerate mistakes. Do you understand?"

Zion nodded. "Of course. I'll keep you posted." He handed George the bag before he turned and walked back to the car.

"See that you do."

He boarded the plane and took his favorite spot in the comfortable, over-sized leather seat as the plane taxied down the runway. Soon they were airborne, and he stared out the window, his mind racing with thoughts he shared with no one. While some were intensely private, others were simply beyond the comprehension of those around him, so sharing with anyone would be futile. He had been, and always would be, the smartest man in any room. Hard to have meaningful conversations when no one could match his mental abilities. Once in a while it would be nice to have an exchange on his level. The curse of being a stable genius.

Josef fluttered around him like a moth drawn to a light. It irritated him, and he told him so. Being the good boy that he was, Josef let only a flash of his disappointment show before he faded into the back of the plane. At times even the most loyal, regardless of how attractive they might be, got on his nerves.

Alone at last, he opened his laptop to log on. No need for Josef to stand hovering over his shoulder. He glanced first at the notes he had entered into his phone before accessing his computer. It only took a few minutes to complete the transaction, and satisfied, he shut down and closed the laptop. The best ideas came to him as they were driving to the airport, and now that he'd acted upon one, he was content. His incredible ability to master any situation triumphed again. He patted the laptop with his fingers and smiled. His shoulders relaxed.

Once more he turned his attention to the view outside the window. "Soon, my love, soon," he whispered as they flew farther and farther away from the lights of Chewelah.

CHAPTER FIVE

Jeni leaned back in her chair and stretched her arms over her head. The way her shoulders ached, she could have been hunched over at the table for a couple of days. Given it was one in the morning, that was sort of true. She snapped the laptop closed, stood, and began to pace. How she wanted to scream. Why couldn't she find what she needed? At first it seemed hopeful, then dead end after dead end characterized the last few hours, and that just plain pissed her off. Something existed here, yet it seemed to be hidden by a shroud she couldn't break through. Her interaction with the vampire validated her belief that a cell of some sort existed here. Yet all her normal channels of information yielded nothing of value. Given it hadn't been that long since she'd turned her back on the path of vengeance that had propelled her to research night and day for the last ten years, it should have been easier to come across something. True enough, she hadn't queried a single database since she moved here, but things couldn't have changed that quickly. Could they?

Well, maybe they could. She'd been chasing vampires. Vampires! Until Avery went missing, she'd considered them creatures of horror movies and gothic literature. Even as she followed their trail and the evidence mounted, she'd still denied their existence. Her denial eventually shattered, the ugly truth right in her face. So, if all that craziness actually existed, how far from the realm of possibility would it be for a major shift to have occurred during her transition from Portland to Stevens County? Not too far.

She glanced at the time again and debated whether to make the call. One other person might be able to help. Becca Farconi lived in Maine, and it would be a little past four in the morning there. To call her right now would be rude, and she tried hard not to be that kind of person. Her success on that front was short lived.

"What?" Becca's classic snap came across as clear as if she stood right next to Jeni. Her terse words would put off those with very thin skin. She'd figured out a long time ago that, as a private person, Becca let in only a few—those tough enough to make the cut. Being tough enough had distinct advantages when it came to her savvy, intelligent friend. One of a kind, a friend and ally like her was a gift.

"I need your help." Might as well jump right to it after she'd dragged Becca out of sleep.

"Hum. Are you saying you didn't call just to say hi and sorry I haven't taken the time to come see you or sent an email or FaceTimed you or…"

Jeni smiled. She'd missed this kind of banter and wondered why she hadn't called Becca lately just to say hi. "Okay. Reprimand noted. I'm sorry. I've been otherwise occupied and promise to do better." It wasn't a lie. When she'd decided to give up her quest and move to a calmer and quieter place, that major life change had become her sole focus. After living her entire life in the Portland area, packing up and starting over wasn't exactly a small task or easy emotionally. Becca had done it by moving all the way across the country. Jeni had no excuse. Or, not a good one anyway.

"Nice try, little sister. You've been otherwise occupied since D-day."

D-day. Becca's reference to the night she'd brought Avery's remains to her in a box, not the invasion of Normandy during World War II that everyone typically associated with the term. D-day seemed like a million years and like just yesterday all at the same time. At the time an investigator with the Multnomah County forensics investigation office, Becca had taken it upon herself to be the one to bring Avery home to her. Together, they'd chartered a boat and gone out on the Pacific Ocean to scatter the ashes of the only woman she'd ever loved. In silence they'd watched as they floated away on the waves.

"Yeah, well, you know how it is. Vampires killing your wife has a way of doing that to a person."

"Ten years."

"Shut up."

"Hey, you called me."

Yes, she had called her, and at this ungodly hour. Kind of rude to avoid telling her why. She drew in a long breath, let it out, and jumped in. "They're here."

"No shit?" She heard the same disbelief in Becca's voice that echoed in her words as she'd been standing out in the field facing the vampire.

"I wish I could tell you something different. Shocked the hell out of me, and on my first official day, no less. Seriously. I mean, what are the odds?"

"That had to suck."

"It gets worse."

In the background dishes began to rattle. Out of bed and making coffee. Good. A little caffeine in the system and she'd have her full attention now. "Do tell."

So, she did. Once able to share with someone she trusted, she relaxed completely. Someone other than a damn vampire, that is. It still irked her that the woman had faced her down as though they were on an equal footing. No, not exactly equal. That one believed herself far above Jeni. Nothing new there. They all thought they were much better than any human alive or dead. Well, they'd see about that, now wouldn't they?

"Jesus, Jen. You're like the pied piper. They just follow you."

"I know, right? It feels like they're trailing me even though I'm pretty sure that's not the case. The vamp seemed as surprised by me as I was by her."

"Tell me again why you didn't dispatch said vamp?"

"Million-dollar question, my friend. The short answer is, I don't know. Something about her was different, like really different."

Even if she couldn't quite put words to the nuances of the vampire encounter, the talk with Becca helped. Her confidence began to surge, and a renewed sense of purpose enveloped her. While she might not be able to change what had happened to Avery, she could do her best to take down as many vampires as she could and maybe save a few human lives along the way. As much as she wished she could wipe every last one of them into oblivious, she had to be content with knocking them off one at a time.

"You shouldn't be up in the boonies by yourself if a pack of vampires has made its home there. Or maybe it would be more accurate to say they've settled into a bat cave there."

She almost laughed at that. The vamps she'd come into contact thus far were not likely to live in the wilds and most definitely not a cave. She'd seen a certain amount of sophistication in them, as though luxury had become their standard. Despite being in a mostly rural county, she'd already seen that wealth and good living were not in short supply. "I can handle it because I came prepared, just in case. It's been a rough decade, and one thing's for sure. I've learned how to protect myself." Big words, and she hoped she could back them up.

"True enough there."

"You do what you have to do."

"Tell you what, little sister. I've got some use-or-lose leave I don't want to lose. Here's how this is going down. I'm coming your way, and we'll kick their vampire asses right back to Transylvania. I'll wrap things up here and get on the road as soon as I can."

Jeni thought about telling her not to come and that she'd take care of things on her own. To put her best friend in danger too was a bit of a dick move. That resolve lasted all of about two seconds. "I'll have a cold beer waiting."

Isa rose well before nightfall. At her age, the sun wasn't as big an issue for her as for the younger ones. Tolerance grew stronger with each passing year, and enough had passed in her life to render her relatively impervious to the harmful effects of sunlight.

Tolerance aside, she preferred the night. More comfortable, though that wasn't exactly the entire truth behind her preference. The cover it gave was more important to her and had been since the day she'd been turned. Embarrassment at what she had become kept her in hiding, and even now, with her mission most noble, she still couldn't shake the shame. No amount of time would change that, and so she supposed it would always be her constant companion.

In the hours after leaving the death field and her mini stakeout, she'd investigated the pretty officer who'd stood up to her, thinking she could arm herself with the details necessary to keep the woman out of harm's way. Instead, her findings made her sick and filled her with mortification. It doubled her over like a bad case of the stomach flu. After being around as long as she had, a situation going to hell shouldn't come as a surprise. This one did.

Even after hours of rest, the guilt did not lessen. How in a world this big could it be possible for her to come face to face with her second biggest failure? First, she had succumbed to the charismatic George. Then, many years later, she met the beautiful Avery, a human who deserved nothing that happened to her. Each time she thought of her, Isa wanted to retch. Avery had been the final straw, as the saying went. The moment when she couldn't plan any more. Action became her sole course at that point.

For so long she planned and plotted as she tried to figure out the best way to bring down the Redcap Society and, in particular, George. She'd be lying to say she hadn't procrastinated, scared that one lone vampire would be incapable of making a dent in the centuries-old organization. It was too strong, too powerful, and George had leveraged all his might to his advantage.

Avery changed it all. Despite her excuses otherwise, the reality always lingered in her mind that she would have to take the first step someday, and as she had watched the life drain away from that one good-hearted human, it had, indeed, arrived. No more rationalizing why the time wasn't right. Her path became set in that moment, and she couldn't turn back.

Still couldn't, even as she faced a woman who knew of the darkness here in the far north, where their secrets should still exist.

Seriously, what were the odds? She'd seen enough in her lifetime to make her believe in fate even if it defied said odds. Some things simply couldn't be explained and were just flat meant to be. Like, perhaps, the meeting with Jeni Denton in the middle of a field in the middle of nowhere.

Unfortunately, this situation did create more than a bump in the road. Jeni Denton, previously a detective in Portland and most likely a deputy sheriff here, would be akin to the thorn of a rose: beautiful and tough, and also able to draw blood. As long the blood drawn belonged to a vampire—besides her—Isa might be able to count her as an ally. She seriously doubted it would happen that way. The probability that Jeni would consider any vampire an ally stretched even her very broad imagination. Might be worth a try though. If, as it appeared, she had joined county law enforcement as a deputy sheriff, it might be good to have her in the back pocket. Cultivating that kind of friendship always helped.

First things first. She got into her car and drove the five or so miles to the address she'd written on a piece of paper. No surprise at how big and beautiful it turned out to be. He would demand only the best and his minions delivered. Lights were on, and several people were moving about. Easy to see in through the massive windows that were the focal point of the house. The inhabitants were not strangers to her. Her fingers flexed. One face in particular made her gaze narrow: Zion. His presence demonstrated one very important thing. George came prepared. So did she.

Their movements also told a story. They were preparing to hunt. She'd spent a lot of her time around these particular vampires, and their every move and facial expression remained consistent year after year. Even from this distance, she understood their purpose. Her plan of action came together as she watched.

Her fingers flexing faster, Isa moved closer to the house. It provided her a better view, or at least good enough to take a better read on the action within. Zion walked past the big picture window, his bearing just as straight and regal it had been for more than a hundred and fifty years. If she were close enough to see more clearly, his eyes were sure to still be the blue of the Indian Ocean. Women and men alike were drawn to him, desired him, and submitted to his every wish. His hand had been the last one laid on Avery, and her screams still filled Isa's ears.

"Oh, my pretty one." Zion ran a finger down Avery's cheek as if to wipe away her tears. Instead, he put the finger in his mouth, tasting as he smiled. "Do not cry. I will make this quick. Merciful."

"Don't do this." Avery dropped to her knees. "Let me go. I won't tell anyone about you."

He touched her cheek again, and Isa resisted the urge to scream. A hundred times or more she'd watched him make that same gesture. He was close to ending it with a dramatic flourish designed for the audience that stood silently licking their parted lips. All except Isa. Energy pulsed in the air, the anticipation a living thing.

"Please, Zion." A compulsion to try one more time came over her. Her plea violated the unwritten rules. This time they needed to be broken.

The eyes he turned on her were not the beautiful blue that melted hearts. Instead, the blackness that defined his soul filled them, and it sent tremors through her. How she wanted to claw those eyes out. Her hands stayed at her sides, her nails biting into her palms. This battle had been lost, just as Avery would lose her life in minutes. The guilt of a senseless death lay on her shoulders.

"Shut up." His words were mean.

Eyes closed, she bowed her head while keeping her back straight. Her entire body trembled, and she clasped her hands together to hide their uncontrollable shaking. Show no weakness.

She wanted to save Avery, to grab the lovely human who had touched a part of her she didn't believe still existed, and run from the room. Instead, she continued to hold her hands together and keep her head down. As the sounds of Avery's screams filled the room, it took all the control she could summon not to sob. Though powerless to stop the slaughter, it changed everything. No more waiting and no more planning. The day had arrived for her to take action.

Isa's head came up, and she now stood right next to the house. The unwanted memory had moved her feet from her spot in the shadows to the front door. Long-suppressed anger pushed her forward, and she grabbed the door handle, intending to tear it free of the wood. Stealth be damned. She would go in like the warrior she had trained to be, and this time there would be no silent inaction. This time, Zion's head would roll, and then she paused. A better idea suddenly occurred to her, and she smiled as she walked back into the darkness, leaving Zion and his buddies to live through another night.

❖

They kneeled before him, and he considered mercy. Their infractions in the larger scheme were minor, yet George worried that any insurrection could damage his hold on the society. Too many years putting himself in a position of sole leadership to risk any threat, whether credible or not. Never before in the society's history had one vampire held absolute power, and he didn't feel inclined to give it up now. Hard fought and hard won.

Besides, no one else possessed the gifts he brought to the position. Born into nobility, he began life a class above all others. A stellar birthright coupled with his innate genius made him a natural to lead all others. Why it took the years it did for him to achieve ascension remained the only unanswered question and one that bothered him greatly.

Dismissing the irritating thought, he returned his attention to the three vampires kneeling before him. "Why?" He did like to hear it from their own mouths.

Olive brought her head up and stared at him with eyes that didn't show fear. "Because you're a bastard."

"Bravo, darling, bravo." A shame she'd be gone soon. Olive always did have spunk, and he liked that about her. If she'd applied that attitude in a better way, this might have ended differently.

"One has to be a bastard in my position."

"Oh, you are a bastard, but you have no right to that position."

"And you think you do?"

Now her eyes blazed with fury. "We all deserve to be at your side, never beneath you."

Not the first time he'd heard that ridiculous statement. It continued to amaze him that they were blind to his brilliance and unquestioned right to rule over them.

"You had everything." He countered with the truth. "Wealth and influence. You, my dear, had a reputation that put you in every important circle all over the world, yet you throw it all away because you believe you should stand beside me? Very disappointing and incredibly foolish."

Olive had turned into an artist whose work sold for millions. Her wealth beyond imagination, she owned homes all over the world. In each successive generation, she reinvented herself, and her body of work grew, as did her talent and influence. Had she made better choices, she wouldn't be on her knees before him, poised for destruction.

She spat on the floor at his feet. "Fuck you."

He shook his head. To lose someone of her caliber was a shame. At times it couldn't be helped. Her loss benefitted the greater good, for him anyway. He ran his hand over her hair. Long and black and smooth, like silk under his palm. As beautiful as the art she made year after year, and she could be counted on never to leave her home unless she personified the same perfection she put into her work. He would miss that about her, as he did appreciate beauty in all its forms, his unchallenged power being one of them.

"Not tonight."

It wasn't necessary for him to be here to witness her demise. The loyal around him would do as he bid without fail. As he walked out the door with his shoulders square and his chin up, he tapped a tall, well-muscled man with long silver hair on the shoulder. "I believe our sister, Olive, would love to see the sunrise from the clearing at the top of the hill."

The man nodded. "I'll ensure that she has a clear view."

He smiled as he continued through the door. Behind the big home with the massive lawns and elaborate gardens, a hill rose. Scattered trees provided privacy but not shelter from the coming dawn. Interestingly enough, some vampires could walk in sunlight, and some could not. Just as some humans turned and some did not. Perhaps one day they would uncover the secret of why.

The hill above the gardens would be a lovely place for a misbehaving vampire not immune to the effects of sunlight to watch her first sunrise since studying under William Merritt Chase right next to Georgia O'Keeffe and Lydia Field Emmet. As an artist how could she fail to appreciate the irony of beauty turning to ash?

In the backseat of the car that had been waiting at the airport when they landed, he put his head back and closed his eyes. One problem solved. Word would travel fast about Olive's hastened demise, and once it hit all corners of the vampire world, he expected no additional troubles. This trip had produced perks he hadn't expected. The thought gave him great comfort, and he readied himself for the flight back to his temporary home in the north tomorrow. Soon the sun would be up, and as he preferred to travel well-rested, a suite awaited him in a nearby luxury hotel. Josef had made all the necessary arrangements.

His jovial mood lasted all the way to the hotel lobby, and then his phone rang.

CHAPTER SIX

Shocked and pleased by how fast the day went, Jeni still sighed with relief when she got into her car and headed home. For a small county, it had kept her hopping since she walked through the office doorway right at eight. Like a murder on day one wasn't enough. Overnight they achieved what appeared to be a break-in at the morgue with the body of yesterday's mutilated victim. Or at least that's the terminology relayed to her. She had a better-than-average idea what the mutilation consisted of because she'd seen it before. A puncture wound, round and about the size of a dime. A wooden stake made from African blackwood would be her bet. One of the hardest woods in the world, it could be fashioned into an easily concealed weapon strong enough to pierce a human's heart, even if small and narrow in diameter. Someone, or something, made certain Rose would never rise from that cold steel table again.

Jeni also had a better-than-average idea who made that puncture wound. She couldn't figure the why of it though. Her experience thus far taught her that the legions of darkness preferred to increase their fold, not destroy potential candidates. Those who did that were like her, the human hunters who wanted to see them wiped from the earth. Each and every one. Did she have company in that department?

She'd have to figure out what that lone wolf had in mind, with a little help from friends, that is. About half an hour earlier Becca sent her a text. She'd pulled off I-90 and onto the Division Street exit, meaning she now headed north. Given she'd hit the city at rush hour, it would still be at least two hours before she would make it to Jeni's house halfway between Clayton and Chewelah. The drive itself wouldn't be bad once she got north of Spokane, where the traffic cleared, and the roads were free of the stop-and-go pattern that defined the city. In fact, Becca would love the beautiful rolling hills, abundant trees, and frequent farms. For someone like Becca, who worked with the dead, the beauty of nature always came as a welcome sight. Good for the soul.

Two hours wasn't long, yet she still willed Becca to drive fast. Now that she understood what had settled here, she wanted to kick ass and take names. Put the old golden rule into practice and do to them what they'd done to her. The drive to take everything that they held dear and turn it into ash was overpowering. She fingered the small vial she wore on a sterling-silver chain around her neck. It held all that remained of Avery, a few grams of ash she'd saved from the cremains scattered into her wife's beloved ocean. Unable to let her go entirely, even as she deluded herself into thinking that coming here showed she'd done exactly that. She might as well have the word denial tattooed on her back.

Maybe if she could destroy those who'd invaded her sanctuary, she'd be able to put her past to rest. A free soul who managed to find the good in everyone, Avery never had a problem seeing the light. She'd been the ying to Jeni's yang, and it had worked in a way that amazed her. Losing her had broken her spirit. No one would ever connect with her the way that Avery had. A once in a lifetime kind of love. Not that she dismissed ever falling in love again. It could happen. It just wouldn't be the same.

That she hadn't been able to save Avery filled her with guilt every waking moment. That she couldn't move on. That she couldn't forgive. Avery would hate all of it. She'd be telling Jeni to pull her head out of her ass and get a life, and that's exactly what she should do. The should-dos weren't exactly her strong suit. Unlike Avery, her head ruled, not her heart, which didn't always result in the kind of happiness that had defined the woman she'd loved. Only once did Jeni take a chance. She didn't regret it, only wondered if she'd ever be able to do it again. So far, it wasn't looking good on that front.

Memories tumbled through her mind as she drove toward home, and when an emergency call came over the car radio, it startled her. A second later her cell phone rang, and Trent's voice held both urgency and irritation. "The old Greenwald place is in flames."

"The Greenwald place?" Like she would know what that meant? "Why call me? There's a fire department around here, right?" Not really a question, given she'd seen the beautiful new fire station built off the highway. The county did a credible job when it came to first responders.

"Of course, and they're on site."

Maybe they did things a little differently here. In Portland she'd never respond to a fire. "So…"

"So, it's arson."

Still didn't make sense. Fire investigators handled arson. "Not a sheriff's department issue, and besides, how could they make that kind of determination at this point?" They might have crack firefighters up here, but making the call this early felt like a pretty bold assumption to her.

"The gas cans sitting in the front yard were the first clue."

"Okay, I'll admit that's a fairly good clue. Still don't get why you want me to roll on a fire. I'm a cop, not a fire investigator."

"Fair enough, though I'm guessing you'll be real interested in the body they've dragged out."

Okay. Now he had her attention. She pulled into the first driveway she saw and turned around. "On my way, if you'll tell me exactly where I'm going."

"Out at the Greenwald farm."

"New girl," she reminded him.

"Oh yeah, my bad."

As she drove, Trent did his best impression of a navigation system.

❖

Isa stood far from the house under the cover of the thick pine trees and watched the fire consume the structure, flames waving from the windows and lighting up the sky. Coming back here tonight instead of charging in last night, had been a stroke of genius, if she did say so. A shame she had to destroy such a lovely piece of architecture. Someone loved the house, given its condition, but there were times when a tragic loss couldn't be avoided. The sacrifice became part of the effort toward something far bigger, although no human would be aware of that fact. They would wonder what happened to the *family* that had purchased the expensive piece of real estate. The single body the beefy firefighter had been able to drag out would provide them not a single clue. No head came with the body, and fingerprints would yield nothing. Zion had been a ghost in this century, and his death would be just as ghostlike.

She had seen it happen before. The big house would remain a burned-out shell sitting black and ugly as the grass turned yellow and the tidy shrubs returned to nature until one day when the county took over ownership because of unpaid taxes. Someone would subsequently buy it in a tax auction and demolish the crumbling walls. Life would go on, the story of the mysterious unidentified victim a thing of local legend.

Just about to turn away, she hesitated when the deputy she faced off with last night pulled in and parked not far from one of the fire trucks. Deputy Sheriff Jeni Denton, previously Detective Denton with the Portland Police Department, got out of the unmarked car. Her appearance at a fire piqued Isa's curiosity. Zero effort had been put into hiding the fact that the fire had been intentionally started. Her fingerprints were all over the gas cans left sitting in full view on the tidy green grass. Careful handling of the cans to preserve any evidence they might hold was in current progress. All their attention to details would be for nothing. Their databases would yield nothing because her fingerprints didn't exist in a single one. No one could accuse her of not being careful or paying attention to the world when it came to personal identifiable information. As things in the world changed, so did she.

The fact that she'd left evidence of the arson in a county this size pretty much guaranteed the response would not be limited to the fire department. It made sense that law enforcement would also show up, though it surprised her a little it would be Deputy Sheriff Denton, given how briefly she'd been part of the sheriff's office.

It pleased her a bit to see the woman with her straight back and athletic body. She wore the tools of her trade with particular ease, and Isa found that intriguing. The way she had stood her ground when they met in the killing field, knowing full well that Isa could have ended her life with ease, impressed her. It had been a really long time since she'd found anyone interesting, vampire or human.

Denton joined another deputy, who had been talking with one of the firemen while gesturing toward Zion's body, or what was left of Zion's body. To see the remains of the powerful vampire tossed on the grass like trash filled her soul with a huge amount of satisfaction she would have missed had she not waited to return with her sword and the gas cans. She hated him for what he'd done to Avery, while at the same time acknowledging that Zion had acted on orders. He might have been the one who killed her, but responsibility for Avery's death lay on someone else's shoulders, and he too would be held accountable. Soon. One down. One to go.

Activities here would go on for hours, and she still had work to do before the next sunrise. She put her phone to her ear and turned away from the now-smoldering house. At first, she held her head down while she talked, and then she slowly raised it. She ended the call and put her phone into her pocket as she stared straight at the spot in the shadows where Jeni stood glaring at her.

It might have been better had he actually gotten some rest. George presumed Josef took that route, as he'd heard nothing from him for hours. Either he rested or he hunted. Actually, as he thought about it, one would be as likely as the other. As the most discreet vampire in his inner circle, Josef had never quite mastered the control needed to be one of the truly great. Actually no one had, except himself. That's why he stood above all others now and forever. That's how he toppled all the arrogant bastards who thought they were better than he.

The slumber he should have embraced wouldn't come to him. Daylight or not, he could have chosen to go home and did not. No great hurry existed to get back to the quaint little community up north. Good to be here in a city where life flowed around him twenty-four hours a day. Though Boise wasn't in the same category as cities like LA or San Francisco, it still held an allure that energized him more than sleep. At his age, he could go for days without the need to lie down. Each day without rest affected his strength in some degree, just not enough to be meaningful. That quality too set him high above all other vampires. He knew of no one else who possessed a similar reserve.

Alone and watching the lights of the city from the comfort of the elegant suite, he pondered his previous actions. Not the order to destroy Olive, for that had been a most appropriate decree. Her demise would send ripples through the vampire nation, as well it should. As he intended it to. The message would be clear and effective. Others wanting to attempt to undermine his authority would think twice, allowing him to return to the north and finish his business with Isa.

Except here, alone with his thoughts, he wondered if he really would be able to end it. Insurrection from the underlings, absolutely. When it came to Isa, his confidence wavered. Complicated didn't even begin to describe his feelings when it came to her. Part of him hated her for her total betrayal. Another part of him, as much as he loathed to admit it, had never stopped loving her. In his human years he had been well-educated, wealthy, and powerful—the son of a very important man from a revered family. After he had been turned, he'd leveraged every advantage available to become a man who played on the same field as kings.

One summer evening late in the eighteenth century, he'd laid eyes on Isa and discovered something magical. Up until that point George believed his status and drive made him immune to pedestrian emotions. With everything available to him, what more could he possibly need? He most assuredly did not fall in *love*. All adored him, and he took advantage of that fact by filling his bed with adventurous partners. Some he turned in order to keep them close, some he fed on, and others he simply killed. It all depended upon his mood and how much each could benefit him either by standing at his side or what he could take from them, willing or not.

What Isa brought to him included wealth. But what drew him to her in the beginning wasn't her money. Plain and simple, he fell for her. He remembered well the first time he watched her as she danced with a young military man at one of the ubiquitous parties nobles like he were obliged to attend. The boredom in her gaze as it swept the room in a way that said she did not want to look in her partner's eyes was familiar to him. A smile crossed his face because he knew exactly what she needed, and it still resonated with him. It hadn't been the cocky young man who guided her across the floor. That one had been an inflated fool with no idea of what a woman like Isa required. She had needed a real man, one who possessed years of life experience, who truly understood the nature of good and evil, pleasure and pain.

In the beginning he believed her to be a perfect match for him in every way. She appeared to accept him at her side as the man destined to be there. The more time he spent with her, the more he realized something in her remained amiss, and he believed he knew what. She came from a rich and powerful family, and yet she stood apart from them, as if she didn't really belong. That dawning realization morphed into an epiphany that she would become one of them. Her destiny would be to stand at his side for eternity.

During the course of his life George made very few mistakes, and those he did, he corrected with ease. All save for one. He wanted to correct that mistake as he had all the others—to destroy her and walk away with the same feeling of vindication he relished on every other occasion. Like with Olive.

He shook his head and turned from the window. All the arguments to the contrary would change nothing. To walk away from Isa and feel anything except anguish would never happen. Despite everything she had done to him, despite her blatant and ongoing betrayal, George loved her and always would.

Even if forced to turn her body to ash.

CHAPTER SEVEN

Jeni waited until Trent walked away, then turned from the fire and started to stroll toward the woods. Though the urge to run hit her hard, she didn't want to attract attention. The closer she came to the deep darkness of the tree line, the more the hairs along the back of her neck stood on end. Like an electrical current ran through the earth beneath her feet to send its charge into her body. No such rational explanation. No downed power line anywhere. Exactly what caused it or, better, exactly *who* caused it wasn't unknown, at least not to her anyway. In the last ten years she'd developed an almost preternatural ability to sense the presence of vampires. Like right now.

The shadows were dark and deep as she moved away from the activity at the smoldering house, wrapping around her as though she attempted to hide beneath a cloak of invisibility. The vamp might have been eluding humans for a long time, but if she thought she could hide from Jeni, she would soon discover her mistake.

"I know you're there." Jeni stopped close to the edge of the property, where the landscaping ended and the forest began. In this part of the country, nature and civilization existed in close proximity. She liked it.

The vampire, who'd been talking on a cell phone, put it in her pocket and turned to face her. Jeni almost audibly caught her breath. Fortunately, she caught herself. An experienced law-enforcement officer and vampire slayer did not publicly display emotion.

She wanted to hate this woman, as she'd hated every night creature she'd encountered in the years since Avery's death. Yet this one, this beautiful one, had an aura about her that she'd never encountered before. To allow herself to be rattled wasn't okay, except she just couldn't help it. Everything about her felt off. The unmitigated evil that she'd experienced in every previous battle didn't exist here. That didn't seem possible, and there it was just the same.

Not the time to be giving a vampire the benefit of any kind of doubt. Act first, analyze later. A good rule of thumb except, once again, she arrived here unprepared. The call that interrupted her trip home brought her here without the specialized tools required to go up against a vampire. They remained at home. Silently she berated herself for not taking five minutes to run to the house and grab her weapons. Regardless of what else happened, she vowed that this would be the last time she arrived anywhere in this county without her special weapons.

"I am not hiding from you."

"Then why stand back here in the dark all dressed in black? Looks like hiding to me."

"I didn't want to get in the way of the firefighters."

"Bullshit."

"Believe it or not. I don't care."

"Yet you care about that." She inclined her head in the direction of the house, or what remained of it. "Otherwise you wouldn't be skulking around back here watching it burn."

"Always have liked a good bonfire."

"Are you always such a smartass?"

A smile ghosted across her face, there one second and gone the next. Or at least that's what Jeni thought she saw. Kind of hard to be sure in the dark. "Yes."

Damn it, she wanted to smile too. Fortunately, she caught herself. No way would she allow this woman to get under her skin. What the hell? A woman? Not hardly. She stood toe-to-toe with a vampire, not a woman. Why then did it seem so difficult to lump her in with the other vampires she'd tracked? The ones she'd used her very special weapons on?

For just a second, she closed her eyes and remembered what had brought her to this path to begin with. She touched the neck of her shirt and felt the tiny vial of ashes through the fabric. Avery. As her name rolled through her thoughts, a chill coursed rippled down her spine. The perfect bucket of water to throw on her odd emotions when in the presence of this vampire. It gave Jeni the boost she needed.

With her eyes still closed, she asked, "Who are you?"

"Isa. Just Isa."

Surprised that she actually got an answer, Jeni opened her eyes. "God damn it," she muttered as she stared into empty darkness.

Isa didn't have a good explanation for why she'd stood there as long as she did. It felt an awful lot like she'd been waiting for the cop to show up, and then when she did, Isa continued to stall. It wasn't clear in her mind if she wanted to see her or bait her. Either way it didn't bode well. She'd never before trifled with someone intent on destroying her or, at the very least, her kind, even if not directed at her specifically. She'd always been a firm believer in a quick dissuasion of those humans who took on the mantle of vampire hunter, their good intentions aside.

From the early days in the society when she didn't belong, she'd been forced to pretend. Smart enough to grasp that if she didn't blend in, she'd end up just like the humans who fought against them or the vampires who publicly refused to conform. Oh, she refused to conform all right, and her only saving grace came in the form of a damn good façade. Until she made her move, no one had been the wiser.

The unfortunate side effect of pretending meant that for a very long time she had been forced to hunt like the rest of them. Unlike her peers, she didn't kill, and she didn't turn a single human. Not once in all her years. She took only what she needed to survive, and nothing more. Of course, saying she didn't turn into a killer might be a bit of misnomer. In truth, she didn't have any qualms about destroying her own kind, particularly those who sat at the heavy wood table in a magnificent room in Moscow. Between George's thirst for power and her mission to destroy the Redcap Society, that table had only one chair left.

If George hadn't yet been made aware of her presence, tonight's barbeque would get his attention. She would like to say all she had to do was make sure she had his notice. That would be a lie.

When she killed Zion, it gave her a rush, which probably made her a bad person. In the big picture, she could live with it. Besides, after she completed her work, everything would be finished, and then she could rest at last. Whether or not she would be remembered as good or bad just didn't matter. No one would mourn her anyway. As the old saying went, that ship had sailed a really long time ago.

Isa glanced back to where firefighters continued to work. Far enough away not to be visible to Jeni, she had heard her curse before she'd turned to rejoin the responders. They all appeared to be in it for the long haul, which made her decide she had enough time to take an unplanned trip. Curiosity pushed her hard, and she didn't ignore it, even as ill-advised as her idea might be. As a rule, she tended to be a little more careful than what she had in mind. Caution went a long way toward maintaining a lengthy, stake-free life. Sometimes, one had to go on a hunch.

The trip to Deputy Denton's house took less than ten minutes, and getting in through the back door a fraction of that time. The house wasn't anything spectacular and lacked the essence of a real home. In short, it didn't look or feel like anyone really lived here. A small table in the kitchen had two chairs, cellophane wrappers from two cupcakes, and a partially empty bag of Skittles. One lone coffee cup had been left on the countertop. The living room wasn't much better. A black leather sofa with several unpacked boxes on the cushions. No attempt at making it a warm and inviting space.

It said cold and transient to Isa. The kind of place teenagers would sneak into for an unsanctioned party.

Upstairs, she first came to a bathroom and ignored it. She doubted anything in there would prove to be of interest. The second door opened into a fair-sized bedroom. Completely empty, the walls were painted a pale yellow, and the hardwood floors were a shining dark walnut. The spacious room had potential, with big windows that promised plenty of light. She suspected, potential aside, it would sit empty for a good long time. The second bedroom surprised her. It featured a queen-sized bed covered with a dark-blue comforter that went nicely with the pale-blue walls, a dark wood dresser, and a single nightstand. The wooden blinds on the windows were closed, shielding it from prying eyes, the complete opposite of the kitchen. This room had more life to it than any of the others she'd seen thus far. She stepped farther inside and stopped. "Oh, damn."

Things had just gotten way more complicated.

❖

George's phone rang as he sat in the comfortable chair staring at the city lights and remembering the good times. Daylight would come soon, and another productive night would end. Those vampires not captured at the house and who'd made the unwise decision to assist Olive had been located and dispatched. His work here now complete. The fact that someone dared to call him came as a surprise. He had important business to focus on and didn't want to be bothered with mundane matters. His underlings would not disturb him. Nothing could be so important that it couldn't wait until he returned to his temporary northern home.

Under normal circumstances he would ignore the call. These weren't exactly normal times. He answered on speaker, leaving the phone on the table next to him. He closed his eyes and barked, "What?"

Vinton's voice was high-pitched, and his words came in frantic Russian. All he made out was *fire* and *Zion*.

"Slow down, Vinton. What exactly are you trying to tell me?" The overly dramatic boy-toy who, a favorite to warm his bed for the last several decades, caused a tic to start in his right eye. Beautiful and entertaining, Vinton could also be melodramatic, which after a while became tiresome. Especially tonight when he had many other things of greater importance on his mind.

"Zion is dead."

He straightened in his chair. "What did you just say?" Of all his soldiers, Zion would be about the last one to meet his demise in that sleepy little town. They all called him the gladiator for a reason.

"Zion is dead, and the house is gone."

"Vinton, you're not making any sense. I haven't been away long enough for a disaster of that proportion to have occurred. Impossible. You are mistaken."

Vinton took several deep breaths that came over the phone so loud he could swear he stood next to him. The familiar drama. "Me and Keller went out for something to eat, and while we were gone, something happened. I don't know. Had to be her. I mean, who else would do something like this? That bitch killed Zion and burned down our fucking house. What should we do, sir?"

His hands clenched into fists. Vinton wasn't wrong in his read of the situation. The only one smart enough to get the jump on Zion would be Isa. How long had she had been stalking him before she made her move? Had she realized the house had become his most recent base of operation? Maybe Zion hadn't been her true target. Maybe she'd made a guess about his arrival in the county and had come looking for him, only to take Zion as a consolation prize. She would do something that vindictive. Her pretty face hid a mean streak he knew well.

Outside the window, the lights of the city sparkled. Oblivious humans walked on the sidewalks below, a steady stream of nourishment, too foolish to realize how vulnerable they were to his kind. A beautiful sight that up until a couple minutes ago, he'd been enjoying. Amazing how a simple call turned everything into shit.

Why did she have to be so troublesome? Why had she always been so contrary? He would have made her his queen, and she would have wanted for nothing. His love, hers for eternity. Why couldn't she just accept what he had to offer? He'd asked himself those same questions a thousand times since she'd left him in such a public way, and the answers never changed. They never would. He could wish it to be different for a thousand years, but it never would be, and that left him only once choice.

Isa had to die.

CHAPTER EIGHT

Jeni blew out her breath as Becca pulled up in the driveway right behind her. The encounter with Isa disturbed her for a couple of reasons. First, because she'd been at the fire hiding in the shadows, and that was just weird. And second, because she hadn't taken off when Jeni first approached her. Also weird. What the hell kind of vampire was she anyway? Given Jeni's calling as a hunter, a smart vampire would give her wide berth.

It all confused her. In other circumstances, how to deal with this would be clear. Right now she didn't have a clue. Inside the house, her custom cases held all the tools she needed to send Isa to the great beyond once and for all. By all rights, she should be anxious to go grab them and get to work. Except she found herself curious enough not to want to follow through on the hunt for this particular vampire. At least not yet. Curiosity about what made Isa so different and interesting pressed harder than the drive to destroy.

Interesting? That didn't sound like her at all. Maybe all the nice dry air up north, a noticeable change from the humidity common in Portland, was getting to her, and thus Becca's arrival came at the perfect moment. She'd get Jeni back on track, and together they'd put an end to whatever happened to be going on around here.

"Hey, sister. Are you just getting home?" Becca opened her rear passenger door and took out a suitcase.

"Long story. Come on inside, and I'll give you the CliffsNotes version."

"As long as you've got beer and chips, I'm all ears. It was a hell of a long flight, although the drive up here wasn't too bad."

She smiled and waved her toward the door. "I got ya covered."

After an hour, a bag of chips, and two beers, she managed to bring Becca up to speed. Becca set her second, almost empty, beer down on the box she'd moved from the sofa to the floor. It made a handy makeshift end table. "So, you're telling me you've come across a nest of vampires up here in God's country, and one of them is turning out to be your BFF. Am I getting that straight?"

"I think best friend is a bit of an exaggeration."

Becca shrugged as she took a pull on her beer. "Doesn't sound that way to me. You've faced her twice and haven't so far dispatched this Isa character. I gotta say, that's not like you. Up until now, you've been the kill-first-and-ask-questions-later kind of girl, if you know what I mean."

Jeni stared at the bottle she turned in her hands. "I've let others go."

"One. You let one go, and he's been our inside man for the last five years. That's different."

Jeni thought about that for a minute. When she'd first met Bob, she'd found huge amusement in his name. Really…Bob the vampire? Even though he was a full-on creature of darkness, she smiled every time she thought of him. Turns out, he was a very unwilling member of the dark clan, and while he found distinct benefit in being part of the society that had taken Avery away from her, he harbored no real loyalty to them. When she found herself in a corner with one of the chosen ones, he became her go-to guy. He would never put himself into a position that might endanger his life, but he didn't hesitate to pass along intel when he could.

"Maybe she's another Bob."

"There's only one Bob, and I sure don't recall him ever burning down a house full of his *family*. He might not appreciate having been turned into a vampire. I also don't see him ever doing anything that might put his life in jeopardy. Beyond helping us, that is."

Becca had a point. Bob possessed a clear survivalist mentality, and he wasn't a killer. Probably one of the biggest reasons they'd been friends for a long time. "I need to think about this. There's just something about her that makes me stop short of putting her down. I always want to put a stake through a vampire's heart, and then when I'm in front of her, I don't. I can't understand any of it. Could be I'm getting tired and soft after a decade of hunting. Maybe I need to do a little more research and find a place to live where I'm not going to run into vampires."

Becca had just taken another pull on the beer, and it went spewing out of her mouth. When she could talk, she looked over at Jeni and shook her head. "Sister, the day you get tired or soft is the day I put away my body bags."

"You know that's weird, right?"

"You know you're never gonna stop, right?"

Isa got back to her house, dropped into a chair, and put her head in her hands. How in the world had something like this happened? Once again, she thought about how the odds of it had to be astronomical.

First Zion's appearance, although that part didn't bother her so much, given the opportunity it provided to do to him what she'd wanted to for a very long time. When she had come in contact with Zion on earlier occasions, the less-than-ideal conditions prevented her from exercising the ability to dispatch the bastard. Waiting until the right moment became the only smart option.

Funny to think on how, at first, she'd liked him. Despite his fight-first tendencies, Zion actually had a quick wit and was, as the saying went, definitely easy on the eyes. Later she witnessed how he used every one of his traits as a lethal weapon. His long years meant he'd had ample time to refine his techniques and, in the end, he became a master manipulator. Everyone, at least at first, fell under his spell. By the time his true colors were revealed, for most, realization came too late. They were either recruited or destroyed. For Zion, no ground in between existed.

She'd committed the ultimate sin by turning her back on George, and Zion took that kind of betrayal personal. He would consider it a badge of honor to be the one to drop her bound and gagged at George's feet.

To see his face tonight brought rage that burned hot. By this time, she'd have thought some of that intense emotion would have faded. Her zero-to-sixty reaction proved that to be a quite wrong assumption. Instead of suppressing the emotion like she would normally try to do, she went with it, her blitz demonstrating sheer beauty in its execution. Zion never had a chance to react, and the silver blade separating his head from his body sang in the air. The fire became like icing on the proverbial cake, even if the first responders were able to pull his headless body from the pyre.

The only disappointing part came when she discovered the rest of the house empty. That confused her as well, considering Zion never traveled alone and they'd been there the night before. Who would carry his luggage? Who would procure his lovely young women? No, his minions were sure to be about somewhere, and imagine their surprise when they returned to the house. That would have been worth sticking around to see.

She'd also thought she might come across signs of George, yet she couldn't find a hint of the arrogant bastard. If Zion had come here, George either had been here too or wasn't far behind. Actually, that thought made her smile. How she would love to see George's face when he was ultimately informed of the recent passing of his dear friend and soldier, Zion. Those two were tight. He'd be royally pissed.

She sobered when she thought of the rest of the night. Tears pooled in her eyes, and she didn't try to hold them back. To let go enough to sob wasn't something she allowed herself to do except in rare circumstances. The sight of that picture on Jeni's nightstand had a physical effect as real as though someone had punched her in the chest. The last thing she'd expected to see when she entered that house was a picture of Avery. Though given what she'd dug up on Jeni, stupid on her part.

She put her hand to her neck and pulled out the heart-shaped diamond pendant she'd worn every moment for the last ten years. The night Zion killed Avery, the beautiful stones had lain sparkling against Avery's pale skin. When she'd taken it from around her neck after everyone left, Avery's blood smeared the necklace. Her tears mixed with the water as she cleaned the diamonds. Isa wore it now as a reminder of both her failure and her mission.

For a long time, Isa had lingered in Jeni's bedroom, staring at the wedding photo on the nightstand. Avery and Jeni, both younger, their faces filled with the kind of joy true love embodies. In one glance, her questions about Jeni were answered. The rage that flickered just beneath the calm and professional surface put everything into context. As she'd left Jeni's house, it hit her once more how cruel the universe could be.

With a deep breath, Isa stood and headed to her own bedroom, where no beautiful photographs could remind her of what she'd lost. Daylight lurked just beyond the horizon, and she needed rest. She'd figure out tomorrow how to convince Jeni they were on the same side.

❖

He stretched out in the bed, sinking into the softness of the expensive mattress. Fatigue finally caught up with him, and he gave in to the need to rest. After he had summoned Josef several hours ago and made his request, his right-hand-man delivered in a spectacular fashion. The three women in his bed were young, beautiful, and willing. Exactly what he needed to take his mind off the loss of a good man.

It would have been fun to satisfy himself fully and drink all three of them completely. He didn't plan to stay long enough to clean up the mess, so he exercised restraint, content to make do with sex and sips. The women accepted his request with an assumption of a run-of-the-mill kinky bent. Some mortals proclaimed themselves vampires wearing custom dentures, black clothing, and god-awful eyeliner. They drank blood as if that would allow them into the ranks of the undead.

He would let the pretty trio believe him to be one of the warped and that his request consisted of nothing more than kink. Being the professionals that they were, the ruse quelled any questions, and besides, when Josef pressed large bills into their hands upon departure, they would be more than satisfied. It worked for him. It worked for them.

Caressing the bare backside of the brunette with the waist-length hair sent a rush of blood to his groin again. Plenty of time to satisfy his renewed lust. As he pushed up to mount the brunette from behind, the door burst open.

"Get up," Josef said as he began throwing clothes at the three women. "You need to go."

"I'm not done," George bellowed. "Get out." How dare he barge in here and start demanding action. Clearly, he'd forgotten his place.

Josef shook his head. "They have to go. Now."

He rose to scream at Josef for his misplaced arrogance, and then something in his eyes alarmed him. "Get up. Move it." He pushed at the women as he too rolled out of the bed and stood unabashedly naked. "What's happened?" He directed his question to Josef. The women were racing out the door, reacting to the urgency and unspoken threat in his words. They understood danger when they heard it. Again, the beauty of working professionals. They didn't hang around waiting for explanations.

"Not now."

He understood. No elaboration would be forthcoming until they were alone in the suite. "I'll shower." He went into the massive bathroom and stood beneath the water, washing away the touch and smell of hours of sex with humans. When he came out with just a towel around his waist, Josef stood alone in the middle of the room.

"We have a serious problem."

"Tell me something new." Josef needed to get to the point. His abrupt disruption of the earlier orgy already made him aware a severe problem existed.

"Three more of our best are dead, and the estate in the Hamptons has been breached."

CHAPTER NINE

Jeni came awake with the same sense of unease as when she'd finally hit the bed about three. As soon as she'd arrived home from the fire, she'd detected something off in her room. Last night, she'd been unable to put her finger on it. Now, as she stood next to her bed and turned toward the nightstand, where a shaft of daylight slashed across the surface, her breath caught. An unreasonable urge to grab her gun tore through her.

For at least a full minute she stared at the line in the dust. The wedding photo that always sat near her bed had been picked up and put back down. It caught her attention because the intruder hadn't replaced it exactly as it had been, and the disturbance in the dust attested to that fact. Had Jeni been one of those OCD housekeepers who wiped down furniture every day, she never would have spotted it. This was one of those moments when her dislike of housework paid a dividend.

She pulled on sweats and a T-shirt and then went out to her car. Daylight hadn't taken over fully yet, and a quiet she'd never experience in the city caused her to stop. She liked it. In a way, it provided a sense of comfort.

Using the light on her phone to illuminate the trunk, she grabbed her fingerprint kit and took it back into the house. Not everyone carried a kit in their car, but with friends who had special skills, like Becca, she had all sorts of non-standard equipment at her disposal. More than once, it had come in super handy, like right now.

Back in her bedroom, she gloved up and picked up the picture frame. Unless the culprit had wiped it down, any fingerprints should still be there. Hers would be present, of course. Her gut told her they wouldn't be the only ones.

Her total concentration bore down on the careful work, and soon she had four cards with prints. She studied them for a long time, pleased with her work and the careful lifts she'd been able to accomplish. If she hadn't decided to be a cop, forensics might have been her next go-to career. It wasn't until she had her tools put away that she noticed Becca standing in the doorway.

"You dust random pictures routinely, or are you just practicing the mad skills I taught you? I like your work, by the way. Pretty clear I'm an awesome teacher."

"Someone was in my house last night."

Becca tilted her head and studied Jeni. "And you know that because of your picture?"

"Damn right."

"You're good, but come on, Jen. Nobody's that good."

She couldn't blame Becca for her skepticism. In her shoes, she'd feel the same way. "You're damn right I'm good. I'm much better at this than I am at cleaning my house, so when someone picks up a picture from my nightstand and doesn't put it back in exactly the same spot, the dust tells the story. That's what we detectives call good investigative skills."

Becca laughed. "Yeah. I stand corrected. I think you are that good. I'm telling you, sister, if you ever decide to give up your cop thing, you have a job in my department. You'd love living in Maine."

Jeni wasn't so sure of that. Her West Coast roots ran deep. "Duly noted, though you wouldn't let me carry my gun, and you're aware of how attached I am to my Glock. Come on. Get dressed. We'll grab some coffee at the drive-through close to my office, and then we can go run the prints."

"They'll just run the prints for you?"

That question stopped her. Becca had a point that she'd let go right over her head until she mentioned it. Being on active duty here for far less than a week didn't give her a whole lot of pull on anything. Marching in and saying "run these for me" probably wouldn't fly or make her very many friends. In Portland, where she knew everyone, she could get away with it as long as she didn't abuse their good will. She grimaced and said, "Maybe not."

"Give them to me." Becca held out her hand.

"I can't ask you to do that for me. Not only is this not in your jurisdiction, it's not even in your state."

"Get over yourself. Give me the damn prints." Becca grabbed the four cards and headed toward her room without another word.

Jeni didn't even try to stop her because she appreciated the focus of a woman who'd just shifted from rolling out of bed to being on the job. She followed and shook her head when she saw Becca pull a familiar tablet out of her case. "You're always thinking, aren't you?"

Becca patted it. "Can't do the job if you don't have your tools. I got three brothers, and I can quote the Boy Scout motto like the best of 'em."

"Always prepared."

"Always." Becca winked.

She watched as Becca powered up the tablet, scanned the fingerprints into an app, and sent them to a coworker and friend in the forensic unit of the Maine State Police, where Becca now worked. "Is there anything you can't do?" It sure didn't seem like it to Jeni. The woman constantly surprised her.

Becca tossed her tablet onto the rumpled bed and grinned. "Haven't found it yet. Now, let's go get that coffee, and you can show me the amazing sheriff's department you left for."

Isa waited with the same patience that got her through all her years with George. The sun would drop behind the mountains, and her favorite time would descend. By that time, George would have been apprised of Zion's demise. How long would she have before he stormed into town? He would rightly see this as a personal affront, and though she always had a problem with Zion so destroying him came with personal satisfaction, her bigger goal had been to direct her rage toward George. He'd been the one to take everything from her, and she'd wanted to return the favor for a long time. Zion's demise brought with it a win-win in her book of accounts. A little gift from the universe.

To protect others like Avery also played into the mix, and she'd do whatever needed to be done to make certain it happened. What she couldn't quite figure out? What to do about Jeni. Once more she fingered the necklace as she considered strategy. While she walked away from their first two encounters alive, she wasn't dumb enough to think she'd be able to every time. Jeni came across as wicked smart and with a giant chip on her shoulder. Isa got why, and that meant she'd have to exercise a great deal of care from here on out. That woman had a score to settle and would never understand the lengths Isa went to in her attempts to save her wife.

In many ways she understood. For anyone aware of their existence, Isa was one of *them*. No distinction needed to be made about her affiliations. Good vampire. Bad vampire. Was there even such a distinction? Could someone who existed on the blood of humans ever really be classified as good? She wanted to think of herself that way, but honestly, even she wasn't sure, so how could she expect Jeni to be any different? Hard to convince anyone of her basic goodness if she wasn't sure herself.

To reach the finish line, she had to let that way of thinking go. It would be in her best interest to stay out of Jeni's sight and quietly complete what she came here to do. No need to convince her of anything. Afterward, she would move on, as she always did. This time she might even find her final resting place. Once George was dispatched to the hell he deserved, the foundation of the society would be on rocky ground, which he could thank himself for. By destroying anyone with the potential for leadership, he had put the society at risk in the event of his demise. It would likely crumble of its own accord. That would be enough for her, and once she had achieved that goal, her work would be done. Changing the world in any meaningful way was not within her power. That much she'd learned in her long life. It had a way of recovering from every catastrophe that hit, and this would be no different. To destroy George and undermine the society would be enough. Her mark made, she could then die satisfied.

With all the players coming into view here in this small northwest community, she had a job to do, and she would complete it regardless of what else did or did not happen. It would be easier, however, to have someone in local law enforcement on her side. Through the years, friends of the human variety had not only been helpful, but they had also made her journey a little less lonely. That idea gave her a thought and maybe a little more time. She picked up her phone and scrolled through her contacts. She did love modern technology. How things had changed in strange and unusual ways since her birth. Many of them good. More than a few frightening.

She found the number she looked for in her contacts list and tapped it. "Well, how's this for a voice from the past."

At the sound of Patrick's lilting Irish accent, Isa smiled. Her accent had faded away over the many years, and to all who met her these days, she sounded a hundred percent American. Fine with her. Thoughts of her origins were not often welcome. It brought too much ache even now. "Hello to you too."

The tall and slender Interpol agent with the thick black hair and dark eyes had been her friend since the night she saved him from a society elder smitten with the intriguing man. She'd dispatched the elder and made a friend for life in Patrick. He could access resources on a global level she'd never be able to touch. Since that day nine years ago, not once had he turned down a request for help.

"What pile of shit have you stepped in this time?"

"Maybe I called to say hello."

"And maybe I'm Colin Farrell, and all the ladies are swooning over me."

He could make her laugh, and while he joked, the ladies did swoon over him, not that he paid attention. For some reason he seemed to be somewhat oblivious. She supposed when the right woman swooned, perhaps he would finally take notice.

"All right. All right. You got me. I do need your help. There, happy?"

"Always appreciate confirmation of my brilliance." He laughed before turning serious. "You've got a lead on George, and you want me to use my mad skills to track his steps."

"Are you using some of your Irish magic?"

"Darling, I am magic. Just ask anyone."

She laughed again. "I have missed you."

"As I, you."

"He has been here, along with Zion, and I want to get to him. There's one thing I have to tell you first."

"What did you do?" He sounded just like her mother when she caught Isa doing something not allowed.

"I might have killed Zion and burned down George's fancy new house."

He laughed harder this time. "God, I've missed you. Tell me where you are."

"Strangely enough I'm in a small town in Northeast Washington state."

"The US?"

"I am still in the US."

"All right. Here I thought you might have come to your senses and returned to the Land of Saints and Scholars. Pity. Well, I happen to have some excellent contacts in America I can tap into. We'll track the bastard down, and maybe this time you'll get lucky."

"It's not luck I need. It's your brand of magic."

"Well, then you are lucky, because that's something I can help you with."

❖

As soon as Josef put the phone to his ear to redirect their flight plan from Chewelah to the East Coast, George's cell phone rang. By the time he put it back in his pocket, his hands were shaking to such a degree that the exit of the human women turned out to be a good thing. He might have torn them into pieces if they still remained within his reach.

Josef put his own phone down and turned to stare at him. "What?"

"My house in New Orleans has been taken over."

Shock showed on Josef's face. "That took some balls."

He sighed. One minute Josef could be commanding and the next, quite simple. The trait became irritating after a few decades. No time for that now. Bigger things to deal with, and his mind whirled as he thought through strategy. "The rebellion that appears to be taking up speed has to be stopped. Olive had more working with her than we knew. We must divide and conquer. Who can we trust?"

Josef seemed to consider the question, and then a light came into his eyes. "Besides you and me, I'd say Sam and Douglas."

He agreed with Josef's assessment. Sam had been a particularly satisfying addition to his inner circle. Active in special forces when he first met him, it had been one of those times when he moved without hesitation. He'd brought Sam over that very night, and the man proved to be everything he hoped: a loyal and dedicated soldier in his army. Douglas came with a brain that would astound anyone at an Ivy League university. While impressive, it could also be problematic in some circumstances. Not in his case, however. Douglas loved him with a passion that he appreciated, and he showed his affection to him on many occasions. That was all he needed to keep the brilliant vampire in his back pocket, as the people here loved to say.

"Yes, excellent. You go with Douglas to the Hamptons, and I will assist Sam in New Orleans."

"Are you sure? Douglas will be crushed that you decided to go with Sam. You know how pouty he can get. Not very attractive on a guy with that big a brain either. Such a prima donna."

He gave Josef a look, even though he shared the sentiment. Douglas would indeed pout. Despite his sure-to-be-hurt feelings, he would also go with Josef simply because George asked him to. Love had a way of making the otherwise defiant become compliant. "Just do as I say, and tell him I'll call for him when I return from New

Orleans." The promise of time alone with George would further cement cooperation by Douglas.

Josef gave him a little salute. "As you wish."

Absolutely as he wished. "Once we've restored order, we'll return immediately to the northwest and take care of the problem there. Now, leave me, and finish making the necessary arrangements."

Josef did as commanded and left the room with his phone already pressed to his ear. It wouldn't take him long to get everything in order. Just as well. The sooner they got things back under control, the better. This recent turn of events distracted him, and that made him angry because he wanted his entire concentration on the Isa problem. Sadly, this kind of thing happened. He ran a tight society and despite his iron-clad control, still there would always be those whose discontent took the form of rebellion. No leader ever received one-hundred-percent blind obedience. The mark of a good leader, however, came in the way he handled the moments of discontent. For him that meant swift and lethal justice. Just as with Olive, the aggressors would find themselves reduced to dust and their hold on immortality gone. If he could, he would channel Vlad the Impaler and put their heads on stakes to warn all the others of what would happen to them if they tried to defy him. The world of today would frown on such a display of absolute power. Pity.

He wished he could have solved the Isa issue before all this happened. When something unexpected upset his timeline, it grated on him. In the old days, his anger would have gotten away from him, and blood would have spilled. A lot of blood. Years of experience and practice made him a stronger and better man. His control of the rage came as a surprise to those who challenged him. They saw his outward calm demeanor as a reprieve. A fatal miscalculation in every instance.

After he boarded his private plane an hour later, he dropped to the fine leather seat and closed his eyes. Sam waited for him at the Lakefront Airport in New Orleans, and it wouldn't take long to reach his property. The dissidents at his estate would be waiting for them. No real concern there. Sam's skills seemed to have no limit. As a human, his talents abounded. Once turned, he'd become incredible. If not for Sam's unshakable loyalty, he might have to worry about him picking up the mantle of discontent. Once a soldier, always a soldier.

His mind shifted away from the problems in Louisiana and to the northwest, where she waited. What would be on her mind as she opened her door and saw the delivery on her porch? He smiled as he envisioned her facial expression. He did so enjoy giving surprises.

CHAPTER TEN

Jeni did as Becca commanded. Always a good idea to keep the forensic specialist hydrated and happy. She made her own cup of coffee and then left her alone with all her high-tech equipment while she went in and showered. When she came back out dressed for work, she'd made a decision. Becca would be coming with her, newbie or not. They would undoubtedly view at it as inappropriate. She didn't see it that way. What was it the folks here didn't understand? A war was rolling toward this beautiful little burg, and she didn't intend to be caught off guard. If that meant bringing in help from her former life, then so be it.

She drank her own cup of coffee and thought about what happened. Despite everything she'd learned about the vampire community, she still found her encounters with the vampire who called herself Isa unusual. Like talking to any vampire wasn't unusual. Funny how her view of the world had taken a shift.

Crime happened here just as it did everywhere. Not like in the regional large urban areas of Portland, Seattle, or Spokane, where it occurred with more frequency and violence. Before deciding to move here, she'd studied the stats for the area, and bottom line, they were good. Those stats were part of what pushed her toward the decision to join the sheriff's office.

Burglary didn't happen regularly, particularly in an occupied home, and people around here paid attention. Within twenty-four hours of moving in, every nearby neighbor had stopped by to introduce themselves, and many had brought baked goods. Not something that would happen in her old neighborhood, and she appreciated the gesture by her new community. Given her new neighbors' level of awareness, somebody would have noticed a break-in or unusual activity around her house.

Leaving the unavoidable question of who could come and go so easily? Only one person came to mind. Correction, only one vampire came to mind. Isa made the trek to her house after she'd left Jeni at the fire, making a calculated bet that Jeni would be there for a few hours. That bet paid off, and she'd had plenty of time to look around to discover what she had no clue. Isa obviously had a game plan, only how Jeni figured into it was a complete mystery.

Perhaps Jeni's awareness of her true nature had precipitated the break-in. Jeni knew about her, so she wanted to know about Jeni. Quid pro quo. Made sense in a way. If that indeed explained the intrusion, it should also explain her interest in the wedding picture. Except it didn't. No one besides Jeni would care about that, because no one here even knew Avery. She'd been gone a long time now, and Avery had been a California native, something she'd loved to tease her about, given the sentiment of many Oregonians about California transplants. The memory of teasing her made Jeni smile. God, she missed that.

She'd just finished her coffee and was still thinking about the home intrusion when Becca rushed in, wearing jeans and a Yale sweatshirt, her computer case slung across her body. "Locked and loaded, partner. Let's get this party started. Lead the way."

Trent sat in front of his computer when they walked into the office twenty minutes later. His attention appeared riveted to whatever was up on his screen, and she wasn't sure he even heard them arrive.

"Good morning."

"Yeah," he said without moving.

"You need some privacy?" The office didn't give anyone much personal space, and judging by the intensity of his focus on his computer, they might be intruding.

"Huh?" He still didn't turn his face away from the computer screen.

"You working on something confidential? We can find some-where else to be if necessary." They could always buzz back to the bright-blue latte stand a couple miles away and grab a couple drinks. While the paint on the stand might hint at color selection by a tod-dler, Jeni already discovered they made damn fine espresso. It im-mediately became her go-to for her caffeine addiction.

"Huh? What? We?" He finally looked up, and surprise registered in his eyes when his gaze fell on Becca. Something else crossed his face. Interest maybe? She didn't know him well enough yet to be able to accurately decipher his facial expression or body language. "Who's your sidekick?"

She smiled. "Trent Whitmire, this is my good friend and investigator extraordinaire, formerly from the Portland ME's office and recently of the Maine State Police Crime Lab, Becca Farconi. Becca, this is my partner, Deputy Sheriff Trent Whitmire."

Trent jumped up and extended his hand. "Nice to meet you. What do you do for the crime lab?"

"I'm a forensics specialist in Maine, and before that I worked as an investigator for the medical examiner's office in Portland. That's where Jeni and I became pals. My cross-country move means I don't get to see her often, but I'm happy to be here now."

"Quite the resume. So, what brings you to our corner of the world?"

Becca gave him a big smile as she accepted his outstretched hand. "Vampires."

Isa didn't want to leave during full-on daylight, even though she'd been unable to rest since putting in the call to Patrick. His trip would be a long one, with several plane changes before he'd finally land in Spokane. He'd be lucky to get by with fifteen hours of flight time, give or take. Then he faced the drive from the Spokane International Airport north to the lovely house right between Clayton and Chewelah. At least traffic wouldn't be a problem because he'd be driving late into the night. Not that it became an issue this far north any time of day or night.

Pacing, she glanced out the window, shocked to see a florist delivery van pull into her driveway. Must be lost, because it had no other reason to be parked there. No one had given her flowers in over two hundred years, and she didn't care to think about the one who'd last brought her some. She'd much rather forget that time in her life.

The delivery man got out of the van and walked around to the back of it. When he returned, he carried a vase filled with red roses. Her stomach dropped, her steps to the door on feet seemingly filled with lead. She could have ignored the doorbell and pretended this wasn't happening. Not her style. She didn't avoid things because they were difficult. In the end, that only created more problems. Better to face things head-on and as soon as possible. Funny when she thought of how long she'd planned her confrontation with George. Not exactly the as-soon-as-possible scenario.

When she opened the door, a youthful man in a black jacket and ball cap with the florist logo handed her the vase. The envelope pinned to the clear wrapping around the roses protected a small card. The sweet scent of the roses sent her thoughts reeling into the past. She shook her head clear before she had time to fully form the memories she loathed to revisit. Instead, she took the vase, closed the door, and carried the flowers to the kitchen. She pulled the card from the small envelope, read the first line, dropped it to the counter, and stared down at the tidy printed words.

When she is absent, I no more
Delight in all that pleased before
The clearest spring, or shadiest grove:
Tell me, my heart, if this be love?

When fond of power, of beauty vain,
Her nets she spread for every swain,
I strove to hate, but vainly strove:
Tell me, my heart, if this be love?

"You bastard," she whispered as tears fell, smearing the ink on the card decorated with a border of delicate flowers. The name signed at the bottom of the card was unnecessary. Only one person would send her the last two stanzas of this poem, "Tell Me, My Heart, if This be Love," by George Lyttelton. George, her Sir George Carew, had beguiled her with the entire poem when he had set his sights on her oh so many years ago. In those early days, she'd found comfort in his refined appearance, lofty words, and chivalrous actions. Tall for his time, and handsome, with wavy hair and eyes so dark they were almost black, he impressed every person he met regardless of their station. Everything about him screamed strong and capable. And oh, how he could recite poetry written by the most talented romantics of her time, as well as sing and play music so beautifully it could bring people to tears.

He had taken her in, just as he had her family. The beautiful poem had provided her a kernel of hope for a life that she could at least tolerate, the best she could hope for. Now he used those same words of love as a warning. In those few stanzas he informed her that he knew where she lived and would be coming for her. Oh yes, the chess match would soon see checkmate.

She wiped away the tears, furious that his games could still affect her. He knew how to wield cruelty. "Bring it on, Georgie boy. Bring it on," she said as she shoved the flowers into the trash. "I'm waiting for you as well."

She stared down at the crushed crimson petals, which reminded her of a night when blood had flowed across the polished floors of the magnificent manor where her life changed in an unimaginable way. The centuries of anger, regret, and frustration all boiled over into resolve. She straightened her shoulders and stood as tall as possible for someone as small as she. The stone floors would run red again, she vowed, only this time the blood of her family would not turn them crimson.

By the time the wheels set down on the tarmac in New Orleans, the fury inside George neared the point of explosion. The flight had taken far longer than he wanted, seeming to happen in slow motion rather than with the kind of compressed time schedule a private plane should be able to deliver. For what he paid for this plane and its top-notch crew, no acceptable excuse existed for the delay. So much needed to be done, and his presence back in Washington State was imperative. This stop, while critical to getting things back on the level, bothered him. Its timing was way too calculated, like she'd orchestrated it all from her perch up in that droll little northwest county. All of it seemed designed to keep him otherwise occupied and off his game. That would be just like her. She liked to screw with him in that way.

Not a young man when he met her in the late eighteenth century, he had still appeared to be a twenty-something lord. It had been easy to play her and her family like a well-tuned violin. In fact, he'd actually played a well-tuned violin for them, and they'd all ooh'd and aah'd at his spectacular skill. One could master anything, given enough time, and by their first meeting, more than a century at honing his skills had passed. Her money and beauty and lands made her irresistible, as they did for a bevy of titled men who also vied for her hand. True, George understood then, and still did, why she would never be in the marriage game. The way she looked at other women told him everything, and he hadn't cared in the least. He'd wanted her, and so he struck a deal with her father, as was the custom. Clean and simple. Regardless of how she felt or what she wanted, Isa would belong to him once the marriage took place.

And then the most unexpected thing happened. He fell in love with her.

He hadn't anticipated that development, which ultimately created a true mess of things. Though he'd pondered it a million times since, he'd never figured out how it came to be like that. At his age, he needed no one, human or vampire, and to find himself needing her had been frustrating and still was. The one failure in his long life had to remain a secret, at least as far as his falling in love with her went. The knowledge of her betrayal of him, and of the society, could not be contained, and that was as it should be. If any of the discontented caught even a hint of his weakness for her, they would test him even more.

That Isa would never love him came as the truth he'd been forced to confront despite all his efforts to make her feel the same way about him as he did her. Instead, she nurtured his hope for love and eternal companionship by a lie she'd perpetuated for years. No one else had ever been able to deceive him as she had, and for that he could never forgive her. The old saying that for every action there had to be an equal and opposing reaction came into play. She put the first action into play, and he intended to come at her with the opposing reaction. Had to be done, though a piece of him would always belong to her. All for another night, however. Currently, other matters demanded his attention before things got worse.

Sam waited for him at the bottom step of the plane. His imposing height would intimidate even the most ferocious monster. Combine it with his exceptional skill set, and Sam emerged the winner in every encounter. He didn't doubt that tonight would end no differently. Together they would quickly restore order to the St. Charles Avenue house. He hoped to return to the plane and be back in Washington before the sun came up again. Imperative to minimize these delays posthaste.

He got into the passenger's seat of Sam's SUV and stared out the dark-tinted windows as he negotiated the streets of the city with a skill that belied the fact he didn't live here. Another of his impressive skills. He could blend in anywhere and make even locals believe him to be one of their own. It would be a sad day if Sam ever turned on him and he had to put him down. To date, George saw nothing except unwavering loyalty. Sam remained one of the true.

"How do you want to do this?"

He glanced over at Sam, whose attention remained on the roads. His profile alone radiated confidence. "Right through the front door." He refused to sneak around his own house. That property and everything in it belonged to him. His largesse allowed others to stay there and tend it for him. Without him, while they might be well off, it was not at the level his properties allowed. Instead of stabbing him in the back, they should be grateful. Using his home like the Alamo didn't reflect a single ounce of gratitude. Their reward would reflect just that.

"You sure?"

"I'm sure."

Sam pulled to the curb when several fire trucks screamed past them. The squeal of the sirens and the whoosh of the air as the emergency vehicles passed them sent an uneasy feeling through him. An alarming thought crossed his mind. "You don't think…"

"No…" Sam said without any real force behind the word.

In the distance, flames shot into the sky. His beautiful Garden District home couldn't possibly be the source of the fire that sent brilliant light into the sky. His eyes met Sam's. "Step on it."

CHAPTER ELEVEN

Jeni had heard the term "swallowed her tongue" all her life, yet she took it as just a saying. When Becca told Trent they were looking for vampires, she nearly swallowed hers, for real. If she could figure out how to recover from that one, she'd be in good shape. The only problem? Her new partner currently stared at her like she'd just been released from the mental-health unit of the local hospital. Well, the first week appeared to be starting off with a bang. Good grief. It had been one crazy thing after another since she got here. She needed to perform a little damage control, quick.

"Okay," she said at the same time she gave Becca the "shut up" look. "It's a little more complicated than that."

Trent leaned back in his chair and locked his hands behind his head. His eyes sparkled, which, like swallowing her tongue, she didn't really think possible until right this moment. "Oh, please, explain it to me. I'm all ears."

Becca didn't flinch or back down. All business. "Yeah, well, you've been invaded."

"By vampires?"

"Indeed."

Jeni threw up her hands. This situation had somehow gotten totally out of control. "Will you two give it a rest and let me explain."

Becca shrugged, and Trent just kept staring at her. "By all means, partner. Explain."

She looked around, grateful for the office they inhabited. In this outpost of the sheriff's office, the two of them shared a small space in the larger building housing several other county employees. She got up and closed the door, making it feel like they were holed up in what could be characterized as a small office or a large closet.

"Easier said than done. How to say this so it will make sense?" Becca had put her in a difficult position and knew it. Typical Becca. She liked to handle things head-on, which helped make her an excellent forensic investigator. That she didn't usually pipe up about vampires to total strangers made this a bit different. In fact, she rarely ever mentioned their existence to anyone besides Jeni, because neither of them wanted people to consider them insane, which was exactly how they sounded like right now. Things could get weirder. Or not.

"I have an idea to make it clear and understandable." Becca leaned against the closed door, her eyes moving from her face to Trent's and back again. "Pretty simple really."

"Becca…" She gave her the *look* again, which didn't seem to faze her any more now than it did the first time.

"You have a nest of vampires in your midst, Mr. Deputy Sheriff."

"Vampires? Like Count Dracula with his big black cape and pointy teeth." The smile he was barely holding back made Jeni cringe.

"Oh, dear God," Jeni muttered as she sank into her chair and closed her eyes. So much for her job here in Stevens County. She'd lay odds on being released from duty about ten minutes after Trent called the sheriff. She'd never been fired before, and this could soon be her first experience with it.

"Yes and no," Becca said while Jeni thought about how her future in law enforcement had just crashed and burned. "No black capes. Lots of pointy teeth."

"So, tell me, partner, is your friend a little on the cray-cray side?"

She opened her eyes and locked onto Trent's. Tempting to agree with him and save her own ass. Unfortunately, just not the way she rolled. "As much as I'd like to say yes, so it explains this entire conversation, I'd be lying. She's not crazy and, in fact, is one of the most brilliant people in my circle. That's why she's here now."

"Really..." The way he dragged out the single word said volumes, kind of along the lines of "you might want to turn in your badge and gun" volumes.

"You don't have to believe me," Becca added.

"And why not?" The look on his face told Jeni he wasn't believing a word either one of them said.

Becca didn't back down. "Because I can prove it."

Jeni swiveled in her chair to face Becca. "What?" News to her, and she'd think if Becca was going to make that kind of announcement, she'd at least give Jeni a heads up beforehand.

Becca shook her head as though disappointed in a particularly dense child. "Come on. You gotta know that girl in the morgue wasn't the first or the last?"

"But, the house..." Jeni still wasn't quite following, so maybe she was that dense child.

"She burned down the house. Do you think for a minute there aren't more?"

"Maybe she killed them all." It's what Jeni hoped, even if she didn't really believe it.

Becca shook her head. "Right, just like in Oceanside and Portland and Bakersfield. Two down and twenty to take their places."

Damn if she didn't have a point. What they'd learned over the last decade told them vampires always traveled in groups, so even if the fire had taken out a vamp or two last night besides the headless body the firefighters carried out, more were either already here or on their way. They'd also learned that vamps didn't do well with the murder of their own kind. They took the eye-for-an-eye thing literally. She'd been watching her own back since she made her first vampire kill.

"What are you two talking about?" The sparkle in Trent's eyes had faded. Now they were narrowed and intent. At least they had his attention, not that she believed for a minute they had his trust. Becca's mention of the fire had done exactly what'd she anticipated.

What the hell, she figured. In for a penny, in for a pound. "Becca's right, Trent. And no, I'm not crazy either. Hate to break it to you, but we're about as sane as you're going to find. What's happened here is you've just inherited as a partner one of the few law-enforcement officers in the world who possesses one very important piece of intel."

"And that is?"

"Vampires are real."

❖

Isa found the day unbearable. More than anything, she wanted to get out and finish this. Several times she walked to her bed and lay down, hoping for the slumber that typically restored her. Oblivion would be a welcome respite from obsessing about killing George and his band of merry men. Today making the effort to get even an hour of rest became futile. Good thing she could go for days without rest or she'd be in a lot of trouble.

While she stretched out on the comfortable mattress, her mind filled with images of George, and despite all her efforts to turn her thoughts to other things, his face refused to abandon her. The third time she tried and failed to banish him, she gave up. Might as well concentrate on more tangible issues, like how to deal with him once he returned to town. She had a good idea where he would be arriving too. He'd always thought of himself as beyond common, which meant he wouldn't travel like most people. In short, he'd have a luxury private plane, and given the existence of a small airport in the area, that's how he'd come and go. So predictable. One thing about George she could always count on: he never changed.

Was Josef still attached to George like industrial-strength Velcro? The man gave new meaning to the term annoying. He stuck so close to George she suspected he even went into the shower with him to wash his back and his balls. Yes, Josef would still be at George's side, so taking out George came as a two-for-one. She'd have to drop them both, not that she minded. George had it coming, as did Josef, through guilt by association.

If the day would just end and she could see headlights turn into her driveway, all would be good. With Patrick's help, they'd clean up the mess here in no time. Zion was already out of the picture and George's command post a pile of charred rubble. She'd accomplished a coup both necessary and enjoyable. She couldn't deny the latter, though that made her just a little bit petty. She could live with that. It'd been amusing to watch George's hideaway burn to the ground. Then when the cute cop showed up, that held its own kind of entertainment.

She still had to figure out how to use the cop. Well, that term didn't quite capture it. She knew how to use her. How to convince her to help remained the only unanswered question. For hours she tried to figure out this situation, and as of this moment, she had precisely nada. Typically, she came up with game plans a lot quicker and easier—her superpower.

Except plans were what had gotten her into this mess in the first place. She'd planned to *let* George catch her back when her family still lived. By her calculations, he'd have been a good bet in the husband department. Handsome, rich, and a decade or two younger than those her parents eyed, George came in as the triple threat and the least objectionable, given she would be forced to say yes to someone. The deal made, her parents were much pleased. George's wealth and property went far beyond their expectations, and he'd shared his riches, at least initially, with her family.

And then one night everything went to hell.

"No, no, no," she whispered to herself as she paced. No more memories. Her focus needed to be on the future. Like, the immediate future, and what would happen once darkness fell and Patrick arrived. Far more important than looking backward at things too late to change. The old Prayer of Serenity actually captured a great deal of truth.

Finally, the shadows outside her window started to lengthen, and the sun made its way toward the western mountains. Armed with research that had helped her get through much of the sleepless day, ready now for whatever the night might bring. Tracking a powerful leader like George would be almost impossible for the average person. If someone knew what to search for—and she did—they could glean a great deal of information. She smiled. When he found out she'd been aware all along that he'd had his minions tracking her too, he'd be furious. The trail left made his search pretty obvious. Wherever she hunted, George hunted too. All over the world.

George's big problem? He always showed up a day late.

George stood on the balcony and stared out over the city. The sights, the sounds, the smells, usually invigorated him. One of the reasons he'd owned the home here for well over a hundred years. Its loss could not be calculated in dollars. Feeling motivated tonight, though not in the way he usually did, he took in a deep breath and turned his back on the night. Things to do and places to go.

They could have flown north even in the daylight. His decision not to spoke to his mastery of emotion and strategy. His anger at the destruction of his home in New Orleans made him want to rush into a course overflowing with vengeance. To send heads rolling and blood flowing through the streets. Tempting as it might have been, a man with his level of intelligence knew better than to give in to that kind of raw emotion. Too dangerous and exactly what the dissidents would be hoping for. He had no intention of giving them what they wanted.

Instead, Sam secured a suite at a high-end boutique hotel, and he cleaned up, satisfied his blood lust and physical lust, and sent the willing, and well-paid, women on their way. In this city, getting what he wanted was never a difficult task. After they were gone, he indulged in some rest. By the time he rose, the sun had begun its descent in the sky. He dressed and readied himself for their ultimate return to the Northwest. The raw anger that consumed him last night had cooled into something far more dangerous. Those who wronged him would find that out.

Before he lay down, he had ordered Sam to forego his own rest in order to track the location of the offenders. As he'd done in Boise, he wanted them wiped out before he left New Orleans. Justice would be swift and final. This rebellion seemed to be taking on legs, and he'd cut them off at the knees before he'd allow an epidemic to spread throughout the society membership or, worse, into the vampire population as a whole. No time for the logistics involved with a full-out war. Prior to his flight home, he'd take the offensive and stop whatever brewed here in this glorious city of jazz and magnificent food.

Back inside the suite, he poured himself a glass of the fine bourbon brought up earlier and left in the sitting area. His hunger sated; he enjoyed the flavor of the thirty-year-old spirits. If one intended to indulge in something besides blood, it might as well be a drink as fine as this bourbon.

At the sound of the lock disengaging, he turned toward the door. As he expected, Sam came in and secured the door behind him. He might have been at work for hours, but it would be hard to discern from his appearance. The suit he wore had been cleaned and pressed, his hair as perfect as always. Outside of his love for George, the other thing that Sam cared about most were his looks and physical prowess. He spent a good deal of time in gyms and in front of mirrors. The old-wives tale about vampires having no reflection held not a grain of truth. Sam could attest to that and, in fact, stopped in front of the mirror just inside the door to adjust his tie, pausing ever so slightly to admire himself.

"What did you find out from Josef, and don't tell me they destroyed the house in the Hamptons too." Time to finish his business here in New Orleans and be on their way.

Sam turned away as if he didn't want to meet his eyes. "Not exactly."

He set down his half-empty glass of bourbon and studied Sam's face. He didn't like what he saw reflected in his eyes. "What exactly did they do?"

"The house is still standing."

"And…" Jesus Christ. He expected more from Sam. At the moment he acted like Josef at his most annoying, and one Josef was plenty. Just spit it the hell out. Obviously, he'd forgotten how valuable George's time was.

"And they killed Douglas."

CHAPTER TWELVE

I'm pretty sure Trent's going to see about having me committed." Jeni took off her gun and placed it in the lockbox she'd installed the day she moved in. Safety remained forefront in her mind regardless of what else might occur around her.

Becca rummaged in the refrigerator, backing out with two bottles of beer. She handed one to Jeni. "You worry too much. He's almost there."

"Oh, right." She twisted off the cap and took a long pull. She'd seen Trent's expression after they'd come clean about everything, and belief wasn't what she'd witnessed in his eyes. He'd probably already called the sheriff to warn him of the mental case he'd hired away from the Portland PD.

"Would I steer you wrong? Did you see him? I'm telling you, my pretty friend, he's intrigued."

"Intrigued by a couple of crazies." They must have been looking at different eyes. She didn't see intrigue. More like "get me away from them."

"Don't knock it. Crazy has its appeal."

She didn't want to go there. She'd seen far too much crazy on the streets. "Not to cops."

Becca waved a hand dismissively. "Don't be a grandma. Nothing to worry about."

Arguing with her was a lot like trying to argue with a teenager. Never give up. Never give in. "I can count on one hand the number of people I've brought into my nightmare, and not a one of them has been a cop. I don't think now's the time either."

"I'm kind of a cop."

Jeni shook her head. "If you mean that you can figure out how people died, like cops try to do, then, yes. You're kind of a cop."

"There you go. So, pulling Trent into the fold isn't all that far-fetched."

"It could be career ending. I'd like to keep my new job, thank you very much. Unemployment isn't on my agenda right now."

"I'm gonna say it again for your own good. You worry too much." Becca smiled as she took another pull from her beer and winked.

Jeni gave up. This conversation just went around and around. She wouldn't win with Becca. No sense trying. Might as well drink. After all, the beer was cold and good.

Besides, better to roll with it now and do the damage control later. Maybe she'd manage to salvage her career, and maybe she wouldn't. Not like she'd be the first person forced to make a mid-life career change. If only she knew how to do something else besides be a cop and investigator. Could vampire hunting turn into a bill-paying job? Probably not, given that no one with a checkbook would back up a "we have wooden stakes, will kill vampires" agency. Would make for an interesting business card and website, though.

Becca took her by the shoulders and stared into her eyes. This time the expression on her face turned serious. "He's going to be an ally. Trust me. I felt it the second I stepped into your office, and that's why I popped off."

It that were the case, it would be the first time she'd seen Becca display clairvoyant abilities. Her considerable skills tended to be more of the scientific type. "You're not a psychic."

"Nope, but I have damn good instincts, and you just have to defer to me on this one. You, of all people, know I'd never put you in danger. It might have sounded like I was just popping off. I wasn't. There is a method to my madness."

"I don't see that I have a choice at this point." Yes, she knew exactly how pouty that sounded.

"That's where you always get stuck, my dear friend. You always have choices. You might not like them, but they always exist."

"Sometimes I really hate you."

"Yeah, it's a curse. Now let's make a plan to wipe these sons of bitches off the planet."

Isa still had a little time before Patrick arrived, and she figured if she ever had a chance to get the cop on her side, now would be it. Might as well give it a go. Better than sitting around here waiting and doing a big fat nothing. Even as a young noble, she'd preferred action to inaction. How her mother had hated that about her. No sitting before the fire in pretty dresses with her hair piled on her head in glossy waves while embroidering delicate little handkerchiefs. In her mind sitting around while servants brushed and pinned and adorned her hair had been a silly waste of time when a single braid took only a minute to do and was far more practical. Another thing her mother hated. Her hand went to the braid she'd needed no servant to complete.

"Sorry, mother," she said in a whisper. "Still more practical."

She parked her car down the road from Jeni's and studied the house just as she had the first time she'd come here. This time, however, a second vehicle, with rental plates, sat in the driveway. Not her new partner, who would be more likely to have come in a county car. One possible scenario occurred to her, as complicating as it might be. Jeni'd called in someone from her past. She'd hoped to make her appeal to the woman *mano a mano*.

Had her great idea just fallen flat? Her gut told her to go for it, while her brain told her to turn around and wait for Patrick. When she'd stopped the car, she'd pulled the key from the ignition, intending to walk the short distance to the house. A quiet approach or, if to be honest about it, a sneaky approach. For a couple of minutes, she fingered the key in her hand and debated. Should she? Should she not?

With a sigh, she put the key back into the ignition and turned it. The car came to life, not with a roar, but with the quiet power of a well-made automobile. One thing she appreciated about this century came in the form of transportation. Air travel might be a modern wonder that she loved. Quick and easy, with overnight flights that suited her well. The miracle of airplanes aside, cars were the best. She loved to drive, and the night roads were amazing. No fighting heavy stop-and-go traffic, and out here, she could push well past the posted limits. Once in a while she suffered a traffic stop, and each time it happened, she smiled. Had her father been around for automobiles, he would have loved them as much as she did and been proud of her daring driving. She paid each ticket without protest. Besides, every few years she got a new driver's license with a new name. Even after all these years, one had never existed in the name of Isa Meyer, and it never would. She didn't try to hide the name given to her at birth, but she didn't leave a paper trail either.

Since the day she left, the Redcaps had hunted for her. They would come for her just as they knew she came for them. Unlike Isa, however, George didn't work very hard to cover his tracks, probably because he believed himself untouchable. He'd been born smart, and centuries of existence had improved upon what nature endowed him with. Give a guy like that hundreds of years of knowledge, and he would be relatively bulletproof. A chink in every armor existed, though, and she'd exploit that chink.

She had news for him and his cronies. She'd been born smart too and also enjoyed a few centuries' worth of education. That was why, right now, she took the high road and decided to give it up. Patrick would be here before too long, and she could return with him at her side. To approach Jeni on an even playing field would be a much better idea. The two-against-one odds didn't work for her. She preferred to go two on two. Assuming, of course, that car with the rental plates had brought only one passenger.

The time to make the wise choice arrived. She put the car in gear and drove past the house slowly enough to get a good view, though not slow enough to attract attention. Not that it made a difference because the blinds were closed. A smart departure from the last time she'd been outside this same house. The people who left their curtains or blinds wide open at night always made her wonder. Anyone trying to look inside could, and that invited trouble. If they really knew about what existed outside in the darkness, they'd not only close the window coverings, but they'd board them up, soak them in holy water, and nail a cross or two to the boards.

Alongside the safety factor also came privacy. She treasured it because, inside the society, it didn't come cheap. It had an "all for one and one for all" kind of mentality, except for those in the highest positions, like George. He'd made the mistake of bringing her into the inner fold. Hard as it had been, she'd found a way to swallow her hatred and disgust for a very long time, the scars of which would most likely stay with her until the end of her days. Her actions concealed a higher purpose, and soon all the sacrifice would pay off. Now if only Patrick would hurry the hell up and get here.

The cool part came when she walked back into her house and realized exactly how long she'd been gone. Sitting down the road from the cop's house watching and hoping for any glimpse had felt like minutes, when in reality hours had passed. A little surprising no one wondered about her and called for a safety check. Must have a little bit of stalker skill inside her, a useful tool in this instance. Kind of creepy in the bigger picture.

Nonetheless, it wouldn't be long now before Patrick would join her. She sure hoped he grabbed some sleep during the very long journey from his house to hers, because she needed him to hit the ground running. She meant that literally. The sooner they could finish this thing, the better. With him at her side, they'd be more than ready for George and any of his entourage.

When the lights of his rental car at last flashed in her driveway, she almost cried. How much she'd missed having someone she knew and trusted close to her. The last ten years had been lonely in many ways. She'd made some friends and allies along the way. No one special and she missed having someone close. Not that she actually needed someone to love. Good friends, yes. A true love, no. She'd reconciled herself to that lifestyle long before she ever left the society to begin her journey of vengeance. Love simply would never be in the cards for her—no time and too much work.

"You beautiful vamp." Patrick wrapped her in his arms. If she were inclined toward men, he would definitely be at the top of the short list. Handsome, with an honest and true spirit, he won big.

She returned his hug. "I'm so glad to see you."

He pushed her out at arm's length and studied her. "You sounded stressed on the phone, but you look bloody fabulous."

He had a way of making her feel good, even when all looked bleak. "You're just trying to get into my pants."

"Ah. Now there, you've done it again. Shot a man down before he even had a chance to make a decent run for it."

"God, I've missed you." She hugged him again.

He kissed her cheek. "Come on, beautiful. Let's get this party started. I slept most of the trip here, so I'm ready to kick some vampire ass. No offense, of course."

Her wish had come true, which made her breathe a sigh of relief. "None taken, of course. Now, come. I have much to tell you."

Following George's earlier orders, Sam tracked those responsible for burning his house down, their current location now known to him. That was the good news portion of the messages he brought with him when he opened the door to George's suite. The bad news made him more irritable than he already was. His intent since rising had been to destroy the assholes who burned down his house and get back on the plane to Washington. They would indeed travel north again, only instead of heading west, they'd fly east. Those who'd killed Douglas must also be held accountable, and they would. He'd see to it personally. A good leader did not allow treason to go unpunished. Examples had to be set, even if that sometimes meant setting them east, west, north, and south. Besides, he'd sent in the soldiers to tamp down the resistance, and it hadn't exactly worked out. Not only were his properties being threatened, but now his best supporters as well. That could not—would not—be tolerated.

The other disturbing piece of the development from the Hamptons made him equally angry. Since his initial contact with

Sam reporting the demise of Douglas, there had been radio silence from Josef. Calls to his phone went straight to voice mail. Not like Josef at all, particularly when the call came directly from him. The phone he held in his hand weighed heavily, and his eyes narrowed as he stared at the silent tool.

"I have their location." Sam held up his phone to show the location app.

George nodded, appreciating the clarity the map provided. "Names?"

"Got them." He swiped to a notes app and then handed him handed the phone for a better view of the list of names. Most he recognized. Several he didn't. His hand tightened on the small device.

"They're recruiting." That development he didn't expect.

Sam frowned. "Looks that way."

He loosened his grip before he crushed Sam's phone. "Shall we put an end to their recruitment program?"

Sam smiled, and he liked the spark in his eyes. He might not be able to count on everyone in the society, but the one who stared at him now with bloodlust in his expression would never betray him. It almost made him hard, and if they'd had more time, it might have. Sam, a man's man who'd made a mark in the human special services, was also a vampire who didn't hesitate to give in to pleasures of the flesh. Tonight, sadly, would not be one of them. Too much work to get sidetracked by pleasure. Well, not exactly true. The destruction of the defiant would be a distinct pleasure.

The blood roaring through his body propelled him forward. His fingers twitched and his breathing came quicker. "Take me to them." Sam did exactly as he asked.

An hour later blood dripped from his hands, and he stood over six bodies, smiling. They should have known better, yet they'd believed they'd weakened him. So foolish and ignorant of his true greatness. Up-close and personal he'd shown them that he possessed not an ounce of weakness or mercy. Strength allowed him to dominate the society and topple those previously in power until he stood alone. In the intervening years his strength only grew until no single vampire could stand on level ground with him. This moment proved that beyond any doubt.

George tipped his head to the sky. The sun would be up in a few hours, and the sunlight would turn the bodies of these betrayers into ashes. He'd like to stay and watch the show. Not this time. By late tomorrow, he could give witness to a much more interesting show, and then once and for all, order would be restored. All future challengers would think twice before lodging campaigns of rebellion.

He licked the blood from his fingers while Sam waited for direction. "Call and make certain the plane is ready to depart."

Sam's expression reflected concern. "You don't wish to stay here and go at sundown?"

"No. I wish to go now. A little surprise for the naughty boys and girls up in the Northeast. They won't be expecting us."

"Us?"

"You're coming with me."

Sam's confusion cleared, and a brilliant smile crossed his face. "You got it, Boss." He put the phone to his ear and started talking.

CHAPTER THIRTEEN

The knock at the door surprised Jeni, especially when she glanced up at the clock. Three thirty a.m. She sat up and stretched, the kinks in her neck crackling like rice cereal. They'd talked until after one, and while Becca made the effort to crash in the guest room on a real bed, she'd fallen asleep on the sofa with her tablet still in her lap and the knitted blanket Avery made for her years ago pulled up to her chin. For a few seconds she breathed in deeply, sure she could make out Avery's scent on the treasured gift. Of course, she'd cleaned it many times during the last decade, so the possibility was remote. Even so, she found it comforting, and that was good enough.

Darkness still reigned outside and that dictated caution. As law enforcement, whether uniformed or not, being on call 24/7 became a way of life. Early on in her career, she'd learned the skill of moving from deep sleep to fully dressed and ready to go in a matter of minutes. One of those moments was right now. At the same time, if Trent or any others in the sheriff's office needed her, they'd have called first. Cell phones had done away with surprise appearances in the middle of the night, meaning whoever waited outside her door wasn't related to her work. Another knock made her jump up.

Before she opened the door, she retrieved her gun. Curiosity took her to the entryway. Professional training told her to act smart. It would be stupid to allow access without being prepared. When she looked through the peephole, she took a step back. Good grief. For a tiny woman, this vampire had some pretty big balls.

Her initial thought was spot on. This had nothing to do with her job. She pulled open the door but didn't loosen her grip on the gun. "What in the hell are you doing here?" Only when the door opened wide did it become clear that Isa hadn't shown up at her house alone. Great, just fucking great. Two vampires. Her earlier decisions to not destroy Isa were about to come back to bite her in the ass.

"I need to talk with you."

"Now?"

"Right now."

"Is that why you're here with reinforcements?" Two humans against two vampires? They didn't stand a chance, particularly considering one of said humans currently slept in a bed down the hall.

A tall, handsome man stepped around Isa and held out his hand. "Inspector Patrick Shea, DCB Dublin." The accent and aura that surrounded him were both intimately familiar.

She didn't take his hand, which would be warm because this man didn't hail from Isa's cohort. He wasn't a vampire. Definitely one from her family. "Interpol."

He let his hand fall as he shrugged. Didn't seem too offended by her refusal to acknowledge the small social gesture. "Yes. Garda as well."

She'd forgotten that the Garda, Ireland's premier law enforcement, staffed their Interpol office in Dublin. She'd known a few in her time. They were good. Very good. "What are you doing here and with her?" Jeni nodded toward Isa without meeting her eyes.

"Can we come in?" He flashed her a smile that would melt resistance, if someone were inclined to fall for male charms. She suspected he used that look routinely to gain trust and cooperation. Barking up the wrong tree here for more reasons than one.

"You didn't answer my questions. Either of them."

The good inspector had failed to thaw their icy confrontation, and Isa stepped in. "We really need to talk with you. Please."

"I don't think so." She started to push the door closed. The last thing she wanted to do was to invite a vampire into her house, even if she did show up with a fellow brother in blue, albeit from across the pond. It stopped short. Becca's hand on the door prevented it from closing all the way.

"Let them in," Becca said from directly behind her.

She congratulated herself silently for not jumping, because when her friend had come up behind her, she didn't hear a thing. Not so good for someone with her kind of training. In fact, downright embarrassing. "No."

Becca put her other hand on Jeni's shoulder. "Let them in." Her voice was soft.

"Why?"

"Because I know this guy."

Isa stared first at the woman behind Jeni and then turned to Patrick. "What does she mean, she knows you?"

"I don't have a clue." The narrowed eyes and lips pressed together confirmed his words.

The woman stepped around Jeni and held out her hand to him. "Hey, Patrick. I'm hurt you don't recognize my voice. Becca Farconi."

His face cleared and he smiled. "Well, shit. You're even prettier than your voice."

"I always thought you'd have red hair."

"Tsk, tsk. Now you're just profiling."

"Guilty, I'm afraid. Black suits you." She smiled, and, like Patrick, the change lit up her face.

What was going on here? This wasn't a meet-and-greet event. Not even close to the reason they were here. "Your date.com hellos can come later."

Patrick turned toward Isa, confusion once again clouding his face. "What in the hell are you talking about?"

"Isn't that what this is? You two met on a dating site, and this is the first time you've seen each other face-to-face." Dating sites were one of the modern marvels that Isa found abhorrent. Probably a bit hypocritical of her, given that she'd spent centuries pretending to be something and someone she wasn't. Still, she found the whole online-dating thing a recipe for lies and deception. She preferred the pure face-to-face meeting thing for anyone she might want to get intimate with. Not that anything like that had happened for her in a good long time. Not likely to happen in the future either.

Patrick's laugh echoed a touch louder than Becca's. "Dear God, no. Do you honestly think all of this…" he waved his hands to encompass his body from head to foot, "has trouble getting a date? "My darling Isa, you've been out of the game too long."

"We met through work." Becca held the door open despite Jeni's clear unwillingness to let them into her home. While she made it clear in their previous encounters that she knew of the vampire world, perhaps she didn't realize the old folktale about a vampire being able to enter a home only upon invitation held not even a kernel of truth. Isa could come and go anywhere as she pleased. If she'd been so inclined, she could have kicked down the sturdy front door and strolled in. Hoping to elicit Jeni's assistance, she opted for the much more polite knock, followed by an equally polite invitation to enter. The first part went fine. The second, not so much.

With Becca's invitation proffered, she didn't wait for Jeni to protest. Isa brushed past both Jeni and Becca and headed directly to the living room to her right. She took a chair next to the fireplace, which afforded a clear view of the front door. It always paid to have a direct route for retreat if necessary. Not that she would be unable to handle herself in a situation like this. Her preference nonetheless would be to take the path of no violence, if at all possible. She saved her aggression for those who had it coming, like Zion and George.

"Okay," Jeni said once everyone sat in her living room. Everyone except her anyway. She stood erect in the doorway with her arms crossed. An expression of distrust clouded her pretty face, and she did have a pretty face. The first time they met, Isa noticed, and it still held true even when the shadows obscured her view. In fact, in the light of this room, Isa decided she might be even prettier. In her uniform, no doubt a dynamo. Who could resist a gorgeous woman in dress blues with a gun at her waist?

But wait. Her thoughts were veering way off course. She'd come here with a mission and might as well jump right into that. What she needed to say would not get easier by putting it off. "I knew your wife."

❖

The first rays of sunlight started to come through the cabin windows to slash across the thick carpet. Sam hurried about closing them while George reclined in his seat as he thought through what they would encounter once they landed. It would turn out to be messy, and that made him smile. He didn't mind messy.

That long-ago night, the catalyst for much of what happened now, had also been a bloodbath. Through the centuries there had been many of them. A few stood out more than the rest. It had been one of the best nights of his already long life, and to share it with her more thrilling than any other. Only in the last ten years had he realized the depths of her hatred for both him and what had happened.

The touch of her hand in his made him grow hard. How he wanted to take her right here and right now. Just beyond the doorway a magnificent bed with a soft mattress and rich covers awaited them. He would tear away her fine rose-colored gown currently hidden by the thick black cloak, tossing aside the expensive fabric until he touched her smooth flesh. The low-cut style teased and promised all at the same time. He tugged at her hand, hoping she felt the same urges he did. They could leave, as the others would finish what he'd started.

She had to be feeling it too. How could she not? Pushing back her hood, he took her beautiful face in his hands and stared into her eyes. She stared back at him, her expression unreadable. She'd picked him. Out of all the suitors who lined up for her hand, she'd picked him. The message she sent was very clear: she wanted him, and now at last the perfect moment had arrived to complete their bond. It would be wrong to ignore the opportunity fate had brought them.

Again, he pulled on her hand as he took several steps toward the bedchamber door. She didn't move. "I want you," he whispered in her ear. "Let them have their party, and we shall have our own. In there."

She dropped his hand and stepped away. Her gaze went back to the great room beyond and the flames that were beginning to grow in the fireplace built for nights like this. Excitement filled all of them every time the fire roared, for it meant a night of plenty. Her face gave away nothing save for the glitter of tears in her eyes.

Once more he reached out and took her hand as he turned his attention to the activities in the center of the great hall. It all played out as he had hoped, and she had to see the majesty of his plan—all of it done for her, the one woman who'd managed to capture his heart. Tonight, their eternity began, with nothing in the way to stop them. "Isn't it wonderful?"

Her words shocked him. "Is it?"

George wondered how he'd missed it back then. He had perceived her tears and her question to be rooted in shock at the beginning of a new and mind-bending reality. She hadn't been the first to find their altered reality startling. The strangeness of it wore off for all of them, and the newly turned soon embraced the freedom of their new lives. It would be that way for her too.

The consummation of their relationship didn't happen that night, despite his hope and anticipation. At the time, he'd rationalized that her reluctance would fade away once she embraced her new life. Ultimately, though much slower than he would have liked, she did warm his bed, and the pleasure it gave him was absolute. With her at his side, his desire to conquer the world became his sole focus. He'd believed they would be together forever. For someone as smart as he, the realization of how wrong he'd been about her remained an open wound. He'd missed every sign, every lie, every deception—all because he loved her. That thought fired up his spirit even more.

"How long before we land," George bellowed.

Sam raised an eyebrow and walked to the cockpit. A moment later he came back. "Pilot says we land in a little more than an hour.

An hour didn't please him. He wanted to be on the ground now. "Have the car waiting."

"Already done."

"We're going to crucify them." George closed his eyes and turned his thoughts away from that night long past. He didn't want to think about her or that night or the fool he had been. What a fool he still was.

CHAPTER FOURTEEN

Jeni's arms dropped away from her body, and her back went rigid. "What exactly do you mean, you knew my wife?" The moment the words left Isa's mouth, electricity raced through her. She'd come up against some powerful vampires before and each time emerged the winner. Not one of them had thrown her off her game like this one managed to do with four simple words.

Isa wouldn't meet her eyes. She'd moved from the chair she'd taken when she first entered the room and now faced the window with her hands clasped. In Jeni's book, classic guilty posturing. This reaction surprised her as much as what she'd said. That she couldn't look her in the eye told a story. Had she been responsible for ending Avery's life? If so, this would be the last time she ever faced a human and came out the survivor. If she'd killed her wife, Isa would die right here, and she'd happily burn down her own house with the bitch inside. The gun tucked into the back of her jeans just happened to hold those very special bullets that could do the job. She'd made the mistake of being insufficiently armed in their previous encounters. After she got home last night, she made certain that mistake was corrected.

"I was there."

Well, now that just cleared it up like the smoke of a forest on fire. "You need to be a little more specific."

This time Isa turned and met her gaze. Pain turned them dark. It made her take a step back. She had yet to encounter a vampire who possessed even a grain of remorse for the taking of a single human life. They were the most arrogant creatures on earth, and she'd encountered more than her share of such assholes in her time. Not just the arrogance either. To vampires, humans were little more than herds of cattle, their lives holding no value beyond sustenance. Nothing about Isa at the moment screamed arrogance.

Isa took a breath. "When Avery was abducted, she was brought to the enclave where I resided at the time."

"You're Redcap." The bitter words tumbled out. Her hand went around to the grip of the gun in the small of her back. Vampires were bad enough. The Redcap Society took it all to horrifying levels, and now one of them stood in her house. This was getting fucking unreal. Her hand shook as her fingers curled around the grip.

"*Was* Redcap."

"You need to get out of my house." Her finger moved to the trigger.

Isa held up both hands and pleaded. "Please. Let me finish."

"You have nothing to say that I'm interested in hearing." She had a ton of files packed with details about the vampires inside that blood cult.

The man she'd called Patrick piped up. "I get why you want us to leave, but trust me. You need to hear her out. It's important."

She swung her gaze to the handsome man's face. She wanted to argue, yet something in his eyes intrigued her. She turned back to Isa and took a few deep breaths, moved her finger away from the trigger. "Okay, but make it quick, or I will shoot you, and trust me, you won't like how that turns out."

"Thank you." No sign that her threat meant a damn thing to Isa.

"Don't thank me. Just spit it out, and then I'll decide if you leave here alive."

Isa nodded, which surprised her. She figured her for more of a fighter. "Fair enough. What you have no way of knowing is that I'd been planning to leave the society since the night they killed my family. It isn't as easy to get away as you might think. Once they have you, it is as though you're chained to them. It took me years of pretending to be something I wasn't to reach a point where I could escape."

Nothing compelling so far that would sway her toward reprieve.

"Whatever. That has nothing to do with my wife's death."

"It does. I promise you. I'd been working to not only leave the society but destroy them. I never agreed with their policies or their goals. They took away everything that was good in my life, and I planned to return the favor. Please believe me when I say that I liked your wife and tried to get her away from them. I failed, and for that I will always carry a great deal of guilt."

"No shit." She should feel guilty, along with every other asshole who'd been in that place. Anyone who had a hand in Avery's death would be put down. Period.

"That failure was the turning point for me. Since that night, I have been taking out the society members one at a time. I came here to destroy the one who stands at the head."

If she thought that would make Jeni feel better, she'd be wrong. None of it had anything to do with her or how she felt about this so-called avenging vampire. She still wanted her out of her house, and to do it right meant taking her out in a body bag or turning her to ash in an impressive conflagration.

"I really wanted to save her because she was special, and the fact that I couldn't has haunted me ever since."

Isa's words echoed with truth, and for the first time, Jeni saw something she hadn't before. Something more than Avery's death haunted this woman, and she instantly wanted to know what brought her here, what drove her to destroy her own kind. Her hand dropped away from her gun, and her shoulders relaxed. Until now she hadn't run up against another vampire that cared one way or the other about a human life.

She made a decision she hoped she wouldn't regret. "All right. Tell me what you need from me." Becca gave her a slight nod. "What you need from us."

❖

Powerful relief washed over Isa at Jeni's words. Upon deciding to come here, the scales tipped in the favor of failure. Armed with the hope that she'd have enough time to make her case, she came anyway. Thanks to Jeni's friend and with her Irish backup, she got her time and something she said swayed Jeni. It made her happy for many reasons, some of which she thought best to keep to herself.

"I want you to help me destroy the one who ordered Avery's death." Now that she had no problem sharing. No need to sugar-coat an absolute truth.

Jeni studied her for a moment, then glanced over to her friend. Some sort of silent communication occurred and a consensus reached that needed no conversation. She looked back at Isa. "On one condition."

Isa didn't do conditions. Yes, she wanted the cop's help, and it would make things infinitely easier, but this would be her show. She'd already waited too long to bring this to an end. Her fight. Her rules. "You must do it my way." Some things could not be compromised.

Jeni shook her head. "My condition or you're on your own, and you'll be watching over your shoulder for Avery's killer and me."

Stubborn. She liked it and she hated it. Spunk was an appealing trait in the women she got together with. Made for some interesting trysts. She didn't care for it in those she needed to follow her. In this instance, Jeni and her friend fell in the latter category. No hook-up here. Only resistance support. From the look on Jeni's face, she would make no ground if she didn't listen. For all she knew, it could be something quite simple and wouldn't affect the final battle. Not a compromise, more of an accommodation. That logic worked for her.

She'd listen to her condition and then make the call. "Go ahead."

"I want to kill the vampire who took Avery's life."

Fulfilling that demand would a little difficult. She'd already dispatched Zion to hell, a place he richly deserved. "I'm afraid that's impossible."

"If I can't kill that one, then I won't help you."

Isa held up a hand. "Let me explain., It's not that I would prevent you from killing him. It's just that I completed that particular job already, and you were there."

"You mean…"

She nodded. "I do. Zion's remains were those pulled from the flames at the house fire you responded to."

"The headless body."

"Yes."

For a moment, Jeni appeared deflated, and then a thought must have occurred to her. "Wait a minute. He wasn't the only one involved, was he?"

Smart woman. "No. He acted on orders." Might as well tell her the whole truth. George needed to be held accountable for all his actions, not just Avery.

Jeni nodded and her eyes narrowed. "I thought that might be the case. So then, I'll take the one who ordered her death. Let me kill that son of a bitch, and I'll help you however I can."

"No."

"Yes."

"He's mine."

The room seemed unusually quiet, given that four people were standing in it. To Isa there were only two: Jeni and her. Their eyes locked, unwavering in a silent stand-off. She would not give on this point. George would be hers. She'd earned the right to send him to hell right along with Zion. He had been the one to order Avery's death, and that should not go unpunished. That crime didn't trump her own need for justice. George had taken everything from her and subjected her to centuries of despair. She had earned the right to take the one thing that mattered to him: his life.

"He's ours," Jeni finally said as her shoulders relaxed. "We'll destroy him together."

She almost said no, her desire to kill George so strong she couldn't imagine sharing it with anyone. Then she gave the possibility a few seconds of consideration, and something in her started to change. It made sense. George had destroyed both of their lives. They should stand together to end his reign. She would still have her moment of retribution, as would Jeni. Isa nodded and held out her hand just as her cell phone rang.

❖

When the car pulled up to the ornate wrought-iron gate at the end of the very long driveway, the blackened spot on the red pavers taunted George. They'd left it there on purpose, their intent transparent: to make certain he'd see it. Douglas had stood there not twenty-four hours ago, and all that remained of one his most loyal followers were traces of ash. Message received.

The rebels that killed Douglas thought they were so smart, that they would be able to unseat him and return the society to the preternatural democracy it once boasted. The time of that kind of rule had run its course. For a few centuries it'd been fine. Not any longer. He intended to keep the new order regardless of how many of the darkness it cost. Besides, they could always be replaced, kind of like trading in a car for a newer, better model. Too many with the old-school mentality continued to walk among them, and he'd prefer to cull the herd.

Sam sat beside him. "How do you want to handle this?"

"Any word from Josef?"

Sam shook his head. "Nothing."

He stared out the window toward the massive house beyond. He'd loved it when he bought it more than fifty years ago, and he still loved it. What he didn't like were the traitors who slept in the seven bedrooms, who drank his wine, who swam in the massive pool. The delusional bunch inside the walls who thought they'd won the war.

In point of fact, they'd won only one small battle, and by now word should have reached them about the demise of their counterparts in New Orleans. He stared ahead and thought about how he would deal with this situation. As he handled those who'd been in power over him, he'd do the same here. His old strategy continued to hold tremendous supremacy—cut off the head of the snake.

His problem at the moment? Who was the snake? At first, he'd thought Olive carried the title, and yet as the events unfolded over the last several days, he'd come to believe she had been but one of the generals selected to go into battle against him. By destroying her he'd put down one small uprising and the same in New Orleans.

The war still raged, as evidenced by the siege inside the walls of the sprawling estate spread out before him.

Despite what would happen soon, his thoughts kept turning to Isa. He wanted to believe he could bring her back into the fold, though he kept that belief to himself for fear of appearing weak. Regardless of the reality, he'd never allow anyone to be aware of how she could undermine him with a simple touch.

Isa had a hand in this, surely the cobra's head he searched for. From the time she'd fled the society, her unwritten agenda included destroying everything he'd worked hard to achieve, all the tangible riches he'd vowed to give her if things had turned out differently. Her actions were the equivalent of throwing all it back into his face.

Those around him would never guess his motivation in achieving the best of every possible possession. Well, he did want it all for himself because he deserved it all. No denying that simple truth. At the same time, from the moment he'd seen Isa, he'd wanted to present her with all the riches and power the world had to offer their kind. He'd never understood how she could turn her back on it all as if it didn't matter. Did she want to be human again? The thought made him want to retch. The rationale behind why anyone would want to return to such a finite existence eluded him.

"Boss?"

Sam's voice brought him back from that solitary place his mind too often turned to these days. It went quickly back to Sam's initial question. For a moment he studied the long brick driveway bordered on both sides by the massive green lawns that cost him a fortune to maintain. His personal kingdom. He'd bought and paid for it all. His hand tightened into fists. "We're going in through the front door, Samuel. My front door."

Sam smiled and pushed the button that caused the massive gate to swing wide. He put the car in gear and pushed the accelerator. The car began a steady forward movement scattering ash into the air as it crossed over the spot where Douglas took his last breath. "I like the way you work."

CHAPTER FIFTEEN

Jeni wished she could see auras. Not that she believed in that kind of thing. If she did, Isa's would probably be full of interesting colors. She really, really wanted to hate her, yet every time they faced off, Jeni did the one thing she'd never done before when in the company of a vampire: she let her walk away.

It wasn't like her to be this way. From the moment she'd learned of Avery's death, she'd been on a focused vendetta to destroy every last creature of the night, bar none. A pretty darned successful crusade too, at least until two nights ago. If she'd held to her credo, Isa would be dust. Instead, she stood in Jeni's front room with a cell phone pressed to her ear, talking in low, urgent tones. From the sound of it, something had gone sideways.

Isa ended the call and shoved the phone into the pocket of her pants. For a moment she studied her feet. Then her eyes briefly met Jeni's before she turned her attention to Patrick. "Olive is dead." Patrick sighed, sounding dismayed. "Damn. I liked Olive."

Jeni interrupted because it all felt relevant somehow. "What does that mean?"

"One battle lost."

Jeni made a come-on motion with her hand. The dots still weren't connecting. "I need more."

"I told you I wanted you help to destroy the one who killed your wife."

"Yeah, got it. Nothing new there."

"There's much more to the story. The one you're looking for is the same vampire who turned me and orchestrated the destruction of my entire family."

That statement hit Jeni hard. Isa was a vampire. Nothing there she didn't already know. The demise of her family, well, that touched an empathetic part of her that transcended the line between human and vampire. She shouldn't experience a connection like this to a vampire. This day already had a very strange vibe, and she had a hunch it would get stranger before it was done.

Her gaze met Becca's, and that steadied her. Thank goodness for her friend. This situation would be intensely weird under any circumstances. To have a strong friend at her side made it a little easier to take.

"Still not enough." Where Isa was going with this remained unclear, and she'd had enough of the veiled references. Get to the damn point, and it better be an iron-clad case, or she'd be done.

"Like I said, I've been working on this situation longer than you can possibly imagine. It's all finally coming together. I have strike teams in place all over the world, which will shake the foundation beneath George's feet. He's not prepared for so many to rise up against him because of his sheer arrogance. He thinks all he has to worry about is me."

Each time Isa tried to explain, things got more complicated. "Back up the pony. This is the first time you've mentioned some guy named George."

"He's the one you're after." She said it in a matter-of-fact way that implied the explanation was obvious. Not so much, though she liked that she could now add the asshole's name to her files. Made it even more personal.

"Well, then let's go get him." She'd been waiting for this moment for a decade.

Isa didn't appear to share her sense of urgency. "It's not that simple. He's far more powerful than just about anyone, and it's not like you can walk up to him and put a stake through his heart."

Clear to her that Isa didn't have a clue as to how good she'd gotten at killing vampires. If her law-enforcement career did end up tanking, she really would have to investigate whether she could make a living from hunting the creatures of darkness. Stranger things had happened...maybe. "It's always been that easy before."

Isa shook her head, and something about it made Jeni feel like a first-grader who'd disappointed her teacher. "No, it is not. We are not talking a garden-variety vampire. This one's been around for centuries. He's smart, he's skilled, and most important, he's brilliant."

Jeni thought of some of the criminals she'd helped put away. Intelligence often went hand in hand with evil. She'd seen more than one genius IQ go to the dark side. Those folks, more often than not, came with an inflated sense of self and always thought they were better than everyone else. More important, they always believed they were the smartest person in the room. In a strange way, many were, at least in terms of IQ points. Raw intelligence without a moral compass had a way of ultimately going up in flames. The prisons were full of those kinds of people. Or at least the human variety. Those of the vampire ilk were the ones Jeni loved to dispatch.

"I've dealt with his type before."

Again, Isa shook her head, and cut her gaze over to her friend. Patrick took the lead. "She's right, Jeni. George isn't like anyone you've ever met. Think Ted Bundy with centuries to hone his craft and an army at his beck and call."

That description finally hit home in the way she suspected Isa hoped, as it also sent chills up her back. She knew some of the team who'd been involved with stopping Ted Bundy. They'd told her things that never made the books or the movies or the articles. That man had embodied an evil no one could fully grasp. She wanted to believe him to be a true aberration and not something she would encounter in her lifetime. "That's hard to fathom."

This time Isa nodded. "That's what I am trying to get across to you. His evil has no bounds, and that makes him very dangerous." Apparently, she'd just redeemed herself with the teacher.

She looked over at Becca, who appeared to focus less on Isa and more on the Irishman. Did she detect a heightened level of interest there? Great. That's all she needed for now—her best friend lusting after the vampire's pal. She didn't think things could get any weirder. She'd been wrong.

Jeni made a decision. How she hoped it would turn out to be the correct one. "All right. You've made your point. It sounds like you already have plans in motion, so what exactly do you need from me?"

❖

Pure relief released the tension in Isa's body. Finally, it appeared she'd gotten through to Jeni, thanks to both Becca and Patrick. Amazing what a couple of humans could accomplish with a few well-chosen words that she couldn't, even after a couple hundred years of practice. Hard to think she'd lost her touch with humans, but sometimes it seemed that way.

It probably had more to do with the isolation she tended to gravitate toward than anything else. Even if she'd still been human, cutting herself off from everything and everyone would have had the same effect. She didn't do herself any favors by choosing to be alone all the time. Too old and set in her ways to change now, and, besides, what would be the point? After this came to an end, social graces wouldn't matter anyway.

She pulled her laptop out of the bag she'd slung across her shoulders and set it where they could all see. "Let me show you the plan, and then it might make more sense. In a nutshell, I am trying to rock his foundation and drive him back here."

"That's why there's been activity here lately."

"Yes. I set the bait. They took it."

Jeni put her hands on her hips and stared at Isa. "You're the one who put the screws to my plans for a little peace and quiet."

Isa nodded, not particularly sorry it'd happened this way. Destiny appeared to demand Jeni be a part of this, as if they were kindred souls. Isa hadn't been parted from a spouse, though, so that level of intimacy escaped her. Just the same, that her family had been taken from her gave her much in common with this intense cop. Love lost, regardless of the relationship, left behind a hole that could never be filled. Unlike Jeni, her pursuit of George wasn't limited to the loss of her family. Her very life had been stolen, and she could never forgive or forget that transgression on George's part. Accountability rested solely on his shoulders.

"George has been looking for me for the last decade. I've kept a watch on him since the night I slipped away from the society."

"Why didn't you kill him before you left?"

A valid and not unexpected question. She would have been disappointed in Jeni if she'd failed to pick up on the obvious. Truthfully, she would have loved to kill him back then. The conditions weren't right in those days, and it had been in her best interest to wait. Besides, in all reality, the society had as much to pay for as George. She wanted to take it all down. "I needed to get ready and put all the pieces into place. Once that happened, I waited for a time and place to draw out George. I have made certain there existed no margin for error. One and done."

"Is he here?"

She shook her head and smiled a little, thinking about those who were putting their lives on the line to upset George. A big job that required unshakable dedication and great peril. Some would die, like Olive, and they all went into this knowing that possibility. For all of them, the end result warranted the risk. "He was. He's been called away. He'll be back. It's not important."

Patrick shook his head. "Bullshit. It's vastly important, and you can't argue that. Just because he's out of the county at the moment doesn't mean we write it off. The guy still has a hard-on for you."

She smiled again. "Yes, he does, and that's exactly the point. We'll use that chink in his armor to separate his body from his head. Everybody has a weakness, and I'm his."

Becca spoke up this time. "You two want to explain the situation to us in more detail? It's a pretty vague picture you've painted so far."

Isa did not care to take a deeper dive into this right now. To be fair, they needed to have all the facts. "George and I have a long history, which I plan to use against him."

Jeni's eyes narrowed as she studied Isa's face. From the first moment they'd spoken it had become quite clear that, beyond beautiful, the woman had brains. It was one reason Isa had been drawn to her, yet it might well come back to haunt her. She was willing to take that risk, and besides, Jeni wasn't letting it go. "What's the rest of it?"

Isa drew a deep breath as Patrick nodded. At least the two of them were on the same page. "Tell them," he said. "They have a right to know."

Yes, they did, and as much as she'd like to keep what she considered trivia to herself, she owed them all the truth. "He's my husband."

While Sam guarded the rear of the house in the Hamptons, George took the front. It'd be a shame to lose this property, particularly after the destruction of the house in New Orleans. Sometimes sacrifice became necessary, and that included the life of Josef. Undoubtedly, if not already dead, Josef was being held inside. The infidels would assume that he would come for his loyal follower, a known favorite of his, and they'd be wrong. A critical miscalculation on their part. Josef would understand because he always did—one reason he remained in favor all these years.

Another of his favorite soldiers just happened to have been a military soldier during his human years. His particular specialty? Explosives. As they were leaving New Orleans, George placed a call to Salvador from the plane. Like the dutiful soldier he remained, Sal met them at the airport in the northeast and brought all the requested items. Without being asked, Sal loaded everything into the trunk of the car waiting on the tarmac. More than once he'd been amazed at Sal's ability to pull together anything and everything at a moment's notice. He never asked him how or why.

Now George and Sam set the pipe bombs around the perimeter of the home. Of course, they covered themselves from head to toe in order to avoid the sun's rays, making it much easier to work. No need to diminish their energy by exposing themselves to sunlight. Much remained to be done, and he wanted to be ready for it all. Inside the walls of the beautiful home, the dissidents slept, thinking themselves safe until nightfall, when they'd expect a visit from him. Too bad they hadn't thought through all the contingencies.

If they truly understood him, they would prepare because he would never wait until darkness fell. Unlike the youngsters inside, his tolerance to daylight made it easier to work now without the need to wait for nightfall. The revenge for killing Douglas and taking control of his property required swift, fatal justice. That they still had no contact from Josef told George he'd no doubt met a similar fate to Douglas, and that too required action.

Too bad for them, and even though he loved this piece of property, he loved black justice even more. With timers engaged on the devices they strategically set, he and Sam got back into the car. The giant gate once more closed as they turned onto the street and started the drive back to the airport. They were at least three blocks away when the first one went off. The flames were shooting high into the sky by the time they were a quarter of a mile away. He laughed, and Sam joined in.

"I hate losing that place, but I must say that was fun. So arrogant as they slept the day away, thinking they were safe. It's as if they don't know me at all."

"Whoever is orchestrating all of this will definitely get the message with that one."

He leaned back against the seat and looked out the darkened car windows. "One would hope."

In the big picture, it wouldn't make a difference. What passed Sam by was the fact that while they won this battle, a bigger war still raged. He didn't mind. So many wars had been fought during his lifetime. In fact, he could count some of the best and most famous generals as friends. Some of the worst too. Lessons to be learned in both the good and the bad. It all combined to provide him a unique skill set he intended to use now.

"Bring it on, my darling," he whispered as he closed his eyes and pictured her face with an expression of sadness once she realized what he'd done to those who followed her. "Bring it on."

Chapter Sixteen

A re you serious?" Jeni heard the words come out of Isa's mouth and couldn't quite make it work for a couple of reasons. Embarking on an all-out war to kill her husband seemed somehow wrong, and she'd have put money on Isa being a lesbian. She didn't really know why she thought the latter and couldn't shake the belief it was true. Somewhere deep down was an interest in this woman she couldn't shake, and that would be as plausible an explanation as any.

It might also explain why she hadn't killed Isa right from the beginning. A lame reason for sure. She'd had to find something that made sense, because otherwise she had no good excuse for not already dropping Isa. She'd never exercised mercy before when it came to vampires, male or female.

Information overload hit her now. To find out the creature who'd killed her love was Isa's husband made her want to throw up. Actually, if she were to believe Isa, he hadn't personally killed Avery. His order caused her death, and in her book that made him just as guilty, if not more so. To order someone else to do the dirty work spelled coward to her, and a special place in hell awaited those people.

Where to go from here was the big question mark at this point. Becca urged her to listen to what Isa and Patrick had to say, and she'd done that against her better judgment. It might have been preferable if she'd been kept in the dark with that little spouse detail. At least then she'd be able to assume that Isa, despite her undead status, still retained her humanity, and that all other vampires were assholes worthy of a stake. In that scenario she could justify her own lack of action when it came to Isa.

"I am afraid, as Patrick is fond of saying, I'm as serious as a heart attack."

"Not funny." This wasn't the time for jokes or sarcasm.

"Wasn't trying to be amusing. I didn't marry George because I loved him. I believed him the lesser of many evils. My father intended to marry me off to whoever had the biggest purse, most of them as old as him or older. I couldn't live with that reality, and then George showed up. The proverbial knight on a big white horse, although the horse he rode in on happened to be black. That should have been warning enough. I ignored all the signs because he was younger and better looking than any man my father set his sights on. I grabbed him and held on tight though I never loved him. With him, I could survive a world that placed no value on my wishes."

"Why didn't you love him?" Her question had nothing to do with anything happening right now. She asked it just the same.

Becca moved toward the doorway. "I need coffee."

"I need whiskey, and don't you dare say it's too early. You know, it's after noon where I come from. What do you have in that kitchen?" Patrick followed Becca out the door, leaving Jeni and Isa alone.

"Why?" Jeni asked again, not surprised that Becca bailed. Pretty sure something in her voice had screamed, *This is getting personal.*

"Because I could never love a man."

Isa had never before uttered the words out loud. In all her years, she'd managed to keep her truth buried even as the world changed around her. She understood her own nature and had for a very long time. Even so, the lessons of her youth were part of her, and some things in the society she came from simply were not spoken of. This was one of them, and thus it stayed inside her without ever having been put to words. Until now.

"I'm a lesbian." She'd had come this far, so she might as well go all the way. Her back straightened and her shoulders squared.

Jeni held her gaze for a full minute. "Well, thank God."

Isa cocked her head. What on earth did she mean by that statement? "Why is that an important point to you?" Saying that during her human years would have been a catastrophe, though it certainly didn't cause much of a stir in this day and age. In most places anyway. Some pockets still remained where it could cause a problem.

Jeni's shoulders relaxed for the first time since they'd met. "It explains why I couldn't put you down."

Isa shook her head. Jeni's face gave away nothing. "I still don't understand."

"I've spent ten years of my life trying to destroy every last one of those like you. I didn't care who they were, where they came from, or how they became vampires. None of it made a damn bit of difference to me. I killed them all, holding each and every one of them accountable for what happened to my Avery."

"You didn't try to kill me."

"Yeah. That's exactly my point. I should have put one of my special bullets through your heart, but I didn't. Not the first time, not the second time, not tonight." She held out her empty hands as if to emphasize the "tonight" statement. "I couldn't figure out why, and then you tell me this wild story that has an ending I sure as hell wasn't expecting. It's that odd ending that suddenly starts to drop all the pieces into place and make sense in a really warped way."

"Not so wild or warped. If you were born in my time, it would make more sense to you. Beautiful young women held great value, but not for their minds or what they could contribute to society. No, we held great value for the money and titles we could bring to our families. We were sold, plain and simple. No one cared what we were or what we longed for. All that mattered was what our bodies could buy."

A shadow crossed Jeni's face. "I'm sorry about that. I can't imagine what that would have been like, and I can at least begin to understand your actions back then."

Isa shrugged as though she appreciated what sounded like sincere compassion. "All of that's on me. I'm not trying to make excuses for why it took me a long time to become strong enough to make my stand, take my life back, and to hold those responsible accountable for their atrocities. I only endeavor to help you understand where I'm coming from. George orchestrated it all. He was, is, my husband, and it is far past time for a divorce."

"A divorce?"

She smiled. "I think 'widow' has a better sound to it."

George sat once more on the plane congratulating himself for constructing such a grand plan. His magnificent demonstration showed what would happen to every last one of the rebel vampires if they attempted to defy him. No one had ever been better at leadership than him.

Yes, the whispers that said he didn't lead, he ruled, reached his ears. They called him self-centered, even narcissistic. A dictator. He didn't see it. Being confident in his abilities and his every decision, and acknowledging the depths of his own intelligence didn't make him a narcissist. Nor did he quite follow where that belief even came from. To be that good came as a blessing, period. Some were simply born better than others. If history taught anything, it was that God never distributed gifts with an equal hand.

Of course, not only had he been born better. He had also taken the initiative to hone his natural skills until he became superior to anyone, anywhere, at any time. To date, not a single individual could match him. A clearer attestation of his superiority didn't exist. Sooner or later they would all learn that basic fact, or they'd end up just like those in Boise, New Orleans, and the Hamptons. A zero-tolerance policy.

It saddened him that these events forced him to lose magnificent properties. He'd get over it because material things could be replaced. With homes all over the world, it wasn't like he lacked premium accommodations. For the last century or so, he'd spent the majority of his time in the United States. He liked it here—big and spread out, with different landscapes and temperaments. Such a large, interesting hunting ground. He could move around from place to place without garnering much attention. While the society had formed in Europe, the headquarters migrated to America when he made it his permanent home. After centuries of flourishing there, Europe no longer offered safety. Too many had become aware of the society, which made it risky to continue to house the core operations anywhere of interest to him on the European continent.

In North America, only a relatively small number of humans was aware of the society's existence, and thus it became easier to live comfortably without worry of detection or trouble. No need to return to the times filled with professional vampire hunters who tried to take his head on a regular basis. The society waged a campaign of its own to discredit those hunters, and for the most part, it had worked. Their discredit made them entries into books on preternatural lore rather than credible pieces of history. A few still existed in the "new world," though they lacked the zeal of their European predecessors. Science took the punch out of the old folktales that came across the ocean with the immigrant families, and few in the general population believed the stories of their grandparents and great-grandparents. Those who did were more an annoyance than a threat.

The real threat, or what they presumed to be a real threat, were the insiders who tried to unseat him. Tried was the operative word. The multiple strikes of the last few days irritated him, but they were not showstoppers. He handled them as he would any and all others that popped up. To be in power for a very long time remained his primary plan, and everyone around him knew that when he formulated a plan, he executed it to perfection.

"The pilot says we'll be back in Chewelah about eleven." Sam sat down in the seat across from him, his long, powerful legs stretched out. His arms, covered with multiple tattoos, crossed over his chest. The only things missing were the multiple silver rings Sam wore during his human years.

"Good." Do we have an alternate location?" His jaw ached at the pressure of his teeth pressed together. Zion's death and the destruction of the lovely home on the edge of the woods remained in the forefront of his mind. Three of his homes destroyed in such a short amount of time caused a tickle of alarm in the back of his mind. At least he knew the responsible party in this instance. No attempted coup in Chewelah would even come close to success, Zion's demise aside.

"Yes. I secured a replacement while we were flying to the Hamptons. The keys will be in our car at the airport. All is ready for you."

"The others will join us?" Several of his soldiers, off hunting during the time of Zion's death, still remained in the area. They'd returned too late to either help Zion or save the house from the flames. He did not hold them responsible for her misdeeds. Had they been there, undoubtedly, they would have put up a good fight. All his soldiers were conditioned to fight until they no longer had a breath.

"Everyone is already there and secure. They will be rested and ready to assist by the time we arrive."

"She probably thinks she's succeeded in discouraging us." He could almost see the smug satisfaction on Isa's face. Many times, when she completed a complicated task, her face would mirror her inner pride. He also remembered her determination when she became focused on accomplishing a particular goal. She didn't give up, ever.

Sam crossed his legs. "I'd like to say yes and that her cockiness will blind her to our approach."

He cocked his head and studied Sam's face. He appeared to be thinking along the same lines as George. "You don't believe it though, do you?"

"No."

He smiled. Yes, indeed, Sam knew Isa too. Not as well as he did, but enough to be aware of the fire that burned inside her that only death would extinguish. "Neither do I."

"We must be ready," Sam added.

Sam's eyes met his and he licked his canines. "Oh, we will be."

Chapter Seventeen

Against her better judgment, Jeni admitted silently that she liked the way Isa thought. It would be a great deal easier to hang onto her anger and simply hate her. Better still, to kill her, just as she had all the other vampires before her. Not so easy when something about Isa made Jeni stop short of taking action, which didn't really jive with her basic nature or given her unspoken vendetta against every single creature of the darkness. Isa made it clear she'd known Avery and liked her. If that were the case, then it begged the question of why hadn't she saved her?

That bit of information didn't match the way her breath quickened and her hands trembled each time she stood near the vampire. Anyone involved with Avery's abduction and murder must be held accountable in a fatal way. Even if Isa hadn't been directly involved, she'd at least been aware of Avery as an unwilling human victim. To give any of her arguments weight, she should have saved her. If so, then none of them would be here now. Jeni liked to think she was a smart woman, who wasn't totally acting like one of late.

Despite her nagging concerns, she nonetheless respected Isa's drive to hold her own kind accountable. She'd never given credence to the idea that not all vampires were bad. Vampires killed people. Good people didn't kill. To wit, a good vampire seemed like a true oxymoron. In front of her now stood one intent on making her case for being exactly that, and damn if she wasn't starting to buy in.

Did that make her a fool? At first, she thought, oh yeah, big time. Something else a little deeper forced her to stop and reassess.

She'd become a really good investigator since starting her career in law enforcement and had relied on gut instinct in more than one case. Right now, that gut instinct screamed for her to pay attention. Against her better judgment, she would. It might turn out to be a mistake. She didn't want to run the risk that it might not be.

As she studied Isa, she made her decision. "Okay, so you want to take on this fight together. Am I getting that right?"

"You are."

"You want a divorce and I want revenge. I would agree that in a way that puts us on the same playing field."

Isa nodded and her posture relaxed. "We can help each other."

"Maybe."

"I'm no threat to you."

"Hard to believe."

"I speak the truth."

Her eyes still on Isa, Jeni said loudly, "Becca, get your ass back in here."

Becca, followed by Patrick, returned. The smile on her face reminded Jeni of the cat that ate the mouse. "All righty, so you two kiss and make up?"

"Not exactly."

Becca sighed and held up her hands. "Why can't we all just get along?"

From the way Becca stood close to Isa's Interpol buddy, she wondered what happened in the other room while she and Isa talked. It didn't take a PhD to figure out that Becca was developing a crush on the cop. If she'd been inclined that way, she'd get it too. He had it all—looks, a fabulous accent, and eyes that should be in the movies. Becca was doomed, and when she gave it a moment's thought, that too might not be a bad thing. Her friend usually picked horrible men. More than once Jeni banned her from making important decisions, like moving in with one of them. So far, so good with Patrick. Her cop instincts said good guy.

She inched close to Becca now and whispered, "Alan, Eugene, Juan."

Becca's eyes narrowed. "Shut up."

"Just thought it worth a mention."

"Too early."

"Yeah. I'm not so sure."

"Later," Becca said her tone low.

Jeni gave her shoulder a squeeze and returned her attention to their guests. "So, you maintain that we're all on the same side here, even though you—" she pointed at Isa "—are one of them."

Isa held up a hand. "Call me a vampire because I am. Do not call me 'one of them.' I played their game for a long time because I felt I didn't have a better choice. I was and never will be one of them. Ever."

The emphasis on the last word left no doubt as to where Isa stood. Yet Isa had been with the Society, by her own account, for hundreds of years. Plenty of time to take a stand. She'd only been hunting her own kind for the last ten years. A bit hard not to classify her as one of them, given those facts. Centuries versus a single decade? "You were one of them for a really long time."

Isa shrugged. "Time is relative. In terms of the length of a human life, that statement would be quite true. In the vampire world, it was the blink of an eye."

"That's what you want me to believe?"

"That's what it is."

"All right. Not sure I buy in one hundred percent, but I'm listening."

Her gaze cut to Becca, who smiled as if she'd just won a big prize. Jeni figured that, in a way, she had. By agreeing, she'd just extended the time Isa and Patrick would be here. More pointedly, the longer Patrick would be here.

Convincing Jeni would be a tough job, and Isa hadn't been wrong in that assessment. Some real ground made here, she allowed herself a moment of hope. Jeni sounded hesitant. She could work with hesitation. At least they'd stepped beyond the out-and-out hostility, even after her admission about Avery. Risky to put that out there. Coming clean equally important. If she hoped to gain Jeni's assistance at any level, honesty had to be front and center.

Besides, she'd spent far too many years living with lies, and she didn't care to do that any longer. To be forced to pretend year after year wore away at the soul. Sometimes it became hard to even remember who she'd been, and she sure as hell didn't know who she'd become. Not a big wonder that she found herself walking the earth alone. If she didn't know who she was, how could anyone get close to her?

Given that this final battle would most likely be her last, nothing left to lose anyway. All her cards were on the table, and there'd be no risk to her. As George went down, so too would she. Her revenge would be complete, and those who, like herself, took exception with the rule of the society, were already in motion. The world that existed just beyond the sight of most humans would soon change for the better. Perhaps even someday the vampires and the humans could co-exist. She wouldn't be around to see it, but she believed it might happen once the Georges of the dark side were sent into oblivion.

"I need your eyes and ears."

"Meaning?"

"Meaning, since I destroyed George's house, he will have to find an alternative. He'll come back because he's dead set on finding me. He's got to have somewhere to stay that will protect him while also coming up to the standards he's accustomed to. No little one-bedroom rental, if you follow me. That bit of information will help narrow the search. I already have three that are possibilities based upon his preferences."

Jeni nodded, and Isa knew she was following just fine. At least on the housing issue. "You seem so sure he'll come for you."

Isa hesitated and wondered how much to share. Patrick hadn't been brought in about the flowers, or the cards that had come to various homes as she'd moved throughout the world. He didn't know about the ruby necklace she'd left in a thrift-store donation box in Omaha. Or about the most recent delivery on her front porch.

She glanced over at Patrick and saw his eyes narrow. At her age, she should be better at a poker face. From the look of annoyance on his face, she was not. "What the fuck are you not telling me?"

She blew out a breath. Might as well share it all. "He sent me flowers."

"Where?" Patrick snapped the single word.

"Here."

"He fucking what?" It surprised Isa that Patrick's voice could go that high. "What the hell, Isa. That's crazy and dangerous."

"I wanted to pretend it didn't happen because, in all truth, I wasn't ready for him yet."

"Sounds like he's ready for you."

Patrick was getting sidetracked, and they couldn't afford that at the moment. "He didn't hurt me."

"Jesus Christ, Isa. He didn't this time because he's just fucking with you."

"I know."

"Well, then you also know he has you under surveillance."

Of course, she knew that. "Let it go so we can focus on the here and now. We can safely assume he has me in his sights, and thus he'll be coming back here soon."

"If he's not already here," Patrick said.

She turned to Jeni and Becca. They probably weren't keeping up since they weren't all the way in the loop yet. Might be a good time to explain the rest of the story. "We've got a bit of a coup in the works, and vampire cells are hitting George from a number of different directions."

"You're trying to take him out somewhere else? First you say he's coming back for you, then you say you've got others trying to kill him. Sounds like the work is almost done, so why do you need me?"

She shook her head. "We're trying to undermine his organization. Vampires in a number of locations are doing their best to kill his soldiers and either appropriate or destroy his properties. As of the last word about an hour ago, he's taken his revenge in Boise, New Orleans, and the Hamptons, meaning we've lost some of our own. Our casualties aside, it cost him two of his favorite locations, not including the house here I burned down, and that had to make him really angry. We're slowly but surely destabilizing him and his faction."

"And you believe he'll come back here?"

"Without question."

❖

Sam put the phone down and rubbed his eyes. "You're not going to want to hear this."

George stiffened. Not one more word about continued problems. Not now. Sam's face told him what he wanted didn't matter. "Another one?" They were over Montana and nearing their destination.

Sam nodded with a grimace. "Vancouver."

He curled his hands into fists, and blood dripped as his nails dug into his palms. He loved the property in northwest Canada, and she'd used that fact to drive the knife in harder. She'd helped him pick it out at the turn of the twentieth century during the early days of the city, part of the reason it became a special spot for him. Some of his most precious possessions were housed there.

"Divert the plane." It galled him to give that command. Given that a better option didn't exist, he viewed it as the wise choice.

Sam stayed silent as he got up from his seat and walked down the aisle to the cockpit. Several minutes later he returned. "Done. We'll land in an hour."

"We have to be more proactive. It appears to me that she's been planning this for some time."

"She's had help. No way she did this by herself."

"Isa's a smart woman, possessing no extraordinary powers. She absolutely had to have had help. That means we must look at all our strongholds and figure out where a weakness exists, because she'll go there next. I don't want to lose anything else, nor do I wish to put any more of our skilled labor at risk. Though it's easier to replace the bodies than my properties."

Sam nodded. "Let me get my laptop, and we can look at your holdings. We can outthink her. She's good. Just not that good."

He would disagree. From the moment of her birth, Isa had been exceptional. Give a woman like that a few centuries to hone her intelligence and skills, and little could stop her. Only his own vast expertise provided the edge needed to put a halt to her vendetta. In his fantasies, he hoped he could avoid destroying her. He knew better. The only way she would ever stop would be to die. That fact made him a little sad because he wanted so much more from her.

Every man possessed a weak spot, regardless of how smart or powerful he might be. In that respect he resembled the human race he left behind. He considered his affinity for Isa his only weakness, and given its insignificance in the overall picture, it wouldn't hold him back. He'd never hesitated to do what had to be done in order to get what he wanted. Now would be no different.

Isa might be one of kind, but it didn't make her irreplaceable, even if he hadn't allowed another woman to take her place thus far. That only meant he hadn't yet come across the proper replacement. In time, he would. He didn't really believe he'd spend eternity alone. No. Someday another brilliant, beautiful woman would show herself, and he would once again have his queen. Another of his virtues: patience.

"Let's look at this situation and determine a strategy to cut her off at the pass." He sat next to Sam, who had his laptop open on the table. He swirled the ruby liquid in his glass, holding it close to his nose and inhaling deeply. "She'll never see us coming."

CHAPTER EIGHTEEN

Jeni couldn't believe how fast the time went. Becca and Patrick stayed in the kitchen, using their laptops to scour various law-enforcement databases. She'd taken the front room with Isa as a place to strategize. Somewhere as the hours ticked by, she'd stopped thinking about her as *the vampire* and began to think of her as a woman who shared her mission. For both, a common goal became crystalized.

The weirdness of the situation wasn't lost on her. By all rights, she should hate Isa as intensely as she'd hated every vampire she'd sent screaming to hell. A different category appeared on the scene when it came to Isa. The fact she'd been there when they'd killed Avery damned her in a way nothing else could.

The hate that sustained her for a decade faded away when she looked into Isa's face. No rational basis for that, and maybe it wasn't important. The help Isa could provide might turn out to be the piece to finally end this quest. It had taken a while to accept that she'd be unable to wipe all vampires off the earth. Part of the reason she was even here came from that realization. Isa now offered her the opportunity to kill the one who'd ordered Avery's death, and to accomplish that would avenge Avery in the best way she could. It would be enough.

She stared at the computer screen. "How can one person amass this kind of wealth?" He had homes in every prestigious area of the country. That they were searching only the United States and

Canada scared her. His life spanned both centuries and continents. If he'd amassed holdings this large in North America, what did he have in the rest of the world? More important, what were his plans? No one with an ounce of intelligence could argue that his push was to take over the world. He didn't try very hard to hide a damn thing.

Isa ran her hands through her hair. "He's had a lot of time, and he started out rich. You know the old saying, it takes money to make money. George is the kind of man who illustrates it."

"It's frightening. I mean, how do we even begin to stop somebody with that kind of power and influence? A damn vampire, no less. It's bad enough we have human politicians and world leaders who buy their way in and then proceed to fuck everything up. Now we're dealing with a vampire who's doing the same. It's just not right on any level."

"Like I told you earlier, I've already put a great deal in motion. You'd be surprised at how many of us in the dark realm have had enough of the Redcap Society and all those who believe themselves to be demi-gods. We didn't ask to become who we are, and we don't want to follow George or those like him."

"But you did."

"I'd argue the finer point of that statement."

"Were you or were you not part of the Redcap Society?"

"I was."

Jeni spread her hands out. "I rest my case."

Isa's expression didn't change. "Your case is flawed. Just because I was part of it doesn't mean I bought into their values. I hated them. I hated all of it, but if I wanted to succeed in taking it down, I had to wait."

"For centuries?" Seriously, Isa couldn't possibly believe she'd accept that argument at face value. Her own quest for vengeance started the moment she learned of Avery's death at the hands of the vampires.

"Yes. As I explained before, it's all relative."

"Doesn't feel relative to me." She'd heard the argument and it didn't resonate with her.

"And if I were in your shoes, I'd most assuredly feel the same way. I'd hate me because I didn't do enough. I should have saved Avery."

She leaned back and studied Isa. Kind of felt like she could read her mind. "You could have saved her, and you didn't?" Rage started to smother the recent leaning toward comradery.

Isa shook her head. "I don't make many mistakes. When I do, they're big. I thought I was doing the right thing by waiting and letting the moment of opportunity be revealed. I really believed I'd be able to get her out of there alive."

"You were wrong."

"So very wrong."

Isa hated thinking about the night Zion killed Avery, let alone talk about it. George did it to hurt her because he'd sensed her compassion for the woman and what she'd not shared with them is that he'd intuited that one death wouldn't hurt her enough. Instead, he'd turned it into a wholesale slaughter. He made sure Avery went first and laughed when her life faded in front of Isa. He'd always tried to bring her into line, make her the obedient soldier, like all the rest of the vampires he surrounded himself with.

Those vampires told him how fabulous he was—how smart, how handsome, how perfect. If any of them perceived flaws in him, they kept their observations to themselves. Only Isa stood up to George, and he tolerated her gall because he loved her.

She knew exactly how he felt about her, had known from the beginning. It wasn't hard to tell the difference between those who lusted after her young, nubile body and those who harbored genuine emotion. Had he been a human, guilt about the way she'd exploited his feelings for her might exist. As it all turned out, she didn't have one bit of remorse about that. Getting sucked into his world, yes. Seeing him as a way out, no.

Charlotte had been a different story, beautiful but born into a lesser class. Isa's family employed her to teach her younger brother.

When the sky turned dusky, Isa and Charlotte would trade kisses in the garden, hold hands while sitting on the window seat, and steal glances when they thought no one else watched. She'd longed to share more and instead kept her desires wrapped up as tightly as the ties that pulled her dresses snug to her body. Isa experienced some guilt over Charlotte because she enjoyed their brief trysts, all the while hiding that she didn't love her. In short, she trifled with Charlotte, and that hadn't been right.

Even now she could still see the men whose faces told her they'd do the same thing to her. Not one of them had loved her, and never would. They wanted to touch her nonetheless, not that they cared about her virtue or what it meant for her. They only wanted their lust satisfied. She sidestepped them all, taking her own pleasure with another young woman while courting the one man who loved her, the one man who could save her from all the rest.

His relentless pursuit of her now didn't surprise her. The way he'd focused on her from the first day they met had been as much a part of him as the color of his eyes. He'd been born with drive, and it had followed him into the darkness. She'd waited a very long time to kick it all out from under him.

"I am sorry," she said after the silence stretched uncomfortably. Jeni's eyes blazed, and Isa feared she'd lost her as much by her words as her silent reflections.

"You should be." The three words were heavy.

"If I could go back, I'd do everything different." Her own words were sincere because she meant them.

"Hindsight's twenty-twenty."

"Indeed."

It was Jeni's turn to embrace a lengthy silence. When she finally spoke, whatever decision she'd made softened her words. "Okay, then. How do you plan to stop him?"

"He's cocky," she said, and the shakiness that came from opening herself up faded as she shifted back into battle mode. "That's what we're going to exploit because he believes it makes him invulnerable."

"I still don't get why you need me. You understand the existing infrastructure and the personalities involved. It seems like you've got the help you need already. So why come here when you know how I feel about those like you? When you know I've done everything I could to destroy every vampire I've come in contact with? When you tell me you didn't save my wife?"

Jeni wasn't wrong. Isa should be able to handle this with those like Patrick, who'd been at her side for years. She'd rallied the forces, and they were taking action as she and Isa sat here studying the computer records. And yes, she understood the vengeance that drove Jeni. She might not have loved in the way Jeni had loved Avery, but she got it.

"I need eyes on, and you're the most logical choice." Sounded lame, yet much of it was true.

"I'm new here. I don't have the kind of in that I would if we were in Portland. In that respect, I won't be a lot of help."

"You have instincts and drive, and most of all, you hate George as much as I do. Those three things alone are powerful."

"I can't argue with that."

"Then shall we kill him?"

Jeni's eyes narrowed and she gave Isa a single nod. "We shall."

They landed in Vancouver and went directly to the hotel downtown near Stanley Park, the beautiful, massive park that provided abundant hunting grounds if one became hungry. Given the ample supplies on the plane, he wouldn't need to avail himself of the bounty the park offered any night of the week. On the flight here he'd formulated an excellent plan of how he desired to handle this one, and unlike in the Hamptons, it would require full darkness. The invaders didn't know, in fact no one else knew, about the system of tunnels that traversed the ground beneath his home there. When he'd established this particular residence, a very real risk of exposure existed, so he'd proceeded to plan for undetectable escape routes.

He'd planned so well, he took a lesson from Dr. H.H. Holmes's playbook when building his very special place. Like Holmes, he used many different architects and tradesmen, and the majority of them simply disappeared upon completion of their work. No one remained alive to tell tales of the eccentric millionaire building the extravagant home on the outskirts of Vancouver. After the work was finished, only one remained who knew the whole story. Yours truly. And his lips were sealed—until tonight anyway. Then he would have to bring Sam in on his closely guarded secret. With their stealthy approach from beneath, the two of them could easily dispatch the agitators and secure his location once again.

The nice part about being in British Columbia was its proximity to Northeast Washington. It would enable him to do the clean-up here, immediately board the plane afterward, and make it back to the Chewelah regional airport in no time at all, even though they were in another country. At least they weren't thousands of miles away from where he really wanted to be.

The more problems he ran into, the more he wished to end it all. He wanted to believe the best in the fantasy he held onto despite all the evidence to the contrary: that she would one day see the proverbial light and come back to him willingly. In reality, the impossibility of the fantasy wasn't lost on him. What he wanted for her and from her she'd dismiss and defy him to the end. At the very least, he gave her credit for remaining consistent year after year after year.

Consistency would also be her downfall because he could track her thought processes as if she'd sent him an email with her plan written out in minute detail. A better strategy would be to at least vary things a bit to throw him off. That never happened. He'd been able to anticipate her moves. Her speed became the problem he'd been unable to overcome to date. She always seemed to be a step ahead of him.

No more. He'd put his own plan into hyperdrive and end this thing. Tomorrow night, he'd stand in front of her and take her heart, one way or the other. The choice rested with her. She could either allow him to possess it emotionally, or he would possess it literally.

His fingers flexed as he thought about the moment he might hold it in his palm. He smiled, thinking about the possibility of preserving it so he could gaze upon it whenever the old longings stirred. Yes, that would be a grand idea. All he needed was a beautiful jar to hold it. The house here in Vancouver had just the shelf on which to display it. A fitting location given they'd picked out the property together.

He was still thinking about the perfect jar when Sam came in with an attractive woman. While he'd imbibed on the flight here, taking nourishment right from the source had a flavor and power that didn't come in a bag. Sam hit the mark quite well with his selection. Her long, flowing red hair fit his tastes well. Her eyes, which were green and fanned by long, fake lashes, did not. He hated women who tried too hard. That didn't much matter, because in a few hours, she wouldn't be trying anything ever again.

CHAPTER NINETEEN

Jeni peeked in and started to enter the kitchen, then backed out in silence. It didn't seem possible that the night could get weirder, but as with several other things, her assessment on that situation failed too. Earlier she'd walked out of the kitchen while Becca and Patrick combined their resources to create a map of the society's holdings. More specifically, the holdings of the noble, Sir George Carew, the vampire who just happened to be Isa's husband. Becca had been typing away on her laptop, while Patrick had been sitting across from her engrossed in his own work.

In the time since she'd left, things had changed. Now, Becca and Patrick sat side by side, her hand resting on his thigh. If Jeni hadn't seen it, she wouldn't have believed it. Her friend didn't exactly move at the speed of light when it came to relationships. While Becca did have a habit of making poor choices in men, and Jeni had never exactly been sure why, quick jumps weren't her style. Smart as hell and with a generous nature, she should have attracted the best rather than the borderline. They weren't horrible men, just no one she should take home to Mom. After the last disaster, Becca had been taking things a whole lot slower, much to Jeni's relief.

Except for now. A vampire shows up in her town, then stands at her door, dragging along some poor Interpol agent from Ireland, and all of sudden Becca couldn't keep her hands to herself. Well, if she had to fall for someone in the weirdness that defined their world at the moment, at least it wasn't a vampire. Patrick appeared to be all human, which made the sparks flying in her kitchen, where boxes still sat on the counter waiting to be unpacked, and the walls she intended to paint were still a cringe-worthy pea-soup green, a little easier to reconcile with. Yeah, real romantic setting, not that it slowed down whatever was happening in her kitchen.

That would be the craziest thing except she couldn't stop staring at Isa. Jeni couldn't help it. The only way to get around Isa's beauty would have been complete blindness. She kept telling herself that the vampire in her living room was a killer who'd done nothing to save Avery. All the self-talk didn't help. She'd gaze into Isa's eyes, and all that logical shit would fly away. She didn't see a killer in there, but a kindred soul, making it impossible to turn and walk away. Crazy, just crazy, and she didn't like it.

"Did they have anything?"

Jeni stopped in the doorway to the living room and stared directly at Isa. Great. Just freaking great. Way to be a calm and collected cop. Not even close. Instead of coming across as a complete professional, she had to look like a teenager pining over an unattainable rock star. So not cool.

"I'm not sure." At least she didn't sound like a complete idiot.

Isa tilted her head and studied Jeni. "You're not sure," she repeated with a confused tone that mocked Jeni's hope that she sounded somewhat rational. "I don't understand."

She shrugged. "Yeah. Neither do I." No lie there. She still hadn't wrapped her head around how or why the attraction in her kitchen appeared to be moving at warp speed. "I think your friend and mine are—how do I say it—getting quite close."

"That doesn't sound like Patrick."

"Trust me. It's not Becca either. Well, not the Becca of late anyway." She wanted to give her friend the benefit of the doubt and not fall back on the woman who'd let too many losers through the front door.

A slow smile pulled up the corners of Isa's mouth, and Jeni sucked in a breath, albeit quietly. "I rather like it. Patrick has needed a good woman for a very long time. I assume your friend is a good woman."

Well, nothing too insulting about that comment. "Of course. Becca's a wonderful person, and he'd be lucky to have someone like her interested in him."

"Excellent. Now shall we talk about our plans? I have to return to my home soon and rest. My people are working to ensure George is kept busy for at least one more night. I want to be ready for him when he arrives back here, and that means I must take my slumber."

Interesting how quickly Isa moved from the rapidly developing attraction between their two friends and their shared foe. What she'd seen in the kitchen gave her more pause than the ten seconds it gave Isa. However, on the scale of importance, George outweighed Becca and Patrick by about a ton.

Questions about Isa's quest still lingered for her. "You've tried to explain and justify, and I still don't get why you've waited to take him out. I have a hard time believing you couldn't have done this years ago." Isa hadn't exactly been forthcoming with her age or how long she and George had been together. Just her speech patterns alone made Jeni believe it had been a very long time. Isa wasn't a twenty-first-century woman. Or a twentieth-century woman, for that matter, leaving her to wonder exactly what century she did hail from.

Isa hesitated, and Jeni could almost see the wheels spinning in her head. With a sigh and a decision apparently made, she said softly, "Fear."

"You were afraid of him. Are afraid of him?"

"Yes. Until your wife, I let my fear of George's power hold me back. When Avery was taken, I realized I couldn't let it rule my life any longer. Every year since, I have grown stronger, and fear morphed into fury. I have used that to get us to this place and to this moment."

Jeni nodded and tried to keep the surprise from showing on her face. Isa came across as a kick-ass, take-names kind of woman, so for echoes of fear to appear in her voice made her more of a believer than anything she could say. "All right. I appreciate your honesty. Never thought I'd hear a vampire admit weakness."

"It is simply the truth. Whatever else happens, I can promise you that I will not lie to you."

Again, the echo of truth in her words landed for Jeni. Isa wasn't like any vampire she'd run into over the last decade. "Why wait all these years? Why didn't you do it when you left the society?"

Isa's face hardened as if a million horrible memories had hit her all at once. "It is true. If all I had wanted to do was kill him, I could have done that a very long time ago."

"But…"

"I don't desire to just kill him. I want to destroy him, and before we send him to the long overdue hell, I want it to hit him like a giant slap in the face."

This time Jeni smiled. The heat in Isa's words fanned the embers of her own anger. They were, indeed, kindred souls. "Atta girl."

From the outside Isa knew her game plan over the last ten years seemed long and drawn out to anyone listening. Or, more particularly, to Jeni's ears. There could be no denying that many opportunities to kill George had presented themselves over the years. All his attempts to try to put distance between them—or himself by believing that's what he was doing—he couldn't. Time and time again, he put himself into Isa's orbit. His deluded belief told him she'd always be at his side despite the fact she never once gave him false hope.

Well, that wasn't exactly true. She manipulated him during that long-ago time when her father put her up for auction. To circumvent her father's plans had been paramount and necessary to make certain her betrothal ended as she wished. Her poor father never realized how she'd played him at the same time she played George. Her deception, with George in any event, ended in the marriage chamber. From the moment the deal was done and the marriage completed, she became boldly honest. She didn't love or desire him, and she told him as much. If he desired intimacy, he'd be welcome to find it outside the marriage.

At the time she believed he'd become enraged. That her truth didn't seem to bother him came as a shock. In fact, the effect on George was quite the opposite. His determination to capture her love became all-consuming, and he did everything he could think of to win her over. That it would never happen, even if he hadn't slaughtered her family, didn't resonate with him. His peace offering at the time came in the form of not taking her family's fortune as his own. He'd graciously, in his opinion, allowed her to retain the wealth due her by family legacy.

Like she would have let him take it anyway. Sometimes, he underestimated her. Actually, the way she saw it, he always underestimated her. Patriarchal laws be damned, the money belonged to her. Unfortunately, her ancestral home did not. Her *husband* had inherited the deed upon the death of her father and brother. That loss had burned a hole in her heart for centuries, even though she'd told herself over and over to let it go.

Now, she looked at Jeni, and something inside shifted. Too bad they lived in such different worlds. This woman spoke to her spirit, and she liked her fierceness. The fact that she found her incredibly attractive didn't hurt either. Why Avery had married her didn't pass her by. She suspected Avery had seen all the same qualities that beckoned to her now.

She continued her explanation, although it might be hard for a woman of this century to truly grasp. "George took everything from me, so simply ending his life isn't enough to balance the scales. He must be held accountable for many things, not just killing my family."

"Avery."

"Yes, Avery, and many others. The only way to get through to someone like George is to destroy all that he holds dear. His properties, his followers, and, most importantly, his power. To outmaneuver him will be the crushing blow to someone with his immense ego. When I strip him of everything that matters and see in his eyes the realization of what has happened, then and only then will I put this through his heart." She pulled out the small carved stake.

"Where the hell did you have that?" Jeni's eyes were wide. Not the first time she'd seen that on someone's face.

Isa smiled. "I have my secrets." Like a small sheath sewn into her jacket so expertly no one ever detected it. One didn't live as long as she did without learning a trick or twelve.

"Sister, you have more secrets than a sheath."

An understatement. "I am afraid I do indeed."

"Do tell."

Strangely, Isa wanted to share with Jeni, and it scared her that this woman, reluctant to speak to her and even more so to work with her, made Isa want to confide things she never spoke of and at the same time made her want to run out the front door. She came here for an ally. Nothing more.

She made a zipper motion across her lips. Despite all that roiled inside her, caution made her stop short of another open and honest moment. Coward. "I think not."

Jeni stepped close and put a hand on her shoulder, the action so unexpected that she froze. Or maybe she froze because the touch sent a charge of energy through her whole body. "We'll see."

Sam had the right idea when he'd brought the tasty treat. He deserved it after everything. He couldn't survive on bagged blood alone. Well, he actually could, but someone like him didn't have to. His position entitled him to the best of everything, and that included a luscious young woman with smooth skin and warm blood running through her veins. She sated his body and his hunger, in that order.

Now he stepped under the spray of the massive shower in the bathroom of his suite and closed his eyes. His enthusiastic activities resulted in a substantial mess. When he opened his eyes, the water ran red as it sluiced off his body. Despite the actions of the traitors at his home, those who were loyal to him were in the next room cleaning it as he cleansed himself. The warm water cascaded down his body, and the smell of the expensive soap replaced the acrid scent of fresh blood. By the time he'd showered, dried himself, and put on clean clothing, the bedroom would be as pristine as it had when he'd stepped through the doors a few hours earlier.

True enough that someone might miss his lovely companion, given her status as a high-end escort. Streetwalkers were of little value to most and as easily replaced as a new pair of cheap sneakers. In the sex-trade hierarchy, tonight's companion held much more value, and at some point, her failure to return would garner attention. His connection to her disappearance would be impossible to trace. They were careful that way. Even if they did connect him to her, what could they do? Arrest him? The thought made him laugh. Above the law didn't even begin to describe his life. Untouchable would be a far more accurate word.

When he stepped out of the bathroom, no one remained in his suite, dead or alive. At the bar he poured himself a scotch. Many of his kind sustained themselves on blood alone. Though he loved blood, the world had so much more to offer, like single-malt scotch. The flavor never got old and, in fact, over the years had vastly improved.

Drink in hand, he sat down in front of his laptop. He logged on and sent an email. Given the hour, it might take a few minutes before he received a response. No waiting tonight. The mail icon popped up in less than a minute, and he smiled as he read.

Flowers received and dumped into trash bin. Reinforcements arrived. Not trying to keep it secret. Your instructions?

Well, well, well. Now wasn't that interesting? Not that she threw his little gift away. He would have been shocked had she done something different. The reinforcements piece more than surprised him. It shocked him. By and large she operated as a lone wolf. That method suited her personality. She'd been that way even as a human and became more so as a vampire. To discover she'd shifted strategy was stunning, though certainly not disruptive in terms of what he had planned for her.

He typed his reply.

Gather as much information as you can about her friends and report back to me ASAP. Make sure new home is stocked and ready when I return next evening. I want all in place, and I want briefed on everything that she is up to. Use every single one of our local resources.

He closed his laptop without waiting for an answer. Didn't need one. Those who worked for him, whether vampire or human, were compensated well, and that meant the best of the best were at his disposal. His directions would be followed to the letter, as no one wanted to suffer the consequences should he be disappointed. Setbacks aside, the win column for him remained in excellent shape. Everything dropped into place, and he could sense a conclusion to years of frustration. He could feel *her*.

Time now to rest. The night ahead promised to be eventful, not to mention fun. He particularly looked forward to the fun part.

CHAPTER TWENTY

Jeni woke up slowly. She breathed deeply, savoring the sensation of Avery's hand holding hers. The touch of a loved one held power like nothing else. It soothed the soul. How nice it would be to forget the rest of the world and just stay here. The thought made her smile. Then reality crashed in.

Not Avery.

She sucked in her breath and froze. Isa continued to doze on the sofa, serene and peaceful. Somehow, some way, their hands became entwined while they slept. The thought that she'd been holding hands with a vampire made her stomach turn and the memory of her sweet little dream wither. She pulled her hand away in a slow, even motion so she didn't awaken Isa. It was disturbing enough to her to find them touching. To face Isa while feeling somewhat violated wasn't a place she wanted to go. Unfortunately, her plan didn't work out. The moment she slid her hand free, Isa's eyes fluttered opened. Shit. It would be nice if just once things went her way.

Isa pushed up. Well, maybe things were on her side a little because Isa appeared oblivious to her revulsion at the intimate connection.

"I am sorry I fell asleep." Her hands went to her head, and she pushed the long, heavy hair off her face. Did Isa sense they'd been holding hands in their slumber? She hoped not.

"Yeah. So did I." She stood, grateful for the distance. "I've got to get ready for work." Her words sounded too fast to be casual.

She glanced toward the window. "Are you going to be okay? It's daylight." Jeni had about thirty minutes to get dressed and to her office.

Isa frowned as her gaze went to the window. "Not ideal. I should have returned to my home at least an hour ago. How could Patrick have let me sleep? This will be a royal pain now." Her brows pulled together, and she bit her lip.

Jeni grimaced and not so much because she felt bad for Isa. More like a vampire in her house would have to be about the last thing she wanted to deal with today. She wished she could tell her to go, daylight be damned. Too many other factors involved to be that kind of rude and abrupt. Somewhere along the line in the last couple of hours, it occurred to her that she could use Isa. Not that she trusted her much. If she led her to the one responsible for taking Avery, then that made all this worth it.

Except for the hand-holding part. That just fucking creeped her out. Sort of. That the touch of her hand had sent Jeni's sleeping mind into pleasant dreams didn't sit well with her. It shouldn't have felt good.

She took a breath and reached for the high road. It was a long stretch. "You can stay here." That the words actually came out of her mouth amazed her.

"I did not come here to impose on you." Isa stood and turned full circle, as if thinking about how to sprint out of the room. Maybe she did know they'd been holding hands in their sleep and Jeni wasn't the only one creeped out by it, which kind of insulted her, double standard and all.

"I believe that, but it doesn't change the facts. You're still here, and it's full-on daylight outside. Better safe than sorry. I want this George guy, and the best way to get him is through you. If you're too weakened or, worse yet, go up in smoke, you won't be any help to me. I need you at one hundred percent."

Isa stopped scanning the room and focused on Jeni. Something in her expression shifted. "I see a great deal of truth in that."

"Hey, I'm a good detective, and truth is my game."

Isa smiled, and once more, a flutter almost made her jump. Once more it pissed her off. She didn't like the way charity toward Isa settled in more and more. She reminded herself that Isa had been there when Avery was killed. She'd let Avery be killed. That line of thought worked, and her stony resolve roared back in. No more warm, fuzzy feelings caused by the smile of a beautiful vampire. Or the touch of her hand. Nice to know she wasn't too shallow.

"Do you have a dark room where I can rest?"

Shit. Becca had taken over the guest room when she arrived, leaving only one other option. Her hesitation had to be noticeable. "My bedroom."

❖

Isa woke slowly, a bit disoriented. Not her room. Not her bed. Then it came back to her. She'd dropped onto Jeni's bed after she'd cleaned up and left for the sheriff's office. As she lay on the bed, now she scanned the room in the filtered light coming from the hallway. It reflected Jeni's personality. The walls were a pale blue, decorated with several abstract paintings alive with brilliant colors. The photograph of Jeni and Avery still sat on the nightstand, just as it had when she'd let herself into the house uninvited.

Were Becca and Patrick up? After the lengthy strategy and research session, the three of them had been intent on grabbing some sleep while poor Jeni headed to work. Patrick picked the sofa and slipped into sleep about two seconds after he stretched out. Becca took the other bedroom and, she suspected, had not been far behind Patrick in the sleep department. She'd left them in peaceful slumber, hoping the same would happen for her.

It did not. Unable to drift off as quickly, she lay in the dim room thinking about the clash between the past and the present. The unexpected nap on the sofa provided sufficient rest to make falling back into deep slumber difficult, her mind whirling with thoughts about her plans for George and his payment for sins old and new.

She smiled at all the trouble she and her compatriots had put him through in the last several days. Wait until he got an up-close-and-personal view of the pile of ash that used to be his house here. She wished she could be there to see his face when he got a good look at what she'd pulled off. Undoubtedly, the loss of Zion would piss him off too, and that pleased her. Emily, her favorite governess, used to tell her to mind her manners, for what goes around, comes around. Zion had missed that lesson. So had George.

Voices drifted down the hall, confirming that Becca and Patrick were, in fact, up and about. Another smile crossed her face. They had certainly hit it off, and quickly too. From everything she could see, the connection ran deep for two people who'd just met. Odd as it seemed, she had witnessed it before, and it convinced her that the love-at-first-sight theory actually held weight. Not that it occurred often. It did happen on occasion, and most likely, the phenomenon had struck again down the hall. It made her happy to believe that even after she finished this deed and met her own demise, Patrick would enjoy love and happiness in the future to come. She'd seen first-hand how he saved many who would never have an inkling of what he'd done. Not the kind to ask for thanks, he would never reach for glory. He didn't seek to be a hero. Simply speaking, he did what he believed to be the right thing and asked for nothing in return. Love should come to him with the promise of a bright tomorrow. Perhaps Becca would be the one to give that to him.

Though she didn't have clean clothes with her, the shower in Jeni's bathroom beckoned, and she decided to answer the call. Tonight would be long and busy. Maybe she would have time to swing by her house to clean up, change clothes, and grab additional weapons, and maybe she wouldn't. She might as well take ten minutes here to shower. At least she'd be clean and alert.

She stripped off her clothes and laid them on the end of the bed in a tidy pile. Five minutes and she'd be back out, or at least that's what she told herself. As the warm water poured over her, everything slowed down. She savored the warm, soothing spray, which gave her a chance to stop and think. While she had heard Becca and Patrick when she awakened, not even a whisper of Jeni's voice. Why? Given the drop of the sun behind the mountains, it had to be closing in on seven, so where was she?

Her answer came as she toweled off her hair and walked naked into the bedroom, where Jeni stopped mid-stride, her mouth open.

Isa dropped the hand holding the towel and smiled. "Hi."

He rose the moment the sun set. Energy coursed through him, and he'd never been more ready to make a huge statement. No further tolerance of the recent bouts of anarchy. He'd make one thing clear to the vampire world tonight: he would not be pushed... ever. Those that tried would perish.

It didn't make sense that someone would challenge him, given his leadership was the best the Redcap Society had seen since its inception. No one had done a better job than he. No one had ever possessed the level of intelligence as he. Top that off with his good looks and charm, and it became clear that no one would ever be as good. So, the fact that there were challengers out there now meant that it would be necessary to remind them of how lucky they were to have him at the helm.

That, and he did not appreciate his properties being trifled with. No more would be lost, even with the challenge occurring here in Vancouver. They might think they had him cornered and weakened. They would be ever so wrong. He continued to hold the trump card, and within the hour, proof of that would resonate throughout the vampire community.

He showered, dressed, and refreshed himself from the carafe that Sam left near his computer. At the same time he drank from the crystal goblet, he logged onto his computer. He didn't want her to think he'd forgotten or abandoned her. With a few keystrokes, he made sure she knew he continued to think of her. He put the empty glass on the table and sent Sam a text. Time to go.

Sam waited with the car downstairs. The directions he gave him as they negotiated the city streets took them to an outbuilding a good quarter mile from the house. The building didn't stand out as anything special, just a maintenance structure for the acres of tended land that surrounded the estate. Designed to blend in with the landscape, it didn't attract attention.

"Park there." George pointed to a stand of trees that would provide good coverage. He didn't wish to attract unwanted notice, and a car like his might, even though fine automobiles weren't uncommon in this area. This wasn't a neighborhood where people drove Chevrolets, Fords, or Hondas.

The key he pulled from his pocket unlocked the door of the building. It might seem odd to carry that single key around with him, given that the number of homes he possessed throughout the world. Yet he carried at least one key with him for every home. To be caught off guard regardless of where he might be at any given time didn't sit well with him. Hence the small bag that accompanied him on every trip. The key he held now was the only one to this particular door, and the lock came from one of the finest manufacturers in the world. When it was originally installed, he had wanted to be certain no one could breach it.

"Motherfucker." Sam whistled as he stepped inside. "You're one sneaky son of a bitch."

Chapter Twenty-one

The absolute last thing Jeni expected to see when she entered her bedroom was a naked woman. Correction...a naked vampire. Isa walked out of her bathroom in all her glory, which stopped Jeni cold. How in the world could a vampire look like that? They were supposed to be vile, ugly creatures, and what she saw right now didn't come anywhere close to that description.

Maybe she'd been too long without a woman, because her blood suddenly ran very hot, and it took an effort to keep her breathing steady. Geez. How had she zoomed right back to high school to come face-to-face with that first awkward crush? She figured she'd gone way beyond that at her age, and the evidence before her right now proved she'd be wrong. Her throat tightened, and any ability to speak fled.

"Sorry," Isa said as she walked slowly to where her clothing lay in a tidy pile on the end of the bed. "I intended to be dressed and out of your way before you got home. I do hope it was all right that I used your shower. I thought it would save time if I cleaned up here."

"Sure. Fine." So smooth. Isa slipped on her form-fitting pants, and the realization that she did so commando made Jeni's breath catch. Nothing too sexy about that...not one tiny bit. No bra either, as she held up her arms and pulled on her shirt. Jeni needed to remind herself of the fact that Isa wasn't human. Yeah. That cooled the fire a little, but only a little, because, dear Lord, she got an eyeful of something she hadn't seen in a long time. How could a vampire be this beautiful? It wasn't right. Oh, hell, it wasn't fair. She didn't want to like Isa, let alone find her intoxicatingly beautiful. Nope, not fair at all.

She turned and left the bedroom. Sure, it came across as rude. Some things couldn't be helped. Standing tall and strong to maintain her composure was a lot more important now. She didn't dare come across as weak or easily swayed by a beautiful body—not to Isa, or anyone else for that matter. Particularly not to Isa.

She breathed a lot easier when she reached the kitchen where Patrick and Becca were at the table with two Belgian beers open. "Really? You think beer is what you need tonight?"

Becca smiled, picked up the bottle, and tilted it in her direction. "Nectar of the gods, my friend, and yeah, I think it's exactly what we need." She cut her eyes to Patrick. "How about you, Patty?"

He rolled his eyes at her. "Don't you think that's a little on the ethnic-profiling side? Every Irishman must be a Patty or a Paddy."

Becca reached over and touched his face in a gesture that seemed incredibly intimate. What in the world had happened while she'd been at work? Their already developing attraction appeared to be moving at warp speed. "No, no, no. Not buying into the stereotypes at all. I like Patty because Patrick is too formal, and you are so not a Pat. So, Patty it is."

His smile told Jeni that she had, indeed, missed something of great importance. The way these two acted, they'd been a couple for a long time. Wow. Just wow.

Before she could comment on their rapid-fire relationship, Isa walked into the kitchen—cool, collected, and fully dressed. Part of her said, Thank God. Another part of her said, Damn.

"What do you have for us?"

"Hey," Patrick said and turned his smile on Isa. "We've been busy little beavers." He cocked his head and said to Jeni, "Do they even have beavers in this part of the world?"

"Not something I've ever checked." And really, why would she care? Wildlife wasn't on her list of important matters right now.

He shrugged. "Just a thought. I like to keep a lot of trivia up here." He tapped the side of his head.

"What have you got? Surely you two did something today beside make goo-goo eyes at each other."

Becca had just taken a drink from her beer and spit it out in a spray that struck them all. When she finished choking and sputtering, her laughter filled the room. "Sweet Jesus, that's hysterical. Goo-goo eyes. Girlfriend, we have to get you out more. Sorry about the beer bath, everyone."

Jeni took a roll of paper towels and set it in the middle of the table. "We have to get out there and kill vampires."

"Yeah, yeah, yeah. All in good time."

"That good time is now." She didn't know what it was going to take to light a fire under them.

Becca got up and slung an arm around her shoulders. "So, you think all my handsome pal and I have been doing today is sitting around the table drinking beer and making eyes at each other?"

She shrugged. No. She didn't really think that, but she also didn't want to say it. What she did say didn't sound too petty. "You got some sleep too, I hope."

Everything felt off today and had from the moment she opened her eyes. It continued after she left here, and the wonky vibes hit her as soon as she walked into work. Some of it she expected after Becca's vampire bombshell. If Trent didn't treat her a little differently at that, she'd have to wonder about him.

He too had been off, and it had been more than the vampire declaration. She hadn't been able to put a finger on why. Not a comfortable feeling at all, and she'd been glad to zip out of there as soon as they'd delivered a domestic-violence arrest to the jail in Colville. Put a little distance between them, and she might be able to figure out what the deal was with Trent.

As if the day at work hadn't been uncomfortable enough, then she'd stepped into her own bedroom to the sight of the naked Isa. Her weird day had just gotten even weirder. She'd thought that would be the end of the strangeness, and once more, she'd turned out to be wrong. The grins on the faces of Becca and Patrick told her they had something interesting. She wished they'd just spit it out.

Becca gave Patrick a wink and then turned to Jeni. "So, how well do you know that partner of yours?"

❖

That teaser of a statement didn't give Isa a clue where Becca might be headed. Who cared about a random sheriff's deputy? In this war, law enforcement wouldn't be much help. Well, except for Patrick and Jeni, that is. She needed them. More accurately, she wanted them at her side. Her friend for years, Patrick would always be welcome as a brother-in-arms. Given she didn't have an over-abundance of friends, she valued him for more than just his skills in international detection and his amazingly open mind.

She wanted to say the same about Jeni, except she couldn't quite yet. Their time together had been short, and they didn't have a relationship that she could point to and say, "She is my friend." The truth didn't look that way at all. Her initial approach to Jeni came strictly in the sense of needing to use her expertise. In a few short hours, that approach changed. Friendship, certainly. But after that moment in the bedroom, she wanted more, and it had been eons since she felt anything even close to desire.

Not important at the moment because anything she felt beyond an intense drive for vengeance needed to go on the back burner. Rather, she had to focus on Becca's statement about Jeni's partner, which she found baffling. No context to put it into except that Becca and Patrick had obviously been busy while she rested, and Jeni had been at work in the sheriff's office.

"Not well at all," Jeni admitted. "I mean, I just started with the department, and beyond a few days together, I've got nothing. Why? He seems like a good guy and a fairly competent deputy sheriff." At least she wasn't alone in her confusion. Jeni's face mirrored her own thoughts.

"Sure is, and he's certainly cute enough, although I doubt you'd notice." Becca laughed.

Jeni shook her head. "Whatever. Get to the point."

Isa studied Jeni a little closer. Interesting comment from Becca, and well, she liked it. A trickle of excitement tapped at the back of her neck. Sometimes she allowed instinct a minute of free rein. She spent so much of her time in warrior mode that just being a woman often got lost. Even if only for a moment, she wanted to remember.

"Okay, so here's the deal." Becca motioned toward her laptop. "Patrick and I—" she pointed to Patrick and winked, "came across some interesting things about your partner today."

Jeni sank to a chair. "Hit me."

Isa sat next to her. Earlier she'd been eager to get going. Something in Becca's voice hinted at a surprise, and now she wanted nothing more than to sit next to Jeni and let her friend lead the charge. Things were indeed getting interesting. "I want to hear this."

Becca smiled. "I think your pal, George," she nodded at Isa, "has been a very busy guy."

Had he been born in this century, George would have been diagnosed hyperactive. Always on the move, always thinking. His intense drive to take over the world fit in well with his hyperactivity. "That's nothing new."

"Au contraire. As a general rule, does he have deputy sheriffs in small, remote counties in his back pocket?"

Becca made a good point, and her attention became riveted. George's influence all over the world couldn't be understated. He typically went much larger and more powerful than a deputy sheriff. He would lean more on the people who held chief-of-police positions in places like New York City, Chicago, or Los Angeles rather than a rural county tucked up in the northwest corner of the country. "No," she admitted. "He wouldn't bother in a place like this."

The smile Becca gave her spoke of triumph. "Yeah. We kinda thought the same thing, so we did a little digging. More like a lot of digging."

And this news illustrated exactly why she'd called on Patrick in the first place. The man simply had skills. She'd been around for centuries, yet he could find out things that were absolutely amazing. Apparently giving him a few hours with Becca equated to pouring gasoline on a fire. Together they were even better.

"What did you find?" A knot settled in her stomach, and she wondered how the news hit Jeni. She'd just started a new job with a new partner, and the proverbial other shoe seemed poised to drop.

"Do you happen to know a vampire by the name of Nelda?"

Isa started to shake her head and then stopped. "Nelly...yes." She thought of the attractive vampire with the bright blue eyes and quick smile who'd come into the fold right before Isa made her exit. The spirited recruit had captured George's fancy. Her mind at the time too occupied with other matters of more importance to her, she hadn't paid too much attention to George's newest pet. Through the years these alluring pets would come and go.

"Yeah. Nelly would be Nelda Schrader."

"What about her?"

"She's Trent's mama."

That revelation stopped her, and words failed her. The news didn't render Jeni speechless.

Jeni stood, shaking her head and clenching her fists. "Motherfucker."

❖

George roared, though he managed to curb the urge to charge forward. At his feet, Sam lay still, a projectile of smooth alder wood piercing his body, a red stain spreading across his pale shirt. What had once been one of his most trusted advisors now lay at his feet, motionless with the offending alder stake pointed toward the ceiling.

He'd come here confident they would surprise the interlopers from the secret escape tunnels. His belief that he was the only one still alive and aware of their existence proved to be almost fatal. For Sam, it turned out to be a death sentence. The bastards had been waiting for them. Not that they stayed around to celebrate their success. Oh, no, they set up their trap, surely expecting him to be the first one to enter through the hidden door, and left. Sam begged to lead the charge after he got over his delight at finding out about the tunnels, and George gave him what he considered to be an honor.

The trap made him furious. That he survived their deadly plan was as it should be. The loss of Sam inexcusable. To lose a second of his special forces was unthinkable. At the same time, it didn't stop him. Triumph over his adversaries without the support of others wasn't out of reach. He could do it easily on his own.

Every time he came here, he walked them door-to-door in order to maintain familiarity in the event he needed to flee. It had never occurred to him that he would need to use them to launch an attack on his own property. Even as old as he was, life still surprised him on occasion.

He stepped over Sam's body to emerge from the tunnel and into the house. His roar echoed. Just inside his library where the floor-to-ceiling bookcases were packed with precious first editions, Josef's body lay slumped in one of the comfortable reading chairs. Like Sam, a single stake pierced his chest, and congealed blood pooled at his feet. His once-handsome face had gone slack.

The next surprise waited for him just outside the library doorway. Before the assholes left, they made sure to destroy his house as they went. As he made a hasty search of the premises, he found it vacated save for the bodies of Sam and Josef. In addition, every faucet in the place had been left running, and water poured from the ceilings, destroying exquisite woodwork and irreplaceable antique wallpaper. It would cost millions to restore. Of course, they knew that. Or she did, which is why she told them to inflict such massive damage. She also knew that water would be the best way to insult him. She had a long memory.

Well, her little plan failed, just as it should have. She would never best him. Beautiful and smart as she might have been on the very first day they met, even then she had never been a true match for his intellect or cunning. A perfect accessory for his extraordinary life, absolutely. His better? Never. Not then and not now.

Certain he walked the house alone, he nonetheless checked for interlopers and found none. Then, he headed toward the basement. While he always had caretakers who tended to the day-to-day maintenance, he would have no issues locating the water main. He wasn't helpless. Not a foolish man, he double-checked before he descended the stairs to make certain additional traps had not been laid. He wouldn't put it past any of them to set up a similar surprise for anyone trying to find the water shutoff. A stake through his body wasn't on the day's agenda. The absence of a second trap told him they believed the first arrow deployed in the tunnel and piercing Sam's chest would be the only one needed. Too bad they'd miscalculated. It had served only to infuriate him more than when he'd first stepped into his glorious home. Or what remained of his glorious home.

Besides, when he destroyed those who rose against him, he would take not only their lives, but their wealth as well. It would be fitting that their money pay for repairing the damage to his property. He smiled as he walked through the basement until, as expected, he located the water main. Near silence fell once the water faucets stopped their fire-hydrant assault. As he ascended the stairs once more, the only sound now was the drip, drip, drip of water as it drained away from the upper floors through the ceiling and onto the hardwood floors and expensive rugs.

He retraced his steps to the hidden entrance to the tunnel. Sam's body lay just inside. Unfortunately, that's where it would stay. No time to bother with him. He stood before the bookcase that served as the door to the no-longer-secret escape route. His fingers touched the tiny button that made the bookcase swing back into place, effectively hiding the entrance and his dead general. No need for it to remain open because he didn't plan to leave the way he'd entered. The fact that they had been aware of its existence made him wary. Yes, the house had been vacated. That didn't mean he trusted they were completely gone. What had waited for him at this end might now be waiting for him at the other.

Upstairs in the master suite closet, his clothing remained dry and untouched. No effort had been expended to destroy his possessions. They probably believed the water assault and the doorway trap would do an effective job when it came to making it hurt. No need to waste time on unimportant things like clothing.

Dressed in black pants and a black shirt, he returned downstairs, where he found a black watch cap in the kitchen closet, something that must belong to one of the handymen he employed. In all black, he would blend into the night. The only glitch was his light hair. It would stand out, and he couldn't risk drawing attention to himself. The cap covered his head down to his eyebrows and over his ears. Problem solved.

Though they most assuredly watched the house, anticipating the results of their handiwork and a celebration to follow, he refused to give them the satisfaction. As he stepped outside, he became one with the darkness and left behind the remains of his treasure and the body of his, dare he say it, friend. He would never have admitted it to Sam, but it didn't make it any less true. Bad enough they were systematically destroying his holdings, now they destroyed one of the very few he considered a true friend. Their actions gave him even more focus than he'd come here with. A dangerous thing.

CHAPTER TWENTY-TWO

O kay," Jeni said as she leaned back in her chair. "Somebody bring me up to speed on Nelly. I mean, I get the fact that if she's truly Trent's mother, then he played us earlier. If he, that is, actually knows his mother is a vampire. Of course, kind of hard to believe he wouldn't be in on something like that. Pretty sure my mom would tell me if she turned into a blood sucker."

Isa studied her like a teacher assessing a student on the first day of school. She could tell she weighed in as to whether Jeni had a clue or if she'd offended her with the blood-sucker comment. Kind of insulting really. Just because she might not have understood her new partner had a vampire connection didn't mean a thing in the big picture. She'd just started working with the guy, and it would take more than a couple days to completely get him. It wouldn't be a stretch to believe that kind of secret would be taken to the grave.

Isa's expression cleared. From the looks of it, she must have decided in Jeni's favor. "He knows." The two words were delivered in a very decisive tone.

"How can you be so certain?" Thinking back to Trent's initial reaction to Becca's declaration about vampires, she had trouble reconciling it with someone who might already be aware of their cohabitation in the world. He seemed genuine in his disbelief.

"I have seen them together since…"

"Since she was turned."

"Exactly."

A thought occurred to Jeni that demanded an answer. "When did you even meet Trent?"

Isa appeared nonplussed. "You forget I've been here longer than you."

Yeah, well, that actually did make sense. Jeni shook her head, trying to clear out the sudden onslaught of cobwebs. Too much information and not enough sleep. In what world did a job change and relocation turn out to be this bizarre? She believed she'd left the world of preternatural creatures behind and that here she'd find some kind of peace and normalcy. That plan had surely gone up in smoke fast. And now the smoke seemed to be morphing into a three-alarm fire. Seriously, her partner's mom turns out to be a vampire? Man, she should take up poker and head to Vegas.

Isa spoke up again. "Nelly caught George's attention while she was in San Francisco. She's beautiful and smart and completely susceptible to the charms of a man like him."

"You mean a vampire."

"Yes and no. Just because someone has been turned doesn't mean they suddenly become a new type of being. It's true that they gain certain enhancements like speed and power and vision. Basic personalities don't much change." Isa spread her arms. "What you see is pretty much what you would have seen when I was human. A pushy bitch a few centuries ago and the same pushy bitch today."

Jeni didn't believe it. Bitch wasn't a word she'd use to describe her. Beyond that, Isa glowed with an energy hard to believe could be human generated. It came across as otherworldly. Not in a bad way, which made her mad. She wanted it to be terrible, just as she'd built up all vampires to be in her mind. It didn't track that a night creature could be anything except evil. This whole thing with Isa seemed destined to upend all her preconceived notions, not to mention her closely held anger, neither of which she felt inclined to give up anytime soon.

As Isa talked, she touched a chain around her neck. Earlier, she'd briefly noted that it was the only thing she'd been wearing when she walked out of Jeni's bathroom. At the time, her shock at finding a naked vampire in her room blurred any other details.

Now she focused on that necklace. A vague feeling of familiarity whispered through her. A memory tickled that refused to gel.

She brought her gaze back to Isa's face. "Say I buy that you're the same as you've always been. Then how can I be sure you're not playing us? I mean, think about it. This George guy brought you into the fold for some reason, so why wouldn't you still be part of his circle?"

Isa shook her head. "You can't ignore the larger picture. I never became part of George's inner circle. As I've explained several times, I used him, thinking he would be the least objectionable horse to tie my coach to."

Yeah, she'd heard her each time she'd made that claim. "You're wrong there. I did hear you before, and I hear you now. But you're asking us to believe that you're not using us now like you admit to using George? Basic personalities don't change." She threw Isa's own words back at her.

She shrugged. "I would be lying to say I'm not, at least a little. Through you, I can get closer to George, and that's the plain truth. I can make him hurt just as he did to me. As he hurt you. It's not so much using you as working with you to accomplish a common goal. Together, we can hold him accountable for what he did to me and my family, and what he did to you and Avery."

Jeni liked her honesty, for a vampire anyway. Was she completely convinced of Isa's intentions? On the fence there. A chance to kill the monster that destroyed her life held an appeal she couldn't ignore. And if Isa could give her that chance, then so what if she was using her?

"All right. Let's get back to this Nelly. How is she going to be a problem? And how do I deal with that sneaky son-of-a-bitch Trent?"

Becca held up a hand. "One more little mystery. Fingerprints you took off your picture came back with nothing in the system, sorta."

Jeni's eyes narrowed. "What do you mean sorta?"

"Well, no match in the system to a name."

"Meaning no name but a match to prints found at another crime scene?"

"We have a bingo."

"Do I have to drag this out of you too?"

Becca's smile grew big. "Same prints on your picture frame were on the gas cans at the fire."

"Say that again."

"You heard me."

Jeni slowly turned to stare at Isa.

Isa thought she'd lost all the ground made earlier with Jeni. Trent's sneaky insider knowledge came to the rescue on that front. Her initial fury at finding out her partner knew about vampires brought her firmly back into Isa's camp. All good until the detour Becca just embarked on looked destined to drive yet another wedge. Not surprising. Making allies of humans didn't come easily. Even the tight relationship she forged with Patrick had taken a good long time to cultivate. At first, he'd been as hesitant as Jeni when it came to working together. Of course, she hadn't broken into his house either.

She did not look away from Jeni's angry stare. "I'm sorry. I needed to know more about you the night of the fire and so I let myself in."

"To my house."

"Yes, and I truly am sorry for violating your privacy. I just needed to know what I would be up against with you. I meant no harm." She hoped Jeni could feel her sincerity. "It doesn't change the fact that I need your help. I can only apologize for a lapse in judgment."

Why it might be different for Jeni didn't go over her head either. Isa and Patrick met on their common journey and soon found they walked a similar path. People Patrick knew had been lost, and because of the nature of his work, he had become aware of similar situations all over the world. The investigator in him demanded more, and that drive ultimately brought them together, despite his initial reluctance to work with a vampire. Jeni displayed the same drive she'd seen in Patrick over and over. Except with Jeni, a great deal rested below the surface. Much more than just losing someone she knew. The wedding picture that sat on her nightstand in her bedroom told a huge story. Isa had never really loved anyone like that, though she could relate to the pain of loss. When she watched George and the society kill her family, she'd experienced the kind of heartbreak that never fully healed. A piece of her would always be missing, and she suspected the same was true for Jeni.

For a few minutes, she believed Jeni would walk away, and then she shook her head. "You're a really fucked up vampire."

She owned that one. "I am."

"Don't do it again."

"You have my word."

"All right, then let's get back to Trent."

Jeni's ability to set aside her past experiences and focus on the future impressed Isa. That's what she had hoped for, and her hope had been rewarded. No question she could do this without her. It would be quicker and easier to do it with her.

At least that's what she told herself. Truthfully, she wanted Jeni to be an integral member of their pack. Something about Jeni drew Isa in, and that wasn't like her. In all her years, she had never been drawn to anyone else. Certainly, throughout her long life she enjoyed lovers now and again. A saint she was not. The first time she fully gave in to her desires and spent a night with a woman doing everything she'd ever fantasized about, her formerly small world burst large. That night she embraced her true nature, and it freed her in a way she would have never believed possible.

That didn't mean she'd gone all lovesick. On the contrary, it made her aware that she could be vulnerable if she didn't watch out for herself. The warmth of love and passion could wrap her up and take her away from reality. Open herself up to another and love could be hers. That would be her heart doing the talking. Her brain told her the opposite. Take pleasure where she wanted, when she wanted, then walk away. No emotional entanglements to drag her focus away from her ultimate goal.

That philosophy seemed applicable, particularly now that she could see the light at the end of the tunnel. That trite saying always made her cringe, until now anyway. The truth of it almost slapped her. She'd worked for so long, sacrificed, and swallowed her pride to reach this point, and it seemed as though she actually could see a pinpoint of light far off in the distance. Once she did what she came here to do, that pinpoint of light would blossom into a spotlight that would turn the night sky into day. The job would be done, and she could easily say good-bye to this world without regret. She needed—and wanted—Jeni to make that happen.

She brought her gaze up to Jeni's face. "Nelly is influential. She's older than George's usual preference for the women he surrounds himself with, but at the same time, she's quite lovely. Combine her beauty with maturity and her son's connections, and she's a triple threat. It allows her to hold a powerful seat in the society."

"What I'm hearing is that Trent's involved with this up to his eyeballs, even though he's human."

"You're hearing right." Becca reentered the conversation. "That fucker has been feeding mama and her boyfriend information like a mega-church pastor preaching to the flock. It took me and Patrick here almost all day to dig up the dirt on him. He's not quite as good at covering his tracks as I'm sure he believes he is. Might be a reason he's on the force here instead of one of the caliber you came from, Jen."

"Bottom line," Patrick said, "your boy has been helping to get George close to you both. This has been a game of chess since the beginning, but we didn't have a complete list of all the players until now. We just put the pieces together in the last hour. I must say, they were pretty savvy in hiding their trail. Their weakness is they don't realize how good we are."

Isa would like to say it surprised her. She couldn't because she'd seen George use anybody and everybody, including her, to get what he wanted. Getting her had been as much about her family's wealth as possessing her body and soul. That night, that awful night she still dreamed about hundreds of years later, proved to her exactly the lengths he would go to in order to obtain possessions, money, and influence.

"We need to be ready for George's return." Her fingers flexed as she envisioned putting them around his throat.

Becca smiled. "Way ahead of you."

As George knew would happen, he made it back to the plane undetected. Those fools didn't stand a chance against him. Certainly, they'd go back into the house at some point and check their handiwork. What they'd discover would come as a surprise. They would expect to find him, or what little would be left of him, and a house destroyed by water. Instead, they would find Sam in the tunnel and water damage that could, and would, be fixed. Their grand plan, or rather, her grand plan had failed.

Now, he sat in the comfortable seat of his plane and made plans of his own. The soft leather, the crystal glass filled almost to the brim, and the lovely attendant helped take some of the sting off the earlier events. Odd to be alone on the flight, and no amount of comfort or nourishment could remove the anger that caused. She'd taken away his property, and that insult would not go unpunished. To murder those closest to him went beyond insult, and he felt it deeply as he sat here by himself. No Josef clicking away at the keys of his laptop. No Sam stretched out in the back appearing to rest but, in reality, on high alert like a mountain lion ready to attack.

Once more, he placed a call and directed another delivery to occur at sunset tomorrow. The night would still be full and dark by the time they landed in the small airport less than an hour from now. As much as he desired to take on the charge the moment the wheels touched down, he wanted a little more time to pull his altered plan together. Perfection wasn't an option in order to ensure that the game-playing would end.

Next, he reached out to Nelly, who waited for him at the airport. A wonderful woman, she possessed preferences that didn't correspond to her previous profession of junior-high-school history teacher. Of course, he liked the fact that in her previous life, she had taught history. It gave her a unique impression of the world he'd originally come from, although no one who hadn't lived through those times truly could. It had been a different world then, and he much preferred the times he lived in now. Creature comforts suited him.

He did, however, miss the deceit and intrigue that made those in power look over their shoulders every single day. In a strange way, that kind of environment made life enjoyable and, in reality, proved to be an excellent training ground for what came after for him. When he had first been turned, he'd been a little lost. That he had been handed immortality didn't much bother him. He'd only needed to find his stride, and he'd discovered quickly that he loved the blood hunt. Along the way he'd met so many kindred souls that his introduction into the Redcap Society became a given. As had his rise to power.

This current situation didn't come as a big shock. Everyone who held absolute power came into contact with the dissatisfied. The great ones, like himself, rolled with bumps and did the things necessary to keep their *kingdom* intact. Just as he prepared to do now. Early in his life, he'd had the opportunity to study some of the best, and in the years since, he'd improved upon those lessons. It made him smile thinking about how things would go down during the next several days.

"Isa, Isa, Isa," he murmured as he gazed out the airplane window and swirled the contents inside the crystal glass. Outside, complete darkness wrapped the plane like a thick black tarp. He smiled. He'd always loved the night, even before he'd been turned. Now he owned it.

Isa wouldn't be expecting what he'd planned for her. She thought she knew him, and in some ways she did. That she overestimated what she knew about him and how to get to him would never occur to her. A smart man always held back, even from those allowed into the inner circle. In her case, he had shown her only what he wanted her to glimpse, and that would be her downfall. She would see the whole picture only when it was too late.

He leaned his head back and closed his eyes. "Soon, my darling, soon."

CHAPTER TWENTY-THREE

Jeni shouldn't have been surprised when Trent called.
Probably more the timing than the actual call. Given their
partnership, calls between them wouldn't be uncommon. They were
sitting around her table talking strategy when her cell phone rang.
She glanced up at the clock. Eleven forty-five. A little late for the
best of friends, and they weren't even close to that. At this time of
night, odd, to say the least.

"What's up?" She kept her tone neutral. He didn't need to catch
on that she knew anything about him that he hadn't shared. She
planned to spring that little surprise on him at the right time.

"Sorry if I woke you."

"It's good, but seriously, what's up? It's a little late for a social
call."

"You alone?"

Why would he care? "No. My friend Becca is still here."

"You hook up with that vampire yet?"

"We've talked." Again, why the sudden interest in Isa when he
hadn't even mentioned her since their initial conversation?

"Good. I've got something I think you and the vamp need to
see. Can you contact her?"

She didn't have a good feeling about the request. Trent remained
very much an unknown player, and given her first impression about
him being a good guy had been way off, she didn't trust much right
now when it came to him. She'd always liked to think she had a good

sense of people, and until now she'd been confident in that ability. Between Isa and Trent, her people radar appeared to be broken.

She glanced over at Isa, who studied her with narrowed eyes. She sensed that she could hear the whole conversation, and who knew? Maybe she could. Since losing Avery, she'd become a quasi-expert on vampires and their supernatural abilities. In fact, she knew way more about them than she'd ever believed possible, outside of folk legends, that is. To find out they actually existed blew her mind.

Now her mind was being blown in another way. A vampire she actually liked was part of her new reality, and a partner who lied to her face without so much as a flicker was the other. Yeah, mind blown. Still looking over at Isa, a tiny shake of the head seemed to be telling Jeni she shared her unease about Trent.

"I'm not confident I can track her down tonight. Can this wait?" She couldn't quite explain why she'd lied. Strangely, she trusted that shake of Isa's head more than the man on the other end of the line. Correction, that cop on the other end of the line. Yes, her world officially turned upside down.

"Maybe, but tonight would be better. I don't want anything lost if we wait another day."

She understood that, with a vampire involved, they'd either have to act in the next few hours or wait until the sun set again tomorrow. Isa mouthed, "Tomorrow." That pretty much confirmed that Isa caught both sides of the conversation.

"Look, Trent, it's almost midnight. I'm exhausted, and I'm not inclined to drag Becca out in the middle of the night. Unless someone's dying, let's do this tomorrow. Is someone dying?"

His hesitation gave weight to the saying "pregnant pause." He didn't like her answer, which made little bells start ringing in her head. He'd never be able to deny what she now knew to be true: he worked with his vampire mother. Her only advantage lay in the fact that, unbeknownst to him, she knew about mommy. She had to believe that would keep her and her friends safe.

"Fine." The tension in his voice told her that it cost him to not press her further. Whatever he and his mother had in mind, they wanted to put it in motion tonight. Her refusal to play along frustrated him. She gave him credit for a good performance. Had she not been in possession of his family history, she'd have been fooled. Must have taken drama in college because his acting skills were impressive.

"We can talk about this tomorrow when I get into the office."

"You sure you can't track her down tonight?" Going down swinging.

"I'm sure."

❖

Isa caught all the conversation with her better-than-human hearing. "His mother has a plan," she said after Jeni ended the call.

"You think?"

Sarcasm. She liked that. Jeni seemed to be getting more and more comfortable around her. Excellent, because they would need to trust each other to bring this whole thing to an end that benefitted them, though to say trust at this point might be a stretch.

This time would be her final confrontation with George. Confidence, skill, and courage would see to that. She also knew better than to under-estimate him. He'd been walking the earth for a very long time, manipulating and playing people since childhood, and he'd become a master at it.

She smiled. How long had it been since anyone made her smile with pleasure? Years. No, more like decades. Many, many decades. It felt good. "Yes. I think."

Jeni put her hands on her hips and studied her. Everything about her screamed cop. It must be the way she looked at those she took into the station for questioning—intimidating in a sexy way. "So, big, bad vampire. What's the plan?"

"She's very good at kicking ass, but her friends with special skills come up with the awesome plans. She's more like the hired muscle, if you feel me." Patrick stood in the doorway with his arm around Becca's shoulders. Well, that was an interesting turn of events.

Becca smiled. "He's right, you know. Same with you, Jeni. It's we techy types that come up with all the good stuff. Stick with us if you want to take this George down."

Jeni raised a single eyebrow. "Really? Since when did pathology become techy?"

"Oh, sister, it's fraught with technology these days. I've got skills I haven't even used yet."

Isa liked the banter between them. This small group was on the bonding track, and that would play well in what would come next. She'd been right about this time being the final battle. All the signs were here. The critical players were all in the same place—or soon would be. The right army assembled. Finally, she could finish this and take a walk into the light. Just as soon as they sent George to hell.

"All right." She waved Patrick and Becca over to the empty chairs at the table. "Lay it out for us. What's your grand plan?" Patrick wasn't wrong about his ability to strategize. Her skills were good. His were better.

Patrick winked, and Isa understood. The game enthralled him. He provided a great service to the world by taking out evil, and he thrived on the challenge. He needed the adrenaline rush.

"Well, you know the old saying about keeping your friends close and your enemies even closer?" Patrick winked. The lure of the hunt shone from his eyes.

Jeni spoke up this time. "Trent."

"Yeah. You and your mate Trent are going to be as close as thieves, if you catch my drift."

"I can somewhat follow your train of thought," Isa told him, and she could, except she still wasn't quite on the same sheet of music. "I'm just not completely clear on the purpose. Explain it in simple terms, please."

"Stay with me here, my darling. Think about it. As long as he doesn't suspect that we're on to him, I'm betting my lunch money he'll lead us straight to his mum…"

Isa smiled as the scenario quickly unfolded in her mind. "And once we have Mum, we'll have the jump on George." She liked the train of thought going on here.

Patrick smiled and nodded. "We're going to need to load up on weapons. We can't go into battle without being armed to the teeth, and I do so love the breadth of weapons you Americans have available."

"I have weapons here," Jeni said as she rose to go to what Isa felt certain would be a gun safe.

Patrick shook his head and Jeni stopped to look at him. "Not enough."

The expression on her face spoke of insult. "I'm not lacking in guns."

"I'm confident you are not. No offense intended, it's just that we will need more than what you might have locked away somewhere in this fine abode."

Isa stood. "I have more at my house." Wherever she happened to live at the time, she always made certain to have a large cache of both traditional and non-traditional weapons at her disposal.

This time Patrick nodded and his smile widened. "That's what I'm talking about."

Isa liked it too. While she rested, Becca and Patrick had made plans that seemed to cover all the contingencies, and that was exciting. "We'll take them all." Jeni might not have the wide variety that Isa did, but more was always better.

He gave Isa a high five. "I like the way you think."

The plane landed in the small airport before the sun began to creep up over the mountains to the east. By the time it crested Mount Spokane, his car pulled into the garage at the new abode. He had liked the other house, and though this one had its appeal, it lacked the majesty of the one she'd managed to burn to the ground. Quid pro quo, he supposed. He'd taken away her home, so she'd finally managed to take away his. Well, one of his, anyway. This one was only a blip in his empire. In fact, losing both New Orleans and the Hamptons, and hit with the substantial damage in Vancouver, still didn't hurt him much in the big picture. When it came to his portfolios of properties worldwide in any case.

Still, any loss created an inconvenience, if not an emotional impact, and naturally, that would have been her ultimate goal. She'd achieved it, even if the inconvenience created might be considered minor. That a backup plan went into motion immediately demonstrated his superiority once again. Someone with his natural high level of intelligence would be extremely hard to best or, in his case, impossible to best. Honestly, by now she should know that, yet she kept trying. Couldn't fault her for persistence.

In the master bedroom, he sat on the edge of the king-size bed topped by one of those trendy memory-foam mattresses. Not quite the feather beds of his youth but he liked it, and soon he would lie back and rest. It had been quite a night. In fact, it had been a hectic few days with the peons trying to put a dent in his kingdom.

Actually, the fail had been epic, along the lines of the battle at the Alamo. Yes, some of his possessions were lost. She'd hadn't accomplished what she hoped. She wanted him weakened. Instead, it had the opposite effect. She'd motivated him. He would do more than rally his own troops. He would call in the chips he'd been coveting for centuries. She thought she knew everything. She would soon learn the gigantic fallacy of that belief.

Earlier, as he had stared out the windows of the airplane, the moon shone its light, gold and bright, to cut through the darkness. The idea had come to him in a flash of brilliance only those as special as he possessed. He had waited to move forward until he reached the house. Patience was only one of his many virtues.

Now, he held his cell phone and scrolled through the contact list. When he found the one he searched for, he tapped it. With the phone on speaker, he held it low and listened to it ring.

"Rather late for you, isn't it?"

Always a smartass. One of the things he liked about him. Not one of his soldiers in the usual sense. Different. In some ways smarter. Handsome. "I'm safely inside. My energy will be preserved."

"You need me."

It hadn't been a question because he never used this number unless he did, in fact, need his services. "Of course." He might appreciate his cunning and expertise, but that didn't mean he wanted him as part of his inner circle. There were some whose trust could never be counted on absolutely.

"It's a full moon tomorrow."

"Precisely." He leaned back against the pile of soft pillows and stared up at the shadows as they danced across the ceiling. Quickly and concisely, he shared his plan before he ended the call and placed the phone on the nightstand. As he pulled his feet up onto the bed and stretched out, he couldn't help but smile right before he closed his eyes.

CHAPTER TWENTY-FOUR

Jeni approved of the plan Becca and Patrick laid out. Her part seemed simple enough. She'd see how close she could get to Trent and find out whatever she could pry from him without tipping her hand. His interest in Isa made her doubly curious. When they'd first hit him with the existence of vampires, he'd come across as skeptical, and now all of a sudden, he'd morphed into Mr. Very-interested. Odd, to say the least, although given their most recent intel, it sort of all fit. The man could give acting classes.

Patrick convinced her to get on board without a great deal of effort. Even Isa appeared amenable, if not anxious, to playing up to Trent. Isa seemed to be holding back more thus far, or maybe she was imagining things because this was all so fucked up. After all, this whole situation wasn't anything she'd expected when she came here. She should have known better than to believe peace awaited her. For the last decade it had eluded her, so why she'd assume it to be any different now was anybody's guess. Peace didn't seem to be in the cards for her.

Tonight, or rather this morning, it made more sense to follow the game plan set out by Becca and Patrick. True, both of them wanted to see vampires wiped out, but they were more objective than either Jeni and Isa. Also, they didn't have a horse in the race. While both had seen the results of the night stalkers, neither had lost their partner or their family. Clarity was important and they both had it.

Her orders included becoming Trent's best friend. If all went as hoped, she would find out what he and his mother planned. He believed Jeni to be clueless, which would play to her advantage. She didn't appreciate people who lied to her, especially someone who should have her back. This wasn't her first rodeo, and he'd find that out when he tried to fuck with her. In the meantime, she'd do her job and keep an eye on him. She could act as well as he.

The night had flown by. Patrick and Isa left a little after midnight for several hours, returning with an impressive cache of interesting weapons. She'd been afraid to ask what they'd been doing. As it turned out, asking wasn't necessary. The cache they returned with told the story. Nice supplement to her own specialty weapons. This could work.

"First things first, Jeni. You have to get a little sleep and then go to work. Play the game." Patrick's job put him in a command position in most situations, and that part of him showed now as he took the lead without it being given to him. She wanted to protest. After all, this was her house and her town. "Isa, you grab some nourishment, and then help us lay out the charge."

That word nourishment stopped her. Jeni hadn't thought about the logistics of having a vampire in her house. Her beauty and intelligence, the curves of her naked body, had distracted Jeni. *Don't think about that whole drink-blood thing.* Too distracting, and she couldn't afford that right at the moment.

Nourishment. That was the word to concentrate on, because the concept turned her stomach. Patrick said it with such ease, as if everyone fortified themselves with human blood. Just the thought of it brought back the horror of ten years ago, of losing the woman who'd promised to be always at her side. She'd thought they'd have a lifetime together. Not even close. A promise broken by another's hand.

"I'll try to get some sleep." She grimaced when she glanced at the clock. She'd be lucky if she got two hours of sleep. "I'll talk with you all later."

"Copy that." Patrick didn't seem to register her abrupt departure. It didn't slip past Becca. She didn't care about Isa. She'd apologize later. Maybe.

Jeni's mood turned quickly. Maybe it didn't surprise the others as much as it did Isa. Their brainstorming brought them all together, and preparing for the evening to come was exciting. They were becoming a solid team, but suddenly, Jeni had snapped rigid and almost run from the kitchen. Isa didn't get what made her take so many steps backward. Of course, she'd been up all night, and fatigue might be the culprit.

"What was that about? Perhaps she's tired?" Surely her friend could shed some light on Jeni's race to get out of the room.

Becca glanced up from the computer with a confused expression. Then her face cleared as she turned toward the hallway and the bedrooms beyond. "We hit a nerve."

Isa spread her hands. "About what?"

Becca shrugged. "That's a really good question. She's been that way since her wife's death. Little things that remind her of Avery can take her mood from happy to depressed in a nanosecond. We said something that must have made her think of Avery. Give her a little time and she'll be okay."

"It was most likely something I said." Patrick's brow was furrowed. "I hurt her and that sucks. I get caught up in a project, and shit just rolls from my mouth. Used to get me in trouble all the time. Oh, hell. Who am I trying to kid? It still does."

Becca put an arm around his shoulders, and again it struck Isa how close the two of them had become. The chemistry between them was undeniable.

Isa spoke the truth. "It isn't you, my Irish friend. I fear it's me, or something about me. Not that I blame her. I represent everything she abhors, and she has every right to feel that way. I'm surprised she's willing to work with me at all."

"Still…" Patrick, always the gentleman, tried to take her guilt on himself. No wonder she loved him.

"Still nothing." Becca waved a hand in the air. "Both of you need to let it go. Nobody's fault. Jeni's the first one to admit that she can be overly sensitive when it comes to Avery. She's a ton better than she was ten years ago. It's just that some wounds never heal completely. Let her sleep for a bit, and she'll be good as new."

Isa understood sensitivity about a personal tragedy better than most. Her heart epitomized an open wound and had for centuries. Even when this struggle ended, and she believed it would within the next thirty-six hours, the wound still wouldn't be healed completely. It never would. That didn't mean the impending battle would be wasted. On the contrary, she looked forward to facing George one last time. At last the perfect moment glowed red on the horizon.

She also took satisfaction in finding herself in the company of perfect partners. Jeni, Becca, and Patrick were the only army she needed. They were smart, talented, and skilled. The trifecta.

Patrick hit on something very important though. It had been a while since she'd fed, and a heaviness in her body reminded her. The earlier rest had helped. Rest alone couldn't keep her at peak performance as much as she'd like it to be so. Like a good athlete, she needed to fuel. Regardless of how repugnant she found surviving on human blood, she couldn't deny the reality of her existence. She either imbibed or she wasted away. Superpowers came with a price tag attached.

"So, about that nourishment I mentioned." Patrick must be reading her mind. Either that or he simply knew her too well.

Chills coursed through her, and the physical reaction made her wonder if she might have pushed it too far this time. Outside, daylight began to edge toward full bloom. Once more, she'd gotten so caught up in their work here, she'd allowed her travel time to slip away. She didn't want to risk going out. "I am in a bit of a fix." If she'd given thought to this necessity even an hour ago, then it would have been safe to return home where a refrigerator held the supplies she needed. Why she hadn't taken care of her needs when they retrieved the weapons, she couldn't say. Not like her to be so distracted. She gazed toward the front room where, through the tall sidelights, sunshine bathed it in lemony daylight.

Patrick smiled. "Then it's a very good thing you have friends."

She snapped her attention back to him. "What does that mean? I can't go out. At this moment I'm not strong enough to handle the light." Memories of the way it would burn on her skin in those early days never fully left her.

"I repeat. It's a good thing you have friends. Like me." He patted a hand to his chest. "I knew you'd get sidetracked and planned for it."

Becca smiled. "He does know you. I'll give him that, and he came prepared." She opened the refrigerator. "Jeni might find it weird to have blood in her fridge, but hey. You have to make do with what you have."

Isa stared at the two bags of blood. "When? Where?" The sight of it made her fingers tingle.

Patrick smiled. "The medical examiner was a champ." He pushed up his sleeve and showed her the wrap on his arm. "So was Becca." She pulled up her sleeve to reveal an identical bandage.

"She didn't ask why?" The chills were growing in intensity and her legs trembled.

"Of course, she did. You forget I can be terribly persuasive when I need to be, and with this accent..." He smiled like an angel. "Now, take your bags and power up."

"I think I love you."

He winked. "I have that effect on women. So many women."

As much as he tried, George couldn't fully reach the restorative oblivion he sought. He decided to rise in order to take care of some matters and then try again. As angry as he'd been over the loss of the first home secured here, he took time now to walk around the replacement necessitated by her actions. As usual, his people had come through.

Upon arrival he allowed everyone to go to their rest, because he had no further need for their services. All had been readied for the night ahead. To be at their best, his army required slumber and sustenance, and a little of both would do him well too, although his age and power gave him extraordinary stamina. Now he inventoried the items he'd assembled and would use after the sun went down.

To have world-class scientists at his command gave him tools the average man—the average vampire—could never possess. Some might think his power had come simply from overthrowing the council of the Redcap Society. They would be wrong. Doing away with those arrogant asses certainly helped. True power came from more than just eliminating competition and entailed more than sitting on the throne alone.

He picked up a vial filled with golden liquid and studied it as he tipped it side to side. The gift of darkness made one impervious to human serums, but this was something entirely different. Power had many advantages, including access to the world's best and brightest. It had taken his scientists more than twenty years to perfect what he now held. He had previously tested it on others, the Redcap Society elders, to be precise, and it worked magnificently. It still made him laugh, remembering how surprised they'd been when the sun came up and their bodies turned to ash. Between their own arrogance and his science, they'd handed him the world. A glorious day indeed.

Now, he prepared the syringe for something a bit more personal. In the back of his mind, he supposed he always knew it would come down to this. That's why he surrounded himself with those who would do his bidding without question. Well, that and because he enjoyed the subservience of others. No one had to explain to him that he possessed a narcissist streak. He'd known it long before it ever had a name, and he embraced it. As this generation liked to say, he could tell the shrinks who wanted to fix him, "Bite me."

"Do you need anything?" Nelly stood in the doorway. "I tried to make certain everything was ready for you."

Why hadn't she gone to her room to lie down? She placed a great value on her impressive good looks—one reason he'd been drawn to her. He preferred to surround himself with beauty, and if someone had that kind of power, why not exploit it? Besides, he appreciated her vanity. He found it an admirable trait. "I'm reviewing my plans for the coming night."

She nodded. "We're ready. We're all ready."

He smiled at her and put the syringe back into the small case. "As I am." He extended a hand. "Let us rest now. We want to be at our very best tonight."

Her smile lit up her face. "I can help you relax."

He patted her hand. "Indeed you can, but we'll save that for another night." While he greatly appreciated her considerable skills in that arena, his thoughts were on another woman.

CHAPTER TWENTY-FIVE

Considering how she'd put him off, Jeni expected to find Trent in a foul mood when she made it into the office. Last night he'd been quite insistent that she arrange a meeting with Isa, and her refusal hadn't seemed to sit well with him. She had zero expectation that he'd be any less irritated this morning.

To find him smiling and acting just as normal as he had each day since she'd started work here made her wary. Now that she knew his capacity for deception, she was aware of his ability to present a convincing façade. His "everything's great" persona was far from trustworthy. No getting around that he had some kind of agenda where Isa was concerned. The trick would be to get through the day without letting on that she knew. Her ability to hide her feelings wasn't quite as smooth as his. Her natural instinct leaned more toward what-you-see-is-what-you-get. The stakes were high, and she'd rise to the challenge.

"We have a call out."

Jeni hadn't even hung her jacket up yet. "Where?" Nothing came over the radio on the drive in.

"Loon Lake. Someone reported a body in the water."

If she wasn't already aware vampires were in the hood, she would be now. In a place this rural and this small, the sheer number of deaths since she'd arrived would most definitely raise an alarm in her brain. Law enforcement would start leaning in the direction of an active serial killer while she'd be doing her own independent investigation of a different kind of killer. She picked her jacket back up and slid her arms into the sleeves.

"Lead the way." Honestly, now that she knew more about Trent, she'd prefer to be the one behind the wheel. The problem arose with her familiarity with the area, which wasn't even close to his. Stevens County was large, and her exploration to date consisted of about a quarter of the county. Better to suck it up and pretend to be comfortable with him in the driver's seat. It would only be for a short time anyway. Tonight would probably bring a giant spotlight to a lot of lies, and by tomorrow there would be no more pretending.

While Trent pulled out onto the highway, she wondered about Isa. So far, she'd seemed pretty open, yet Jeni guessed that, just like with Trent, far more existed beyond the curtain. Secrets nestled behind her beautiful eyes, and Jeni couldn't deny her curiosity. She should be repulsed. Strangely, she wasn't. Damn it anyway.

"What's on your mind?"

Jeni turned to Trent. "Nothing really." The last thing she'd share with him would be her thoughts about a beautiful vampire, even if she did trust him. Given that she didn't, she'd keep her all her thoughts to herself.

"You've been in la-la land since we left the office. I can tell you've got something on your mind. See? I'm starting to get the partner spidey senses. All signs are, this is going to be a good partnership."

Not even close, but she'd play along. "Yeah, like the fact that we're on our way to another murder scene. I mean, really, Trent, what are the odds this would happen so quickly after the last one in a place like this? You won't me convince this is business as usual for Stevens County."

He gave a little shake of his head. "A little out of the norm. You should be used to this. I mean, where you came from, violence wasn't that unusual, even for the Rose City."

"I am conditioned, to a certain extent. At least in relation to a metropolitan area with hundreds of thousands of people. Different dynamic. Different demographic. It would make sense in Portland. It doesn't out here."

"Unless there are vampires…" His snicker wasn't exactly coy. A couple days ago, she might have bought it. Not now.

She wanted to call him out. Wanted to smack him up alongside the head. She didn't do either. "Let's stay focused."

"Whatever you say, but come on, vampires? You gotta admit it's a wild theory. Your friend might need some serious professional help. I can give you some numbers."

"Didn't you call me last night and try to talk me into tracking one of the vampires you're calling a wild theory?"

"Yeah, I did." He laughed. "You didn't produce, remember?"

She kept her eyes forward. The way things were going, the day would be a couple of years long. "How about we concentrate on our job and the dead body? How much longer until we get there?" It would nice to establish some distance before she said something she'd regret. Her task of cozying up to Trent might prove harder than she thought.

"Ask and thou shall receive. We're here."

He pulled off Highway 395, and a quarter mile later, they were on a dirt road, where the ruts gave new meaning to rattling the teeth. Somebody must have really wanted to hide their handiwork. "Who found the body?" This sure didn't seem like someplace a person would just happen upon a crime scene.

"A runner. Apparently, the woman who found him runs trails every day with her dog, and they stumbled upon the corpse. She routinely comes down to the water to let her dog swim midway through her run. If they hadn't been out here, who knows when this guy would have been found."

Once out of the car, they joined the uniformed officers standing just inside yellow tape strung between four pine trees. She could see why someone would pick this area for an energetic run. The slightly rolling hills and scattered pine, aspen, and evergreen trees were beautiful. Beyond the trees, the lake glistened in the morning sunlight. The tranquility of this area would be a great start to anybody's day.

"What have we got?" She pulled out the small book she always used to keep notes in, ready for the responding deputies' briefing. As the young deputy, Geoff something-or-other, started talking, she glanced down at the body that had been left in the tall grass about thirty yards from the shoreline, and barely managed to stifle her scream.

❖

Earlier, Isa had intended to nourish herself with Patrick's surprise and then get to work side by side with the two seasoned investigators. Following Jeni's all-nighter, she too had no time for rest. She could stay in the interior of the house, safe and sound from the daylight, and prepare for the coming evening. Given what they'd learned last night, going back to her house might not have been the best idea, even with Patrick at her side. They'd come back with the weapons now laid out on a long dining-room table, and that pleased her. She wanted the three humans to have the best armaments she could provide. The other thing she didn't do while at her home, besides taking nourishment, was to slip into clean clothes. She felt that oversight acutely right now.

Fortified by the blood Patrick had procured for her, she bundled up and drove back to her own home. She could work at home just as easily—no easier—than at Jeni's. Once there, her good intentions to work went by the wayside. Her body demanded rest. She stretched out on her bed, thinking she'd give herself an hour and then jump back into planning and preparing. When her eyes opened, darkness had started to push away the daylight.

"Damn it." She jumped from the bed and sprinted to the bathroom. She'd wasted too much time sleeping away the day, and why in the world hadn't Patrick come to check on her? That he would leave her here all day pissed her off. Now George would have had an entire day to prepare an assault, and knowing him as well as she did, that's exactly what the arrogant monster would do.

After she got out of the shower and dried off, she punched in Patrick's number, putting the phone on speaker so she could dress while she talked. The moment he answered, she bellowed, "What the hell?"

"Easy, my dear." He spoke softly, as if to a tantrum-throwing child. That made her even angrier.

"Easy, my ass. How could you let me sleep all day?"

"You're no good to anyone if you're not at a hundred percent. By the looks of you this morning, you were running on empty. You needed to rest, and since you snuck out like a naughty child, it serves you right."

"I was fine."

"Beg to differ with you, darling. You were not fine."

"Beg to differ with YOU!" The love for him she'd felt earlier faded into the kind of annoyance she used to get when her brother was acting like an asshole.

"So, do you think this conversation is getting us anywhere or wasting precious time?"

God, how she hated it when he was right and flaunted it. Her annoyance factor jumped up some more. The day slipped away while she slept, and ranting and raving wouldn't change the fact. She needed to let go of useless emotion, regroup, and get ready for the charge. Her body buzzed like never before, a sure sign tonight would be the one. She took a long deep breath and let it out slowly.

"Fine."

He chuckled low. "You might be an old bat, but you're predictable."

She bit off a childish comeback. Like her brothers, Patrick liked to bait her. "What have you got?"

He laughed before telling her, "Put on your dancing shoes and get back over to Jeni's. We have a battle plan all ready to kick into action."

Patrick had skills, and he used them more than once to help her. He also had an ego that made him a royal pain in the ass. Still, as much as she represented the driving force in this mission, she also understood the importance of sometimes following the lead of another. Isa could be a powerful foe in any situation. Her power multiplied when she welcomed the kind of help Patrick provided. Throw in Becca and Jeni, and the chance for success quadrupled.

"I'll be there soon."

"We'll be waiting with our boots tied and our guns loaded."

She punched the end button and turned toward her closet. Hanging inside were a pair of beautiful leather pants and a matching jacket. She could slip them on and become a vision in black. That wasn't pride. She knew the impression she made when she pulled on the custom-made garments. She didn't need or want to go for sexy gothic.

Tonight called for functional and lethal. Black jeans, a sweater, and Doc Martens would serve her far better. One thing she appreciated about this century was the variety of clothing available for females. The frilly and pretty still hung on racks in every store—the kinds of things her mother would have foamed at the mouth over. All the better to turn her daughter into a peacock that could attract the attention of every eligible baron from eighteen to eighty. At the same time, pants and boots as functional and comfortable as anything available to a man were there too. She'd worn enough dresses in her long life to last her for infinity.

The belt she strapped on held the tools of her trade: a sheathed silver knife, a Smith & Wesson loaded with specially made wood-tipped bullets, and a spray canister most would mistake for pepper spray. Hers held holy water. Though holy water wouldn't kill a vampire, it would definitely blind one long enough for a final, dispatching strike. A very useful result.

Her gloved hands made certain none of the substances fatal to her kind ever touched her own skin. She patted the items on her belt, performing the same mental exercise she went through each time she began a hunt. It wouldn't be long now.

Time to head back to Jeni's house. As much as she'd love to face down George one-on-one, she'd be a fool to ignore that power that came with numbers. Four would be a great deal better than one, especially considering George's propensity toward throwing others into the fray before he ever considered getting his own hands dirty. He'd have a crew at the ready. Well, so would she.

Besides, Jeni deserved to be there as much as she did.

Isa reached for her keys and headed toward the back door, stopping only at the sound of a knock on the front one.

❖

George felt great and looked even better. It tended to happen that way when big nights rolled around, and this one certainly qualified for that category. After he dressed, he picked up his cell and scrolled through his contacts until he found the one he wanted. He tapped the number and waited. The conversation was brief and to the point. Then, he ended the call and walked downstairs to the great room.

Her back was to him as she stood before the two-story windows staring out into the darkness. Her long flowing hair never failed to make him want to reach out and touch it. "Is everything ready?"

Anyone else might take his abrupt question as an insult. Not Nelly. He had yet to find anything that offended her. Another thing he liked that about her. Steady and dependable. Unflappable. She turned and gave him a tiny nod. "Of course. Your plane is fueled and ready. Everything you need is on board."

"Your son?"

"He's ready as well. I talked to him ten minutes ago, and he's on the way. All is in motion."

"I want to be out of here no later than midnight."

"Trust me. He won't let you down. He's a clever boy."

"You mean he's a werewolf salivating for his prize. A big motivation for him to deliver."

She chuckled, and underneath the pride she could never suppress with regard to her only child echoed. The love for her son transcended their separate paths in the world of preternatural existence. "Well, there is that. He's really taken with that bit of a human from Maine. He'll do whatever we ask to get at her."

"She's of no importance to me. He's welcome to her."

She gave him a slight nod. "He will be most pleased."

"As he should be. It's a most generous gift."

"And the Irishman?"

"Like the woman, his life is of little matter. Take them both. Tell him to have a banquet. My people will make certain nothing links back to him, and he may continue as the hick deputy he seems to so love to be."

"He'll be most grateful."

"I don't give a damn about his gratitude." If he didn't do his job, George didn't care how useful he'd been so far. Mistakes had no place in his plans for tonight.

Nelly turned to glance at the vampire who stood just outside the room. He made a motion to her, and she nodded before turning back to George. "Your request is waiting in your room." She bowed her head and took a step back.

Without another word, he turned and walked away from her. No need. She understood everything said and unsaid.

Back in his room, the young woman with the strawberry-blond hair sat tied to a chair, a gag in her mouth and terror in her eyes. That worked for him. Made the flavor so much more enjoyable. Besides, the agenda for tonight needed spice. He smiled as he crossed the room.

Chapter Twenty-six

Jeni had gone into the field with Trent confident they were about to investigate yet another vampire victim. She hadn't been wrong on that score. The rulers of the night were all here, killing as though open season on humans had begun. She wished it were that simple.

To see the face of a friend, pale and bloodless, dumped like garbage, one hand resting in a pile of deer scat, took this from a day on the job to personal anguish. To be honest, anything that involved a vampire had become personal the moment they targeted Avery. This nightmare showed how much the ante had been raised, and her instincts told her it wasn't by accident.

The real question as to how and why Sandi had ended up hundreds of miles from Portland and dead at the hands of a vampire baffled her. This George that Isa chased would know nothing about her or the family and friends she left behind when she came here. Yet Sandi's dead body seemed to say otherwise. No coincidence here; she didn't believe in them. If Sandi had intended to visit, she would have called. No. This bastard sent Jeni a message. He knew about her and wanted to hurt her, again.

Managing to stifle her scream and keep her face neutral had taken more willpower than she believed she possessed. Trent's focus on her gave her a clue that he'd been in on this particular move. How exactly he'd found her friend and set her up for slaughter, she'd probably never be able to find out. All she knew, without any doubt, was that he'd done this. Somehow, some way, she'd make sure he paid for this senseless act of cruelty.

That resolution aside, she'd seethed all day. It took effort not to let her anger show because she refused to give Trent the satisfaction. He couldn't push her either, because if he did, he'd tip his hand. An unusual murder, yes, and that fact she could express. Her tenure so far might be brief, though her knowledge of the criminal dynamics had been well researched before she'd made the move. The murders over the last few months were highly unusual. She knew why, though many in the county claimed ignorance, including Trent. He lied.

For hours a game of cat and mouse ensued. That he waited for her to say she knew the victim seemed clear. His body almost vibrated with anticipation of the moment she would admit her connection to Sandi. No way did she intend to give him anything. She undertook the process as if Sandi were any other victim. She crossed all her *t*'s and dotted all her *i*'s.

When she kept to business as usual, he finally resorted to his first ruse once the workday grew near completion. He needed to meet with Isa. An edge of frustration sounded in his demand disguised as a request. She still made him wait. Two could play his game. Until she'd entered every single one of her notes into the computer, she didn't move, and by then, darkness had fallen. The wait made him fidget like a five-year-old who'd had way too much sugar, and that reaction pleased her.

Now they stood on Isa's doorstep, and he pushed the doorbell. She'd called Becca earlier to tell her about Sandi and found out that Isa had gone home right after Jeni left for work. One thing about this time of year—it didn't get really light until well after she reached the office, giving Isa plenty of time to drive to her house in the shadowy light of dawn. She'd still probably have to bundle up, but at least it wouldn't turn her crispy.

At first, Jeni thought it odd that Isa had left at all, given the timeline they were up against, but then it actually made sense. She probably wanted to change. After all, didn't vampires like to wear clean clothes? Isa had jumped into Jeni's shower, so she knew she preferred to freshen up. A shower she could offer, clothes not so much. They were not anywhere close to the same size. But, more important, why was Trent so hot to get to Isa's house?

He'd gone quiet earlier in the day when she'd refused to play along, with not another peep about the urgent get-together he'd wanted last night. Like Jeni, his demeanor for the benefit of everyone else around them wasn't unusual when investigating a murder. She was the only one who caught the charge of energy that rolled off him. As a friend of hers was fond of saying, the player was being played. She knew his game at the crime scene. She didn't quite get his game when it came to his desire to face Isa.

And now here they were at Isa's house, and she had a hunch he'd soon play the hand he'd been holding close to this chest since his late-night call. She told herself to be ready for whatever it might be. Isa's expression when she opened the door told her she thought the same thing. Good. Nice to know battle ready was the tone for the night.

Their eyes met, and something inside her clicked. It scared her. She hadn't felt anything even close to it since Avery had been taken away from her. Everything around here had been going sideways, and still, she wanted to reach out and take Isa's hand for strength. It was as if together they could fight anything that came their way, even hordes of vampires and lying deputies.

Talk about fucked up.

Isa didn't have to guess who rang the doorbell and now stood outside her front door. It surprised her more that he'd waited this long. Of course, at this time of year, darkness took its time, leaving later in the morning and falling early at night. Barely five o'clock and heading toward pitch-black outside her windows. She appreciated this season because of the comfortable environment for her. Humans grumbled about the time change at nauseating levels, preferring the longer days to the darkness. Had she still been human, she would too. Then again, had she still been human, she would have turned to dust centuries ago.

"Come in," she said to Trent and Jeni when she pulled open the door. No need for a polite greeting. She'd let Trent make the first move. She held the advantage while he would be blissfully unaware.

She turned her gaze to Jeni, and her eyes narrowed. Something wasn't right; she could see it in her face. Had Trent discovered they knew his connection to George? Judging by Trent's swagger as he entered her home, she didn't think he had a clue yet. Something else put a shadow over Jeni. As much as she wanted Trent to show his hand, she had a greater wish for him to go away. He continued past her and into the living room, his back straight and shoulders square. *Make yourself at home.*

"We have to talk," Jeni whispered as she walked by and touched her shoulder.

Great. Now her curiosity ratcheted up about tenfold. "Do you know what he wants?"

She shook her head. "He's been tightlipped all day."

His back was to them as Isa and Jeni stepped into her living room. He'd turned on a single lamp that cast low light into the large room. She hadn't bothered earlier, as she didn't plan to be back here until late, if ever. Once she put a stake through George's heart, what happened to her after that no longer mattered. Besides, how much light she did or didn't have was of little consequence. Her eyesight in the dark didn't diminish from the clarity of full daylight—another of the enhancements brought to her courtesy of George.

His posture caught her attention more than anything else about him. A flicker of something familiar nagged at her. It clicked for her in an instant, and her breath caught in her throat. Why didn't she see it earlier? She'd opened her mouth to call him on it when he turned around. The full-face respirator he wore sent every other thought fleeing right before she dropped to the floor.

❖

The call came as the plane moved out of the hangar and onto the tarmac. Things had gone as well as had been expected, and they awaited his arrival. George directed the pilot to be on standby as he got back into his car, with Nelly sliding in beside him. They sped through the quiet streets and back roads that would take them to their destination. He smiled in the darkness.

Trent met them at the door to the home he'd seen many times in the file compiled on her. Astonishingly modest for a woman of her high birth. Every once in a while, she surprised him, like the night she ran.

He studied Trent, impressed by the illusion of calm he projected. That he held on by sheer willpower was clear to him, although not to others who lacked his superior senses. The man possessed an impressive amount of inner strength. He liked that about him. Wasn't awed by his uncontrolled bloodlust quite as much. After all the time he'd walked the earth, he understood the importance of control in every aspect of one's life.

Trent accomplished his assigned task, as evidenced by the two unconscious women in the floor, nicely bound and ready for transport, without losing his composure. Well, one of them was ready for transport. The other held no importance to him. For all he cared, Trent could have her the second they were on the way back to the airport.

Yet a look in Trent's eyes as he kept a booted foot on the one called Jeni made him wonder. "What is it?"

Trent rolled his upper lip, revealing the gleaming white canines that could tear flesh from bone even in his human state. "They like each other."

He didn't track. "Like each other? Explain."

Trent's eyes narrowed. "I could see it in her face the minute Jeni and I came inside. She's got the hots for her. I'd bet Mommy's life on it." His gaze flickered to his mother, who stood dutifully behind him.

"You're willing to wager your mother's existence on your assumption?" He found that possibility interesting. He'd always believed them to be as close as a mother and son could get. Or would it be more accurate to say vampire and werewolf? Their family tree made for interesting reading and was quite rare in the community of preternaturals. Another reason he loved having them both under his control. Unusual pets.

"He'd wager my life on anything that would secure his freedom. That's what he's really angling for here, isn't it, darling?" Nelly's eyes cut to Trent.

And the truth comes out. Both mother and son were indentured to him, and they knew they could never escape his control. With nothing formal, no need for pen and paper, they all understood their eternal duty to him, and should they break it? The failed incidents of the last few nights were excellent examples of what happened to those who broke their bonds. They damaged his property. They displayed impertinence. They sent a message. The last word, however, belonged to him. It always did. It always would.

Trent bowed his head. Good boy. He might walk with a big stick in the human world. He might run as an alpha in the pack. Yet he knew better than to try the same bluster with George. "What do you want me to do with her?" He licked his lips as he pointed down at Jeni.

His eyes narrowed as he thought for a moment. He cared little about the cop, even as he came to learn she was the one who'd taken down more than a couple of his loyal followers and thus the reason for killing her friend and leaving her body near the lake. He opened his mouth to tell Trent he could have her, and then a thought occurred to him. A better idea. His adaptation skills were truly amazing.

"Load her into the car. She will go with us."

CHAPTER TWENTY-SEVEN

Jeni tried to open her eyes, and the simple motion of moving her eyelids almost caused her to throw up. What in the bloody hell happened? One second she was standing in Isa's living room, and the next, her head pounded as though someone had taken a baseball bat to it. Reminded her of the time she ended up with a concussion after a foot chase in Portland. She'd been on mandatory desk duty for two weeks after that one, and the only satisfaction she got from it was that the guy who hit her was currently doing six to ten in the state pen.

She hadn't been chasing anyone this time, which made the headache far more frightening than a convicted felon whacking her with a tree branch. Slowly she managed to get her eyes open, thanks to the dim light in the room. Had it been broad daylight, the pain might have been more than she could suffer. A two-day bender couldn't feel this bad. A few slow blinks, and things started to come into focus while making her want to scream.

Except that focus didn't much help. Things weren't quite right. She didn't lie on the thick area rug covering the dark hardwood floors in Isa's house. Beneath her the cold stone made her shiver. It smelled too, like the room had been closed up for years, though not tight enough to keep out the dampness and the mold. Something definitely not right here. Might have been an early call on the not-throwing-up thing.

As she blinked to try to clear her vision, her head continued to pound. Migraines weren't her thing. In fact, she rarely had a headache. She didn't think she'd been hit in the head again, and she certainly didn't remember anyone else in the room besides Isa and Trent.

Trent. It came back to her a flash. He'd had his back to them when they walked into the living room. She'd thought he was studying the lovely painting that hung above the fireplace. At first, the black straps around his head blended in with his black hair. He'd been turning around when they caught her attention. By then it was too late. The sweet scent that filled the air had already done its work. Her knees buckled as she saw the mask he wore. She didn't even remember hitting the floor. Everything after that until right now was a big nothing.

The cold air that slapped her face brought her more fully awake and pushed away the cobwebs created by the pain. She tried to reach out to push herself up in order to assess her situation, and it would have worked if it hadn't been for the fact that her hands were restrained behind her back. Nobody had to tell her that her own handcuffs were wrapped around her wrists. Her feet were likewise restrained, and only a downward glance showed her that duct tape did the job there. The feeble light in the room, provided by several candles on a table near her feet, didn't offer her much help in figuring out her location. Most of the room remained shrouded in deep shadows.

As she pushed herself into a seated position, all she could say was thank goodness for power exercises. She'd be stuck on the floor like a beached whale if she hadn't developed enough strength in her core to pull herself up. Next, she managed to get her knees to her chin and work her arms around to her front. Not exactly a quick or easy process, and most assuredly not graceful. From there, she could reach her boots and the hidden handcuff key she kept tucked inside. After she'd declared war on those who'd destroyed Avery, she'd learned a lot of new tricks. Way more than the standard ankle-strapped handgun, which, of course had been taken.

No one had thought to check the inside lip of her boots, and the key remained where she'd hidden it. *Thank you very much.* She had herself freed from the handcuffs and duct tape posthaste. Another wave of dizziness hit when she stood up, and she touched her head with her fingertips. Had Trent whacked her over the head with something? No lumps. No bumps. No, the ever-efficient and deceptive Trent had used something else, and she believed it to be something of the chemical variety. Sneaky bastard. But why? This seemed way over the top even for her deceptive, soon-to-be ex-partner.

She'd get to him later. Right now, two important goals lay before her: figure out where in the world she'd been taken, and find Isa, not necessarily in that order. She picked up a candle from the table, wishing like hell she had her mega light from her patrol car, and walked to the only door in the room.

First problem came with the lock. She got down on her knees and studied it. Old and relatively simple. All she had to do was find something to pick it with. That took her about five minutes of searching. Thick, long hairpins in a drawer held definite potential, even if they were old and from a bygone era. Luck was on her side and they worked slick. The lock disengaged. The thick wooden door didn't want to open easily. Aged and heavy, it too made her wonder again about her location. Though she hadn't been in the area long, she didn't recall hearing about any dwellings as old as this one. For that matter, she hadn't seen any on the West Coast that had the authentic old-world feel this room possessed. She managed to pull it open despite the resistance, and another wave of cold air hit her in the face.

The hallway didn't offer any ready answers. Her candle cut only the smallest sliver through the cold, drafty darkness, because in order to keep it lit, she had to cup her hand around the flame. She really, really wished she had her flashlight. She hurried to the end of the hallway, thinking the big window there would give her a view of the surroundings and help her get her bearings.

She stepped close to the thick, wavy glass and peered out. "Son of a bitch."

❖

Isa shook off the cobwebs and opened her eyes. It took a few seconds to hit her, and when it did, she jumped up. She hadn't been restrained. Not that it would have been easy to accomplish. The strength of the gift of darkness made it almost impossible. Anything put on could be easily broken apart. As she scanned the room, the truth about why no effort had been expended on attempted restraint slapped her. Of the several ways used to control a vampire, silver blessed by a priest was one, and the lock she spied on the door undoubtedly qualified.

The second method, and the one used on her back at her house, involved chemicals. Some kind of toxic agent had incapacitated her. Several came to mind that were more than efficient. That son of a bitch, Trent, had blindsided them.

Them. Her and Jeni. What had they done to Jeni? What most likely had happened while she slept in a dark and numb state made her want to retch. They would have killed her, or worse.

The earlier flicker of recognition had told her Trent's true nature: werewolf. The rarity of a werewolf and a vampire in the same family made it easy to miss the danger Trent presented. No wonder energy rolled off him. A full moon rose in the sky this night, and while the moon didn't entirely rule werewolves, full-moon nights gave them greater power than at any other time. He could have easily torn Jeni to pieces with great joy and abandon while she'd been taken here.

No. She couldn't think about that right now. She'd deal with Trent later, much later, given where she stood now. It boggled her mind that she could be here again and while darkness still reigned. The trip alone would have been long enough for daylight to return. The possibility existed that more time had passed than she knew. All he had to do to keep her under would have been to administer more of the agent that first incapacitated her. She glanced down and saw a mark on her hand. Clever of the bastard. Easy enough to keep her under control with an intravenous stream of drugs.

She walked to the carved table and put her hands on the wood. Beneath her palms the subtle effects of age rippled with texture. Today they would call this table an antique. She remembered when it had been brand-new. A draft from the windows sent a chill through the room, and the fireplace, large by modern standards, seemed somehow smaller than she remembered. She'd been around the world many times, and that had a way of making everything seem smaller.

Leaning forward on her hands, she closed her eyes and willed herself not to cry. It would be exactly what he wanted, and she refused to give him anything. Some of the fear that had kept her chained to his side for so long tried to come back—tapping, tapping, tapping at her mind. Instead of allowing it in, she took several deep breaths, letting them out slowly through parted lips. "Stay strong," she told herself on a whisper. "Stay strong."

A sound made her turn back toward the door. The silver lock turned, and the door moved. Not surprisingly, a human pushed it open. George would be just as affected by the blessed silver as she. Old and powerful as he might be, even he couldn't develop an immunity to that. Once the door opened fully, the human, a beautiful woman with black hair and dark eyes, stepped back into the hallway. Cold air flowed in just as she remembered. The hallways here were always chilly, even in the summer months.

"I hoped you would be back with us." Contrary to popular folklore, vampires did age, albeit very, very slowly. The centuries had been kind to George, and he had retained the sort of looks Hollywood actors willingly paid millions for.

The moment she saw his face, the old fear fled. Her resolve returned tenfold. This would end. Tonight. "What is this?"

"Full circle, my darling, full circle." She didn't like the smile that crossed his face.

❖

God, this situation made him feel more alive than he had in eons. Definitely since Isa left the fold. Now it all came around in one beautiful big circle, and what she didn't realize yet was that her fate, as well as the fate of the cop down the hall, rested in her hands. Delicious.

He hated when those he cornered told him they had no choice. People always had a choice. But people didn't always like the choices they were presented with. Hence, the sickening excuse of having none. Well, Isa would have one, and it would be highly entertaining to see what side she came down on.

When the plane touched down on the private airstrip a few miles from here, the night had waned, and not enough time remained in which to have this little face-to-face. He acknowledged his own choices when they arrived here and had decided to keep both women medicated until the sun set again. Trent's gas had knocked them out long enough for his much stronger serum to be injected. Very effective for both humans and vampires, alike. It wouldn't hurt them to have a little more of it pumped into their veins. He wanted as much time as possible to enjoy the night, whichever way it went. For him, it would be pleasurable regardless of the direction. Live or die? Fun and fun.

The best part lay spread out on the bed. The seamstress had done an exceptional job with the dress he'd ordered. He'd expected the best from her, and she hadn't disappointed. He had been so pleased, he'd directed Hannah, his human housekeeper here, to reward the seamstress handsomely. He would definitely avail himself of her services again, based on this piece of work alone. On occasion, humans did have uses other than serving as a tasty meal.

As of yet she hadn't spied the dress. She would have been certain where she stood at this moment, and with her quick mind, she would have scanned every inch of her surroundings. That didn't seem to be the case. Maybe the drugs still dulled her senses to a degree she wasn't yet seeing with clarity. Not an impossibility, given the serum strength needed to keep her subdued. He could wait her out. After all, he'd been waiting years for this moment. A few more minutes, a couple of hours, didn't matter at this point.

And then there it was, the sound he'd waited for. The sharp inhale of breath when realization dawned. He smiled as he moved his gaze from the dress to her face.

He could swear she grew pale as the words tumbled from her. "What the fuck is that?"

His smile grew, as did his pleasure. It was better than he imagined. "Are you saying you don't recognize it?"

"Of course, I do. It isn't possible. Not after this much time. It should be a pile of dust by now."

He laughed. "Good, is it not?"

"It can't be."

"Well, of course, it's not the original. You're quite correct. Sadly, it didn't make it, although that survived." He pointed to the portrait hanging above the fireplace. One more thing she hadn't noticed. This just kept getting better and better.

"You sick son of a bitch."

The pleasure that her facial expression caused to wash through him was almost orgasmic.

CHAPTER TWENTY-EIGHT

This wasn't coming together. Jeni stared out the window and tried to sort it out, except she couldn't. What spread out before her made it impossible to put the puzzle pieces into place. "We're not in Kansas anymore, Toto," she whispered. Not Kansas and not Washington. A sinking feeling in her stomach screamed this place didn't exist anywhere in the United States, and that was just fucking insane.

Moonlight illuminated acres of green grass, beyond which lay water as far as she could see. The house was massive, and she'd seen pictures of estates like this. Places, as people liked to say, across the pond, but how far across she couldn't fathom. The disorientation almost made her sick.

Stay calm and think. This couldn't be as bad as her mind told her it might be. Or maybe it could. Either way, she couldn't risk standing here trying to figure it out for long. Whoever left her in that room would surely come back, and she didn't want to be standing here like a lost puppy when they appeared. If they'd taken the trouble to bring her here, then Isa had to be here too, right? They'd keep them at the same place. No, not a question. She *had* to be here.

Where were they? She cupped her hands around her eyes as she pressed her face to the glass. She'd seen a lot of mind-boggling things since losing Avery, and this was right up there on the weirdness scale. Before, she'd believed her mind had been wide open. After, she couldn't unsee how small a universe the human population functioned within. Her understanding of the world had been blown wide open, and now it appeared to have gone international.

She dropped her hand to her side and began to pat her pant leg. Excitement flashed through her. Strangely enough, her phone remained in her pocket, and she pulled it out. Thank the Lord for small favors.

"Yes!" All she had to do was call Becca. Help would be on the way before the call even ended because that's how good Becca was. Only one small problem—no service. "Damn it." She almost threw the phone. It would have been a mistake, and she caught herself before she made it. The little device had more magic than call and text. She activated the flashlight feature. The candle she set on the floor while she stared out the window produced light so low it bordered on near uselessness. The phone did a way better job of lighting up the space where she stood, although the enhanced illumination didn't go very far in helping her put her current circumstances into context. Well, that wasn't exactly true. She could tell right away that this structure hadn't been erected as a replica of an old-world castle. This was the real deal.

Her previous suspicions were reconfirmed. No Kansas. No Washington. No good old USA. So freaking unreal. If she didn't negotiate her way around this place before her phone died, and the flashlight feature along with it, she'd be screwed. She had to find Isa.

First things first. Push back the panic. She turned off the light, stilled, and closed her eyes. Odd sounds, a house—scratch that, a castle—made unique noises when one quieted enough to allow the ears to hear. What she didn't hear made her hopeful. All the sounds were the moans and groans, and whistles of air through cracks and crevices that she would expect to catch from a very old structure. No footsteps and no voices. She liked that. To be alone allowed her time to explore and, hopefully, for those who'd brought her here to be blissfully unaware she'd freed herself. Perhaps if they believed her secure in the cold room, they wouldn't come for her for a good long while.

Jeni turned the flashlight feature back on and started slowly down the hallway, stopping at each door to put her ear against the wood. The uneven stone floor had her stumbling each time she caught the toe of her boot on a protruding edge. How many people crashed and burned on this floor after a night of hard drinking? Plenty, she guessed.

The doors lining the corridor were thick and old, making it hard to catch any hint of sound through them. Not exactly the same style in her home. Those babies didn't block noise in a meaningful way. Of course, since she lived alone, putting an ear to one of them in hopes of catching the sound of activity inside hadn't been an issue. She rarely bothered to close them.

In this place, every door was closed, and she wished she could hear better because it mattered. Gut instinct became her fallback as she pressed her ear hard against door after door. She had to trust that the lack of sound meant the rooms were empty. Good and bad. She'd hoped to find Isa sooner rather than later. Making her way down the corridor, it became clear that it would be later, if at all.

After twenty minutes of nothing, she once more stilled and gathered into herself. Frustration opened the door to panic, and it would be dangerous to lose her focus. Time to draw on her namesake, the goddess of war. It had been her father's idea to give each of his children the middle name of a Greek god or goddess. In her case, Athena. For a cop it had always seemed appropriate. Far too many times the job resembled war, the nature of the law-enforcement beast. When Avery had been taken from her, war had seemed appropriate for the unofficial job she'd been compelled to take on. And now? She faced a final battle and could use the strength Athena brought more than ever. *Thank you, Dad.*

Power gathered around her, or so it seemed, and when she opened her eyes, she no longer felt like Jennifer Denton, the deputy sheriff who'd been kidnapped and currently held hostage in a strange place. No, she had become Athena, goddess of war.

Isa wanted to rip the painting from the wall and throw it into the fireplace currently blazing with a fire big enough to burn a body.

If anyone were to stumble into the bedchamber, they would see a beautiful room, resplendent with all the best money could buy during the years of her youth. She remembered sitting for that painting as if it had been only yesterday. She also remembered hating every second of the experience. The expression on her face, captured by the ever-capable hands of the artist, whose name escaped her now, didn't portray even a hint of her revulsion. There were certain expectations when it came to the engagement portrait, and being the ever-dutiful daughter and bride-to-be, she did not disappoint. What would have been the point? Of course, had she known the truth then, things might have gone in a different direction.

Now gazing upon the face of the oblivious human she used to be, she wanted to scream, pull the portrait from the wall, and shred it. "You're a sick son of a bitch."

He smiled, his eyes shining with the same expression of glee they'd contained the night he killed her family. "One of my favorite memories. Me and the woman who promised to love, honor, and obey me."

"Fuck you."

"I cannot believe you don't cherish that memory." He pointed above the mantel. "Our engagement, the talk of the land. The mysterious nobleman and the catch of the country. The elusive Isa. Every man, old and young, wanted you back then. Only I captured you."

She whirled on him. "Is that what you think? You captured my affection? And here I thought you were intelligent." She shouldn't have laughed, but she couldn't stop herself.

"Shut up." His voice held a razor's edge, and she liked that she could still get under his skin. The oh-so-powerful Sir George didn't possess the steel exterior he tried hard to make everyone believe he embodied.

"Really? So, you brought me home just to tell me to shut up. You don't want the truth?"

"The truth is, my darling, you have one chance to save your life, and this is it. Take it or die."

"I've given you too many years already. I'll give you no more, and if that means I die, so be it." Peace settled over her as the words left her mouth. She wanted to be the one to turn him into dust, yet if she couldn't do that, her own death would be the next best thing. As she stood here in the room where she had grown from a child into a woman, weariness bore down on her. Perhaps the time to join her family had arrived at long last.

"Tsk, tsk, tsk. Giving up? I don't believe it. Besides, I brought along a little insurance in case you decided to be difficult. In fact, I knew you'd resist. It's just the way you are and one of the reasons I love you. No matter what happens or where you are, you have remained you. Consistent. Admirable."

She sputtered. "Love? What the hell are you talking about?"

He put a hand under her chin and tipped her face up. "I've always loved you. I think you know that deep down. It's what this is all about." He waved his hand to encompass the room. "Put on the dress, and we will finally finish what we started back when your father promised me your hand. You must honor that promise. I've been patient long enough. Do this, and I'll send your little friend home."

The man was insane. The engagement painting. The exact duplicate of the dress her father had paid a fortune to have made for her. Her childhood home. Insane.

Wait? Her friend. "What friend?"

His smile scared her. "Why, Officer Jeni. Do you think I'm not aware of your feelings for her? You can't hide a single thing from me. You never could."

He deluded himself on that score. She'd hidden more than a little from him, and he knew it. "I have no feelings for her."

His laughter came off brittle. "I also know when you lie."

"Do you?" It was her turn to laugh. "I lied to you from day one. I lied to you when I said 'I do.' I lied to you until the day I walked out. I hate you, George, and I did then, and I always will. You'll never make me love you, even with this absurd charade you've orchestrated."

He shrugged. "Then it should be of no consequence that the one you profess not to care for will die."

❖

George would have paid a million dollars to see her expression when she recovered consciousness in the bedchamber of her youth. Disappointed that he'd missed that moment, he was nonetheless pleased by her reaction when he walked into the room, and it had cost him only some time and a Learjet ride to Europe. The epic payoff he'd anticipated, however, didn't quite have the punch he'd hoped for. He'd expected fireworks and got more of a sparkler. Not acceptable.

His experience told him this would be the place and time she would join the family she'd moaned about for hundreds of years. Listening to the same story over and over had become wearisome, but because she was special, he'd endured the monotony of it. He would have ended the whining of any other the first time through.

Things were different now. Time and distance strained his patience. Well, to be precise, she'd changed things. Her defection put all of this into motion, and the responsibility for her future rested in her hands alone. Her bitter words changed nothing about the choice ahead.

The future for her new little friend too. Despite what he'd told her earlier, he hadn't quite made up his mind about the deputy's fate. She served a greater purpose here. The truth shone clear in Isa's eyes. She cared for the human. Kind of like she'd cared for the one before. He tilted his head as he studied Isa's face. This one was different, more, somehow. She'd cared for the human called Avery as a friend. Perhaps even loved her as one would a close friend. This went beyond friendship, although he wasn't convinced she got the whole picture yet. Better for him if she didn't. He could use it. Love often served as a mighty weapon.

Of course, that didn't mean his own love for Isa would cripple him. He had come prepared to do whatever he needed to. His power in the society, indeed in the world, could not be compromised even by one he had loved since the first moment he saw her. He had waited for her all the years she'd stayed at his side, believing that one day she'd come around. He gave her much time to reconcile her family's demise with the reality of their existence. He always believed that one day she would see things his way, and she would open to the eternity of life at his side.

When she defected, he could no longer deny the truth. She would never come willingly to his cause or his bed. By the time that truth hit him, it no longer mattered. He loved her, and that was enough. In the last decade his love hadn't diminished. Only his plan for her had changed.

Tonight, he demanded a pledge from her to be loyal and to consummate the promise she'd made to him on that bright summer day, all while wearing the beautiful dress he had recreated for her. If she could do those things, all would be forgiven. Not that he would blindly trust her. No. He would always have to keep an eye on her. He could deal with that inconvenience. The presence of her naked body in his bed, the touch of her skin beneath his hands, and the taste of her lips upon his were all the reward he would need.

"I'll kill you if you hurt one hair on her head." Fire glowed in her eyes. He liked that. It reminded him of the young girl she'd been the first time he saw her. At that time, she'd been an innocent eleven years old, so he waited almost nine years before he began the process necessary to secure her as his wife. While some were anxious to take her much younger, he preferred a touch of maturity over nubile flesh. In those days, suitors had to face many hoops to secure the hand of one as coveted as Isa. He jumped through each one with ease. Her parents never stood a chance against him, although he allowed them to believe the decision had been theirs.

"It's all up to you, my darling. Say I do, and mean it this time, and your friend is safe. If not…" He shrugged and raised an eyebrow.

"It will never happen. Not then and not now."

He shrugged again. "We shall see. Why don't you slip into that beautiful little frock while I retrieve your friend, and we'll talk more then. I always did like you better in a dress than those." He pointed to her pants and grimaced. She resembled a boy in that outfit, and while he had enjoyed his fair share of trysts with handsome men, he liked his men to look like men. His women like women. Call him old-fashioned.

"Fuck you."

"Tsk, tsk. Such a foul mouth you've developed. Your father would be quite disappointed." Frankly, he did not care for her manner of speech either. Again, he preferred that his woman display elegance and refinement.

"Do not speak of my father, you bastard."

He enjoyed being able to taunt her. "Let us have no more of the vulgarity. It does great injustice to a beauty like yourself. Now, do as you're told and put on the dress." He clapped his hands several times, and the human who waited in the hallway opened the door. He gave Isa a last once-over, laughed, and walked out. His human servant closed the door behind him and turned the silver lock. If Isa understood the stakes, and he believed she did, she would be dressed and waiting for him when he returned with her little friend. This promised to be to be a very enjoyable night. Even better than he imagined.

CHAPTER TWENTY-NINE

W hat kind of hell is this?" Jeni muttered as she moved through the hallways. After she'd called on the strength of Athena, she'd been moving with purpose and determination from hallway to hallway. She didn't have a clue how long she'd been checking room after room with nothing to show for it. She hadn't heard a thing or seen a soul. Finally, the gods began to smile on her when a flickering light coming from a doorway far down yet another of what seemed like never-ending corridors caught her attention. She couldn't believe how big this place was.

The murmur of voices made her slow down and move with caution. That they spoke a language unfamiliar to her wasn't totally unexpected, but it made her uncomfortable just the same. Where in the hell had they been taken? How she wished she could translate. They might give her an idea where to find Isa.

As she moved closer, she clicked off the light on her phone and hugged the wall. Best to move on silent feet toward the voices and the light that spilled out of the open door and into the hallway. Her pulse pounded when she peeked around the door frame and into the occupied room. Only when the two women turned toward her did she actually say out loud, "What the fuck?"

When they rushed toward her, she thought they were vampires and that she was screwed. But when her fist connected with the larger woman's face, nope. All human. The big one went down at the force of her fist, and a roundhouse kick took out the second. Sweet. Athena had her back tonight. With both women on the floor unconscious, she stopped once more, hoping the noise of their bodies hitting the floor didn't bring reinforcements racing her way. Hearing nothing, she scanned the room. Personally, she hated drapes, especially big, heavy, ugly ones. An unexpected bonus presented itself with those old-fashioned window coverings that brought gifts in the form of thick cord. Plenty of it, and exactly what she needed to tie up her new friends. The fabric of the drapes tore easily too. Perfect for the gags necessary to keep them nice and quiet. It would be easy enough to dispatch these two to the great beyond. Not her style. Her vendetta didn't include humans, even though she understood how many of them helped the masters of darkness. She might be a crusader. She wasn't a killer. Some might argue the distinction existed merely in semantics, and she was okay with that. In her head, the distinction remained clear, and she could sleep easy because of it.

With her captives incapacitated, she slowly turned and surveyed the room. Unbelievable. Over the fireplace hung a painting, very old, judging by the cracks evident in the paint. Isa, young, carefree, and beautiful as she stood in a field with her arms outstretched. It appeared more like a candid snapshot than a portrait she'd posed for. The artist had been talented and way ahead of their time in terms of style. She liked it very much.

Other, smaller paintings were scattered throughout the room. Again, while no art historian, she judged them to be nowhere close to recent works. The most interesting décor of the room that, in her professional opinion, looked an awful lot like the lair of a stalker, were the framed photographs decorating the walls nearest the doorway. Now those pictures were recent. As in Washington State recent. Her eyes narrowed as she walked through the room again, assessing the shrine of Isa. She couldn't be sure, though she suspected she'd nailed it dead on. A subtle gap existed between the last painting and the framed photographs. One had to peer closely to make the time connection.

It tracked with what Isa had told her about George, the society, and her departure after Avery's death. If she were a betting woman, she'd place one on the last painting having been created more than a decade ago, the first framed photograph taken within the last several months or about the time Isa had moved to the lovely country home a few miles from Jeni.

She'd been motivated to find and destroy the vampire responsible for taking Avery from her. Now that motivation crept up. She knew about stalkers and the dangers they presented when unable to possess what they wanted. In this case, Isa. She also knew, or at least understood Isa, and the last thing she'd agree to would be rejoining the society. Jeni had been skeptical about Isa at first and didn't want to believe that vampires could be anything beyond evil. Isa managed to change her mind. She couldn't point to anything specific beyond gut instinct. She didn't think a cop existed who didn't put a good amount of stock in gut instinct.

It went beyond believing Isa. It also applied to what would undoubtedly happen here tonight. This crazy SOB would kill Isa if he didn't get what he wanted, and that wouldn't happen. True stalkers didn't take well to the word no. Throw in the fact that George combined immortality with being a stalker, and what he might do boggled the mind.

Now that she'd taken her own death off his twisted agenda, she intended to disrupt the rest of his plans. The way she'd been trussed up and left made her believe that, while his primary focus lay on Isa, he had something designed for her as well. Besides dying, she didn't know what else and was pretty sure she didn't want to. Even now, armed with what she did know about the creatures of the night, the thought of becoming their next meal made her sick. She refused to think about what he would actually do to Isa or what he'd done to Avery. That was a rabbit hole she couldn't afford to go down.

Still, the thought of Avery spurred her on. Her beautiful wife, trusting and open, had been helpless against their deception, and they'd used her innocence to destroy her. At least Isa had power and history on her side. She would be smart and capable in this type of situation. It didn't change the way Jeni felt right now. The reality that she and Isa had been overpowered and brought to who the hell knew where made her cautious and also gave her purpose. Neither of them was an easy mark, and this never should have happened. But it did, and now she had to deal with it.

Time to call on Athena again. If she had any hope of making it through this night, she would need to be the goddess of war every second of it. Starting now. She studied the room again, with a different eye this time, and she finally saw it. Ready.

"I'm coming, you son of a bitch." He had taken Avery away from her. He wouldn't take Isa.

❖

"You fucking bastard." Isa screamed at the closed door. She clenched her hands at her side and resisted the urge to go over to the hated dress and rip it to shreds. In fact, she decided to give in to the urge and do it. Then a noise made her halt. Her head snapped up as the door opened again.

George stepped back through, a single raised eyebrow. "Really, my dear. A fucking bastard? Hardly. A practical man would be a much more accurate characterization. I get things done."

She didn't let her surprise show. It wasn't like him to respond to an insult, yet he'd not only responded. He'd heard it through the thick closed door and returned. She held his gaze, hoping her own revulsion shone through. The days of pretending she cared for him were long gone. "No need to brag. I learned that lesson quite young, when you killed my family to get me."

He shook his head. "You missed the greater purpose of that night. I did want you, and I never made a secret of that desire. That is not why your family perished. I killed them to possess this." He waved his hands to encompass the estate she'd grown up in. "Don't misunderstand me. I wanted you too, but let's face the truth once and for all, my darling Isa. As much as I loved you—still love you—your family's wealth has always meant more to me. You see, I want it all and always have. You, the land, the money, the power. I have all, save for one thing, and I'll have that as well."

"You're sick."

He shrugged. "So an esteemed professional might say. I would respectfully disagree. I am simply focused on getting what I want. I don't care how long it takes or how many I have to kill to get it.

All great men throughout history possessed a similar drive. I see nothing wrong with doing whatever it takes to succeed."

His last words weren't lost on her, and they were chilling. She'd been aware during her years with the society that he wanted more from her. With some effort, she'd deflected much of his unwanted attention without generating his ire. She'd always believed he'd given her space because of her clear grief at the loss of her family. Not any longer, because he'd been playing her all along.

Once, his mastery at deception would have filled her with fear. Not any longer. Instead, determination made her bold. "It must have pissed you off when I left." She lifted her chin and held his eyes.

Darkness flowed over his features, pushing away the smugness he'd been displaying since returning to her room. "You will pay for that move, regardless of the decision you make."

"Really? A decision? You have me locked up in my own bedroom and surrounded by garbage from the past. What kind of decision needs to be made other than to get out of here?"

His smug smile returned, making her shoulders tense. She hated how he could embody arrogance so easily. "Simple, my darling. Return to me and live. Deny me and die."

She'd heard that tone of voice before and had witnessed how he dealt with those who betrayed him, whether they actually had done so or not. That he hadn't turned her to dust yet made her wonder what he really had in mind. The words he spoke to her sounded simple enough. However, with George nothing was ever simple. The only thing could she discern for certain: he loved her and he hated her.

"I'd not be with you back then. I won't debase myself to be with you now."

"You might want to think your decision through." His calmness alarmed her, though she refused to let him see her reaction.

She decided instead to push him. She laughed. "Like I haven't thought about you and all you've destroyed over the centuries? Sir George, Earl of Totnes, I really did think you were smarter than that." To use his full title would get under his skin just as much as her insult would.

She didn't think his expression could turn darker, yet it did. With a speed that would be impossible for anyone except a very old vampire, he stood inches from his with his hand on her neck. "Respect."

It took every ounce of strength she possessed to stand tall and continue to stare into his dark eyes. "Fuck you."

❖

His hands flashed out, and George tightened his fingers around her neck. God, how he craved to squeeze until the defiance faded from her eyes. As much as he wanted to, he couldn't. He refused to lose this battle to her, a woman. Superiority belonged to him, and giving in to base emotion was unacceptable. In the end she'd give him what he wanted, and the deputy-sheriff insurance he'd brought along, convinced she would resist, would make certain it happened the way he envisioned. Through the years he'd learned that he possessed the ability to control his emotions, while she consistently gave in to them. He would make that distinction work to his advantage now.

"In good time, my dear." He let his hands drop away from her neck. Not before they left red marks on her pale skin. In a human, they would turn black and blue. For Isa, they would be gone in moments. He relished the sight of them while he could.

"Never." He gave her points for not blinking. She had learned strength since she left him. Just not enough. No one would ever be able to match him. Isa included.

"We will see. Now, do as I instructed earlier, and prepare yourself for our, shall I say, renewal of vows. We'll have our lovely little ceremony in just a bit. Slip into that spectacular dress, and darling, please don't forget your hair. You remember how I always preferred it up. You look far too common with it down, and these—" he waved toward her clothes "—will be burned."

Cold day in hell, she thought. She said, "Again, fuck you."

"Again…in good time."

He walked to the door and clapped. This time Henry opened the door and held it for him. A favorite of his, Henry had been in his employ for over twenty years. Isa would be sure to remember him, and that pleased him. She hated this particular human, who had as little regard for the general population as any vampire, which was only one of the reasons he had become one of his most trusted human servants. He wasn't bad in the bedroom either, and on occasion, George indulged in pleasure of the human variety.

George stepped into the hallway before turning back to her. "I almost forgot to ask. Do you like the small touches I've added to your room?" He smiled at her as he saw the disgust cross her beautiful face. No one could accuse him of being naive. If given the chance, she would bolt. The intricately carved doorknob, along with the silver latches on the windows, would ensure she stayed within the walls of the bedchamber until he returned with her special friend. He left nothing up to chance. Brilliant.

"You will not break me."

He raised a single eyebrow and smiled slowly. "Really? Is that what you think?"

"It's what I know." She did not return his smile, not that he really expected her to.

"My turn, my darling. I thought you were smarter than that." He motioned for Henry to close the door and turn the key to lock it. She wouldn't touch the silver. It still didn't hurt to be thorough. He knew better than to trust his beautiful Isa.

"You stay at the door," he commanded. Henry could keep watch on Isa, just in case. He didn't need any help with the human cop, because her skills, even as considerable as they might be in her world, would be no match for him. If a gaggle of motivated vampires couldn't overthrow him, one measly human didn't stand a chance.

The hallways were cold and dark as he walked away from Isa's childhood room toward the east corridor, where he'd stashed Jeni upon their arrival. George didn't need the light to find his way to the makeshift cell where he'd stashed the cop. He'd spent many a year walking through these hallways and sitting in the spacious rooms.

By today's standards, the rooms themselves might be considered average. When Isa's father built the estate, they had been seen as quite large and luxurious. The best money could buy in the era of Isa's youth.

They comforted him by reminding him of a time when he had achieved the strength and power he needed to attain command of his life and the Redcap Society. He didn't want to say that he had peaked, because he stood on the top of the world looking down upon those who were common. That went for both vampires and humans, and any other creature of the preternatural variety. In time, he would command them all.

As he walked through the drafty corridors, few lights broke the darkness. A handful of human servants lived on the estate year-round in order to keep it in perpetual readiness for him. Over the centuries, he visited here frequently, and more so during the last decade. He didn't need a shrink to tell him why. The condition of her room and the re-creation of that dress pretty well said it all without anyone uttering a single word. Those who worked in this place knew better than to ever speak of it. They did as they were instructed, and they did it without discourse. Wise on their part. That he paid them well also ensured their silence.

In truth, he didn't care what a shrink might say about his fixation on Isa. The way he figured it, he simply focused on a problem that needed a solution. She owed him, and he intended to collect, tonight. He lengthened his stride. The room with all the likenesses of her wasn't a shrine. He viewed it as more a flowchart, which was the hallmark of a fine strategist and not a representation of an obsessive-compulsive disorder.

The air cooled as the darkness grew deeper. In this part of the estate, fires didn't blaze in the large fireplaces. No need. The staff kept the rooms clean, and that was enough. No one occupied this wing any longer, at least not after the demise of Isa's family. The room he'd left the deputy in had once upon a time belonged to Isa's governess.

After this night concluded, he would either turn this place into his base of operations or destroy it. Isa held the key to that decision.

The former would be his preference, given the special significance this estate held for him. That Isa held no regard for anything he might desire pretty much guaranteed it would be the latter. A shame.

He pulled a key from his pocket and slipped it into the lock on the door to the room where he'd dumped the bound minion. This room didn't have the silver so necessary in Isa's case. Only a plain lock, old yet well-oiled. No sense replacing something as well-crafted as the hardware on most of the doors. Except as he turned the key, he realized it wasn't necessary. The lock had already been disengaged. Pushing the door open, he stopped just inside. No flickering candlelight. No even breathing. His acute vision didn't need a light to breach the darkness. Rage filled him as he stared at the overturned, empty chair. "You colossal bitch!"

CHAPTER THIRTY

George almost scared the shit right out of her. He didn't see or hear her as he marched past, and she gave silent thanks to the universe for that small favor. Plastered back into the shadows of an alcove, she wondered why he didn't at least smell her when he buzzed by. Judging by the speed he moved, maybe it wasn't too shocking. Talk about a man on a mission, or rather a vampire on a tear.

It didn't take a genius to figure out where he headed. The path he appeared to be taking mimicked the one she'd just traversed, except he moved along it a lot faster. It also wouldn't take him long to figure out she'd escaped his best effort at restraint. Seriously, not a very impressive effort Not only did she have specialized training, but come on. She'd been chasing assholes like him for more than a decade. She didn't go down easy, ever. And in the good-over-evil battle that was her chosen career, her record for good triumphing was pretty damned stellar.

"Surprise," she whispered as she slipped out of the shadows and hurried in the opposite direction. Urgency had just kicked up a couple of notches, and she answered the call with a fast pace. Finding Isa before he figured out she'd slipped by him made her move with a quickness she could have used in her soccer-playing years. She'd like to say that once she found Isa, they'd get the hell out of here. Except she couldn't lie, even to herself. For a decade she'd been waiting for this opportunity, and walking away now wasn't going to happen. She didn't intend to leave this place until one of two things happened: she killed George or George killed her.

Confidence made her certain George would be the loser, though this wasn't exactly the way she'd envisioned this going down. Of course, she also hadn't envisioned being at this point in her life without Avery.

Or feeling drawn to a beautiful vampire.

Or sneaking around some medieval castle trying to save said vampire.

Life sure managed to surprise her at every turn. Since the moment Avery had been taken from her, things rolled forward with the momentum of a snowball zipping down a steep mountain. Even trying to run away to a small town not only didn't work; it also turned the snowball into an avalanche. So much so that now she raced down a castle hallway trying to save the beauty and kill the beast.

Her booted feet slid on the stone floor when she saw the thin man stationed outside a closed door. No brain surgeon required to tell her what or who was on the other side of the door. The momentary inaction almost cost her. Fortunately, she made a quick recovery and leaped right into motion.

The skinny dude didn't stand a chance. She hit him hard with an uppercut to the jaw, and he dropped, as her mother liked to say, like a bag of rocks. Just for good measure, she kicked him. On the job, they'd call it excessive force. In a castle owned by a vampire and run by his human suck-ups, she called it due process. Yeah, yeah, yeah. She knew all about the old judge-and-jury argument. She just didn't care. If this piece of crap threw his lot in with the likes of George, he got what he deserved. She kicked him again.

Turning her attention to the door he'd been guarding, nothing happened when she tried to turn the fancy silver doorknob. Son of a bitch. Locked. The bastard George had probably taken the key with him. That's what she thought until it hit her...the silver on the doorknob. No way would George touch that and risk damaging his precious flesh. That she really didn't know him didn't diminish her conviction that he would take his own self-preservation above anything else. That left one other option access to the room.

Kneeling, she checked the pockets of the man on the floor and was rewarded by a key. She patted his head. "Thank you, scumbag."

The key went in smoothly, and the lock turned with ease. The door—big, old, and heavy—swung open on silent hinges. A whole lot different from the door on the room she'd been held in. Georgie-boy spared no expense here. After seeing his shrine to Isa, it didn't come as a surprise. He would have only the best for the object of his obsession. She put one foot inside and stopped. What in the world?

"How fucked up is this guy?" Her eyes met Isa's. Wow, when did this happen? All she wanted to do was grab her in a hug. Plant a big old kiss on her lips.

If Isa was surprised by her entrance, she couldn't tell. She smiled and answered what had been a rhetorical question. "On a scale of one to ten, he's at about a fifteen."

Not a bad answer either. She'd agree with that about three hundred percent. "Wait until you see the room with the giant fireplace."

Isa raised an eyebrow. "Doesn't narrow it down much. There are a dozen or so giant fireplaces here."

"Didn't have time to check out the digs. Too busy trying to save our asses. Still, what's with this?" She waved her hand toward the room that seemed to be a shrine to a princess. Dolls and music boxes and a beautiful dress spread out on a big four-poster bed. A huge painting, Isa in her late teens, hung over the fireplace.

Isa turned her head and sighed. "I grew up in this room. It looks just as it did the last day I spent in here. Well, except for that." She pointed to the portrait. "That came from the gallery. All the family portraits hung there. He moved it up here for effect."

"He's got a hard-on for you."

"Understatement."

"We need to get out of here." The open door beckoned, and she became anxious to get rolling. Jeni didn't want to get cornered in this room regardless of how nice it might be.

Isa shook her head. "No. We need to stay."

"No. We need to leave." What in the world was Isa thinking? Staying equated to suicide. Not the way she planned to go out.

"It's time to end this."

"I say we get out of here and then figure out how to take down your buddy George. You have a better plan?"

Isa smiled. "I do."

Isa gasped when Jeni charged through the door. To see her alive and not in George's hands gave her hope. Her flushed face, beautiful and powerful, the most wonderful vision Isa thought she had ever seen. How this woman managed to creep into her heart baffled her. Never once had she shared anything close to intimacy with a human. Too dangerous, and while she held her own life in little regard, she protected it, so that she could survive long enough for this very day.

She still retained that goal, and tonight she planned to make it happen at long last. At the same time, she would protect Jeni at all costs. She couldn't bear to lose her or to risk any harm to her. Avery had entered her world and become her friend. Then fate brought Jeni into her orbit, and she sang to her soul. She couldn't resist the song and didn't want to. She only wished that the universe could have brought them together sooner. Who knew what might have happened? Most likely she never would find out.

When declaring they should leave, Jeni put forth a very valid point. That would probably be their wisest move. The problem for Isa lay in the fact that she'd grown very weary of leaving. It didn't seem fair either.

When Isa left this house so long ago, her soul had been crushed. Two choices had stretched before her that night: die along with her family or accept the fate handed to her and become a creature like George. In the intervening centuries she'd questioned her choice repeatedly. Suddenly, she no longer questioned. The bigger picture crystalized at last. She'd saved herself all those long years ago so she would be ready for this moment.

She'd saved herself to stand in this room with this woman and take on the final battle against the darkness that had destroyed her world. Maybe they would win, and maybe they wouldn't. But they would stand together. She could avenge her family, and Jeni could avenge Avery. The grand plan of the universe brought them together, and she would see it through regardless of how it ultimately ended. If she went down, the song would go with her, and that prospect filled her with peace.

"We have to defeat him. Here. Tonight."

"Yeah. Big words coming from the woman locked inside her bedroom. I don't even know how many others are roaming around this mausoleum. This place is freaking huge, by the way. Your childhood home, I presume?"

"Yes, I grew up here, and the truth is, it doesn't matter how many others are here. Not that I believe there are many. All we need to worry about is George."

"Again, he has the advantage. I'm not sure why you're not seeing that important fact."

"Think about it. I can make my way around as well or better than George."

Jeni still looked worried and Isa couldn't blame her. The odds weren't good, at least at a cursory glance. "I don't even know where he is, and sister, I don't know how to break it to you, but we've got nothing to fight him with."

Isa smiled at Jeni once more. "That's where you're wrong."

The empty room made him want to finally give in to rage and destroy everything. He caught himself and took a deep breath. They'd underestimated the human. Those around him should have done a better job anticipating what she would do. That she'd try to escape and might succeed should have been a given. Heads would roll over this, and he meant that threat literally.

He would deal with the sloppy underlings later. Right now, he needed to find her before she caused him any additional trouble. She remained the key to getting Isa to cooperate. His little Isa had a soft spot for this one. That came as a new and interesting development. During her years with the society, she'd been a solitary figure when others routinely hooked up. Some for fun and games, others as lifemates. Not Isa. She'd turned to no one, and that included him.

Now he would use her pretty little friend to force her hand. Patience hadn't worked, but he was most excellent at the use of force. All he had to do was find the bitch. That shouldn't be terribly difficult, given the size of the estate. She would wander for hours, without any idea where he'd stashed Isa. Unlike her, he'd committed every inch of the massive structure to memory and could easily traverse it in total darkness.

Besides, he had staff scattered throughout, and they would detain her without the need for him to chase her down. They all knew better than to let strangers roam. It would be an easy matter to round her up again and drag her down to Isa's room. She would surely be ready to make her choice by the time he delivered Jeni to her room. Still, he'd bring the bait just to be sure she made the right choice.

He spun and left the empty bedchamber. In the hallway he breathed deeply, and as expected, her scent filled his senses. Berating himself for being so caught up in the game he'd missed this clue when he came charging down here, he followed the trail she'd unwittingly left for him. Her scent was both heavy and unique, making it easy to follow.

Inside his special room, he shook his head. Two of his staff were tied up on the floor, their eyes were wide with fear. They should be afraid. The price for this transgression would be high and payment swift. Later, however, as he needed to get this situation under control before he bothered with them. He didn't appreciate errant detainees roaming his property.

It did make him smile when he thought about her seeing this room. He loved it here with all the various stages of Isa. The young girl she had been when they met, the young bride who had managed to hide her dislike for her new husband, the older and wiser Isa standing on the porch of her hideaway in Washington. How many times over the years had he stood in this room and gazed upon her precious face? Too many to count really. His own special sanctuary.

He gave himself a few minutes to fill his spirit with the images of his love. Yes, she belonged to him and always would. It didn't matter how it all ended tonight. Nothing could ever take her away from him. This room made certain of that.

Glancing down at his restrained servants, he briefly thought of taking them as nourishment. Not his preferred meal for they were middle-aged and far from attractive. He did so love the young and beautiful, their blood alive with energy and desire. These two wouldn't provide those specific qualities, although the fear he could see in their faces did have its own appeal. He flexed his fingers and took a step toward them, then stopped.

No. He didn't need their blood, for his own coursed with righteous indignation, and he didn't want to do, or taste, anything that might dilute the feeling. How dare Isa and her human defy him. They didn't understand the force and weight of his power. They would soon.

He left the servants tied up and continued his search. They would be there later should he still require nourishment, and depending upon how this all turned out, he might be full by the time he returned. He picked up her scent and his speed.

Chapter Thirty-one

A ll right. Lay it on me then." Jeni still thought their best chance was to break out of here, make it somewhere where they could get service on her cell phone, and then figure out how to take down the vampire obsessed with Isa. Calling in reinforcements in the form of Becca and Patrick would make the latter a lot easier. It was that power-in-numbers thing.

"I am done avoiding him. I am done with him, period. I've waited a very long time to finish him, and this is my Armageddon." Isa's shoulders were squared and her chin up. Standing her ground.

Jeni couldn't help the frustration that colored her words and didn't even try. "We don't have anything to finish him off with." She understood Isa's desire to stop the guy who'd fucked up her life. She didn't get her wanting to do it with nothing to defend themselves with. Dying cornered didn't sit well with her, and she wished like hell she had her weapons.

"We are not powerless."

"Yes, we are, and we need real firepower for this guy. I mean, look what he did to you and me. He got us…well, I really don't know where he got us to or how, but it sure isn't Washington State. Not to mention I don't have a single weapon on me, and I sure don't see your nifty belt of goodies. I don't think I'm going to be real effective against a vampire with my bare hands, if you get my drift."

"I do get your drift, and just to put all of this into context—you're in Poland."

"Excuse me?" No freaking way could they be in Poland. He might have been able to keep them in la-la land for a few hours, but fifteen or sixteen hours? Not a chance. Isa had to be wrong.

"Poland. The Eastern European county nestled between Germany and Lithuania."

"I get where it is. I passed world geography. I'm saying there's no way we're in Poland."

"Well, unless George dismantled my family's estate and moved it stone by to stone to the United States, we're in Europe."

Jeni's knees went weak and she sank to the velvet seat of the chair nearest to her. "Europe. That's so messed up."

"It is."

"Fuck. We're on our own." No calvary would be on its way, even if she could make a call to Becca and Patrick. They were alone in this. Just one tiny vampire and one cop without a gun. Still, if they could find someplace where they could get cell service, at the very least, they could summon help of the law-enforcement variety. Why Isa couldn't see that astonished her. Up until now, she'd been pretty reasonable.

"Yes. We are on our own. We are *not* weaponless."

"Yeah, and what are we gonna do? Beat him to a pulp with one of your fancy little dolls?" As far as she could see, nothing here would be a good weapon, so her comment wasn't snarky. Okay, maybe a little snarky. Her only excuse: fear.

Isa's eyes lit up. "I have a much better idea."

Isa hoped George hadn't dismantled her room. It looked well-maintained, though original, as if he'd taken effort to keep it that way. His obsession with her former self might well play to their advantage. "Trust me."

Jeni threw up her hands as her eyes swept the room. Isa could see the dismay that filled them. Jeni neared the point of giving up. All she had to do would be to keep her in the game a little longer. A tall order. "Right. Trust. That's helpful."

Isa smiled at her. "Back when I lived in this place, molding me into a proper lady so that I could attract the richest prospects in a husband was my mother's primary goal, and she was relentless. Don't misunderstand. She didn't mean to be cruel. That's just the way things were in those days."

"I hear a 'but' in there."

"My father, bless him, went along with my mother while keeping his own agenda." She smiled as a barrage of memories flooded her mind. "What we managed to keep from my mother was how he allowed me to train with my brothers."

"Train, as in?"

She went to the window seat, where thick velvet pillows waited for someone to sit upon them. Moving the pillows aside, she lifted the cover to reveal the storage space below. Jeni quickly moved to her side and peered down. "As in how to use a sword and fight with a knife. How to protect myself in any situation. In that way, my father was ahead of his time by many, many years. He believed if it was good enough for his son to learn, it was good enough for his daughter as well."

Jeni's sigh was loud in the empty space. "Not much use when there's no sword or knife in sight."

Again, Isa smiled. She could almost feel her father standing next to her and whispering in her ear, "*It's our secret.*" Isa patted her hand while resisting the urge to hold it tight. "Don't believe everything you see."

"Are you always this vague or just doing it to irritate the shit out of me? It's not like we have an abundance of time. As soon as George figures out I'm gone, he'll haul ass right back here."

"He will, indeed, be coming back." She reached in and let her fingers trail along the side of the window seat. The motion took her back centuries and filled her with the same anticipation as the first time she'd reached into the space. Simultaneously, sadness flowed over her. Even after all this time, she still missed her father.

"Come on. You're killing me here. What the hell's in there?"

"After my mother discovered what father had done, she tried everything she could think of to stop him, including searching my room for the weapons he allowed me to keep. Father didn't like her interfering and so he built—" Yes. There it was. She pressed the hidden button that released the false wall. "This. She moved the false wall aside and laughed. Yes. Yes. Yes.

After all these years there they were, just as she'd left them. She grabbed the hilt of the sword and pulled it out. How wonderful it felt in her hand, just as if she'd held it only yesterday. Tears pricked at her eyes as she remembered how proud her father had been the day he'd given it to her and then shown her the secret hiding place. Her mother would no longer be able to confiscate her precious weapons.

"Whoa. Now that's a sword."

Isa smiled. "Your turn. You're going to need to grab the knife. The handle is bone inlaid with silver, so I'd prefer not to touch it. You're going to love it. Father had it made especially for my small hand."

"Silver? Now you're talking, sister."

Jeni looked natural with the beautiful knife in her hand, as if it had been made for her instead of Isa. When her father had given it to her, the beautiful craftsmanship had been undeniable, and she'd expressed her gratitude while never telling him it hadn't felt natural in her hand. Perfect, undoubtedly, only not for her. Now she understood why. It had always belonged in Jeni's hand.

The sword, though, was a different matter entirely. She had been a master with it then, and the power of it hadn't diminished now. Bless her father for giving her the gift of skill. How she wished she could tell him that.

Jeni's head snapped around at the same time Isa caught the sound of footsteps. "Get ready."

"You have a plan?"

Isa nodded. "You slow him with the silver knife, and I'll take care of the rest." On impulse and just in case her plan failed, she leaned over and kissed Jeni.

George didn't hesitate. She'd run straight to Isa. For such a short time together, the two women seemed to be inseparable. That made him even more furious. She should run to him, not some twenty-first-century woman who pushed her way into a man's world. Their centuries of history should count far more than her brief time with a human she'd just met. In fact, their closeness insulted him.

As he closed in on Isa's bedchamber, he could see Henry crumpled on the floor, a small pool of blood at his head sending a metallic taste into the air. The fool had let a woman take him down. Why did finding good help in recent decades continue to be a problem? Men had been much tougher eons ago. Everyone these days had gone soft.

A dead human wasn't difficult to replace. A shame all that blood would go to waste. Another time he would have stopped to determine whether death had taken him. If not, and he still clung to life, a snack would be in order. Not now. He had another matter to attend to. His bride awaited on the other side of the door, while his staff on the first floor readied the venue for the renewal of their vows. He reached into his pocket and curled his fingers around the special syringe, just in case.

He smiled as he stepped through the door. He would overpower them both if necessary. Isa was tiny, even given her vampiric strength. And the cop? Well, she was human, after all, and no human could ever hope to match him in strength or intelligence. That wasn't bragging, simply fact.

His smile disappeared because Isa stood exactly where he'd left her, still dressed in those awful trousers, her head high and her arms at her back. Did he or did he not instruct her to put on that dress? He'd gone to a great deal of trouble to have it made, and he expected her to wear it for their ceremony. If he had to, he'd put it on her himself.

All along he'd been telling both himself and her that she had a choice to make tonight. As he stood in her doorway, realization dawned that he'd fooled them both. He had already made the choice for her. She'd put on that dress and she'd commit herself to him. She would be at his side for eternity. Period. That was the only choice available to her. He let go of the syringe and pulled his hand out of his pocket.

"I told you to put on the dress."

"And I told you to go to hell."

"And I'll help you get there." He smelled Jeni only a second before she stepped behind him. His hand flashed out to grab her. She side-stepped him in a fluid movement he didn't expect. Sneaky cunt.

The pain that shot through him at the same time was unlike anything he'd ever experienced. Silver. That bitch had just pressed a silver blade into his flesh. Not completely made of silver, or he'd be on his knees. Still, it had enough to make his breath catch in his throat and his attention waver. Only for a second, and then once more he flung out an arm, this time connecting firmly with her head. He took great satisfaction in the sound of her body hitting the cold stone floor. Hopefully the bitch cop never got up, though he hoped she hadn't died yet. He'd feast on her blood when this was all over, and he'd do it in front of Isa. Just as he'd been forced to teach her a lesson once before, he'd do it again, and he'd smile as he did it.

He heard her before he saw her. As he'd glanced down at Jeni, Isa moved toward him. He presumed she would be going for her friend now that he'd smacked the hell out of her. That's what he expected anyway. The time it took for her to reach him turned out to be the exact amount of time it took him to register that she'd uttered the single word checkmate while she swung a gleaming sword. The swish of it through the cool air turned out to be the last sound he ever heard.

CHAPTER THIRTY-TWO

Faint sounds that she couldn't place made Jeni blink. Boy. She hadn't slept this hard for a long time. She stretched a little and thought that maybe the time had come to get a new bed. This one had gotten super hard, and now her body ached from a long night sleeping on it.

The sounds grew clearer and it registered. Isa, repeating the same thing over and over. "I'm sorry. I'm sorry. I'm sorry."

Things started to come back to her, along with a pounding head and a screaming back. She remembered. "Why are you sorry? You didn't hit me."

"I got you into this." Regret sounded clear in Isa's voice. "It's all my fault."

Jeni pushed herself into a sitting position and blew out a long breath. Talk about a kick in the head. She'd never felt this way before and hoped she never did again. "He, not you, hit me. He owes me an apology, and by God, I'll wring it out of the bastard too, even if I have to light a torch to his ass."

"Not going to get it from him." Isa put a hand on her back and stared into her face. Her dark eyes were filled with something Jeni couldn't quite define.

"Did I kill him?" She didn't think one thrust of the knife would have been enough, unless she hit something vital. Did vampires have vital organs? Somehow, she didn't think so. Or maybe she did, because that would mean she'd actually taken him down, and that would be a very good thing.

Isa inclined her head to the left, and Jeni glanced that way. "Oh." Now she understood what Isa had meant when she'd said to leave the rest up to her. "Where's his head?"

"Over there."

She moved her gaze to the left. It embarrassed her that something quite like happiness filled her. In her profession, killing was always her last option, yet in this instance she took a certain amount of joy in seeing his total destruction. No more would die at his hands. Like Avery.

"Thank you."

"I would never have let him hurt you." Isa put a hand on her cheek.

"I didn't mean for saving me."

For a moment Isa studied her face, and then her expression cleared. "I owed it to her. I owed it to you." Isa reached around her neck and undid the clasp of her necklace. She pulled it free and took Jeni's hand, dropping it into her palm. "I've been wearing it every day since they took her life. I promised I wouldn't take it off until her death had been avenged. It belongs to you."

All of a sudden, it clicked. The necklace had struck a familiar chord in her earlier, and now that she held it in her hand she understood why: it had been Avery's. Why she didn't put it together earlier, she'd never figure out. "Avery's…"

Isa nodded. "I'm sorry. It should have come back to you years ago."

"But you needed it to remind you."

Nodding again, Isa closed her eyes. "Yes. I never wanted to forget her or the promise I made."

Jeni stared at the necklace and then curled her fingers around the precious piece of jewelry. Tears were rolling down her cheeks as she leaned in and took Isa in her arms.

❖

Isa didn't want to break out of Jeni's embrace. She didn't realize how much belonging meant to her until it happened. She could stay here forever. Unfortunately, her long-awaited vengeance wasn't the end of this nightmare.

"We have to get out of here."

Jeni leaned back. "How exactly are we going to do that? I mean, I'm not even sure how we got here. We're halfway across the world with no passports, no plane tickets, no nothing."

"And in a house filled with those loyal to George."

"Oh, yeah. Don't suppose they're going to take that very well." She leaned her head in the direction of George's body.

"Not a chance."

"So how good are you with that sword?"

"Good enough…if we work together."

Jeni squeezed her hand and kissed her. "I'm on your six."

"What?"

Jeni laughed. "It means I've got your back. Come on. Let's get this done and go home. Where the hell did that knife go."

"It's still there." She pointed to where it remained embedded in George's side.

"Gag."

Isa couldn't help it. She laughed. "Some kind of tough cop you are."

"I shoot. I don't stab."

Still laughing, Isa retrieved the knife for her. "Come on, let's get out of here."

It didn't turn out to be quite the battle she'd expected. Two vampires and one human life lost. The rest, including the two Jeni had restrained earlier, were quick to surrender. Not quite as loyal to George as she'd expected. He believed himself to be an absolute ruler with absolute power, that all bowed to him in unquestioned obedience. She had news for him. He had existed in a bubble that had little in common with reality. Many hated him as much as she and Jeni did. That made their departure in good physical condition a great deal easier.

Once the estate had been secured, Isa turned to Jeni. "Do you still have your phone on you?"

"Never leave home without it."

"How about we give Becca and Patrick a call?"

"Yeah. I suspect they're frantic trying to figure out where we are. The only problem is finding a spot where I can pick up a bar or two. I've been trying since I woke up in that room. I still have the no-service message."

"No doubt they're frantic, and I'm quite certain Patrick can get us home without any red tape."

"As in no passports."

"As in."

Jeni pulled her phone from her pocket. "I don't have an international calling plan." Then she smiled and winked. Walking down the long driveway, she kept her eye on the display until bars started appearing. "Yes!"

"You have service?" Isa sounded hopeful.

"Nope."

Isa frowned. "Isn't that a problem?"

"Only if I want to make a call."

"I'm lost."

Jeni smiled. "No cell service, but there's a hotspot around here somewhere, and that's all we need to get our asses home." She typed quickly and hit send. Her message to Becca was on its way.

EPILOGUE

Poland
One year later

Jeni dropped her bags inside the grand entryway. Hard to believe she was back here. And even harder to believe she'd come here to stay. Never thought she'd become an expatriate. Life sure had a funny way of working out. Kill one vampire to avenge her wife, and her world changed in ways she could never have imagined.

When Patrick had flown them back to the United States, changes were already in motion by the time they landed. First and foremost, she no longer had a partner. Trent, the werewolf, had made the mistake of going for Patrick. A very bad choice. Sure, as a werewolf, Trent had been powerful and lethal. But Patrick, as an Interpol officer and a crusader against the creatures of darkness, came with an extraordinary set of skills. Trent hadn't been prepared for that or Patrick's silver bullets. He'd gone down on the first leap.

Next Patrick and Becca had cleared out George's retreat, including Trent's mother. They'd managed to locate where George had taken them right before they turned Mommy to dust. They were already at the airport getting ready to come to their rescue when Jeni had finally been able to send them a message.

Yeah, funny how things turn out.

Isa had made the trip back here weeks ago. She'd come ahead to make the preparations necessary to turn her ancestral home into their new base of operations. It became clear to all of them how well they functioned as a team and how effective they could be if they continued to work together. If they could take down George, they could take down the Redcap Society once and for all. They'd crippled it when they ended George's long life. Now they would crush it.

At the sound of footsteps hurrying her way, Jeni dropped her jacket on her suitcase. "Hey," she said when Isa came into view. A little flutter went through her, which made her smile. Ten years ago, she'd have sworn love wouldn't come to her again. Sometimes it was very good to be wrong.

Isa came into her arms and she kissed her deeply. "I missed you."

"And I, you."

"Are Patrick and Becca here yet?"

Isa shook her head. "They stopped in Paris for a quick honeymoon. They'll be here Saturday."

She smiled. Patrick turned out to be the perfect match for her friend, and she couldn't be happier for them both. "Good for them."

Isa took her hand and led her down the hallway. "Good for us. Wait until you see the bedchamber I prepared. You're going to love it."

"None of those creepy porcelain dolls, I hope."

Isa laughed. "Not a one, but how do you feel about swords mounted on the walls?"

Jeni laughed this time. "Oh, baby. Now you're making me hot. Lead the way, my love."

And she did.

About the Author

Sheri Lewis Wohl lives in NE Washington State where she's surrounded by mountains, rivers, and forests. It's a perfect backdrop for her stories of danger, romance, and all things paranormal. When not writing, Sheri enjoys cycling and training and working with her search dogs, Zoey and Deuce.

Books Available from Bold Strokes Books

Aurora by Emma L McGeown. After a traumatic accident, Elena Ricci is stricken with amnesia leaving her with no recollection of the last eight years, including her wife and son. (978-1-63555-824-1)

Avenging Avery by Sheri Lewis Wohl. Revenge against a vengeful vampire unites Isa Meyer and Jeni Denton, but it's love that heals them. (978-1-63555-622-3)

Bulletproof by Maggie Cummings. For Dylan Prescott and Briana Logan, the complicated NYC criminal justice system doesn't leave room for love, but where the heart is concerned, no one is bulletproof. (978-1-63555-771-8)

Her Lady to Love by Jane Walsh. A shy wallflower joins forces with the most popular woman in Regency London on a quest to catch a husband, only to discover a wild passion for each other that far eclipses their interest for the Marriage Mart. (978-1-63555-809-8)

No Regrets by Joy Argento. For Jodi and Beth, the possibility of losing their future will force them to decide what is really important. (978-1-63555-751-0)

The Holiday Treatment by Elle Spencer. Who doesn't want a gay Christmas movie? Holly Hudson asks herself that question and discovers that happy endings aren't only for the movies. (978-1-63555-660-5)

Too Good to be True by Leigh Hays. Can the promise of love survive the realities of life for Madison and Jen, or is it too good to be true? (978-1-63555-715-2)

Treacherous Seas by Radclyffe. When the choice comes down to the lives of her officers against the promise she made to her wife, Reese Conlon puts everything she cares about on the line. (978-1-63555-778-7)

Two to Tangle by Melissa Brayden. Ryan Jacks has been a player all her life, but the new chef at Tangle Valley Vineyard changes everything. If only she wasn't off the menu. (978-1-63555-747-3)

When Sparks Fly by Annie McDonald. Will the devastating incident that first brought Dr. Daniella Waveny and hockey coach Luca McCaffrey together on frozen ice now force them apart, or will their secrets and fears thaw enough for them to create sparks? (978-1-63555-782-4)

Best Practice by Carsen Taite. When attorney Grace Maldonado agrees to mentor her best friend's little sister, she's prepared to confront Perry's rebellious nature, but she isn't prepared to fall in love. Legal Affairs: one law firm, three best friends, three chances to fall in love. (978-1-63555-361-1)

Home by Kris Bryant. Natalie and Sarah discover that anything is possible when love takes the long way home. (978-1-63555-853-1)

Keeper by Sydney Quinne. With a new charge under her reluctant wing—feisty, highly intelligent math wizard Isabelle Templeton—Keeper Andy Bouchard has to prevent a murder or die trying. (978-1-63555-852-4)

One More Chance by Ali Vali. Harry Basantes planned a future with Desi Thompson until the day Desi disappeared without a word, only to walk back into her life sixteen years later. (978-1-63555-536-3)

Renegade's War by Gun Brooke. Freedom fighter Aurelia DeCallum regrets saving the woman called Blue. She fears it will jeopardize her mission, and secretly, Blue might end up breaking Aurelia's heart. (978-1-63555-484-7)

The Other Women by Erin Zak. What happens in Vegas should stay in Vegas, but what do you do when the love you find in Vegas changes your life forever? (978-1-63555-741-1)

The Sea Within by Missouri Vaun. Time is running out for Dr. Elle Graham to convince Captain Jackson Drake that the only thing that can save future Earth resides in the past, and rescue her broken heart in the process. (978-1-63555-568-4)

To Sleep With Reindeer by Justine Saracen. In Norway under Nazi occupation, Maarit, an Indigenous woman; and Kirsten, a Norwegian resister, join forces to stop the development of an atomic weapon. (978-1-63555-735-0)

Twice Shy by Aurora Rey. Having an ex with benefits isn't all it's cracked up to be. Will Amanda Russo learn that lesson in time to take a chance on love with Quinn Sullivan? (978-1-63555-737-4)

Z-Town by Eden Darry. Forced to work together to stay alive, Meg and Lane must find the centuries-old treasure before the zombies find them first. (978-1-63555-743-5)

Bet Against Me by Fiona Riley. In the high stakes luxury real estate market, everything has a price, and as rival Realtors Trina Lee and Kendall Yates find out, that means their hearts and souls, too. (978-1-63555-729-9)

Broken Reign by Sam Ledel. Together on an epic journey in search of a mysterious cure, a princess and a village outcast must overcome life-threatening challenges and their own prejudice if they want to survive. (978-1-63555-739-8)

Just One Taste by CJ Birch. For Lauren, it only took one taste to start trusting in love again. (978-1-63555-772-5)

Lady of Stone by Barbara Ann Wright. Sparks fly as a magical emergency forces a noble embarrassed by her ability to submit to a low-born teacher who resents everything about her. (978-1-63555-607-0)

Last Resort by Angie Williams. Katie and Rhys are about to find out what happens when you meet the girl of your dreams but you aren't looking for a happily ever after. (978-1-63555-774-9)

Longing for You by Jenny Frame. When Debrek housekeeper Katie Brekman is attacked amid a burgeoning vampire-witch war, Alexis Villiers must go against everything her clan believes in to save her. (978-1-63555-658-2)

Money Creek by Anne Laughlin. Clare Lehane is a troubled lawyer from Chicago who tries to make her way in a rural town full of secrets and deceptions. (978-1-63555-795-4)

Passion's Sweet Surrender by Ronica Black. Cam and Blake are unable to deny their passion for each other, but surrendering to love is a whole different matter. (978-1-63555-703-9)

The Holiday Detour by Jane Kolven. It will take everything going wrong to make Dana and Charlie see how right they are for each other. (978-1-63555-720-6)

Too Hot to Ride by Andrews & Austin. World famous cutting horse champion and industry legend Jane Barrow is knockdown sexy in the way she moves, talks, and rides, and Rae Starr is determined not to get involved with this womanizing gambler. (978-1-63555-776-3)

A Love that Leads to Home by Ronica Black. For Carla Sims and Janice Carpenter, home isn't about location, it's where your heart is. (978-1-63555-675-9)

Blades of Bluegrass by D. Jackson Leigh. A US Army occupational therapist must rehab a bitter veteran who is a ticking political time bomb the military is desperate to disarm. (978-1-63555-637-7)

Guarding Hearts by Jaycie Morrison. As treachery and temptation threaten the women of the Women's Army Corps, who will risk it all for love? (978-1-63555-806-7)

Hopeless Romantic by Georgia Beers. Can a jaded wedding planner and an optimistic divorce attorney possibly find a future together? (978-1-63555-650-6)

Hopes and Dreams by PJ Trebelhorn. Movie theater manager Riley Warren is forced to face her high school crush and tormentor, wealthy socialite Victoria Thayer, at their twentieth reunion. (978-1-63555-670-4)

In the Cards by Kimberly Cooper Griffin. Daria and Phaedra are about to discover that love finds a way, especially when powers outside their control are at play. (978-1-63555-717-6)

Moon Fever by Ileandra Young. SPEAR agent Danika Karson must clear her werewolf friend of multiple false charges while teaching her vampire girlfriend to resist the blood mania brought on by a full moon. (978-1-63555-603-2)

Quake City by St John Karp. Can Andre find his best friend Amy before the night devolves into a nightmare of broken hearts, malevolent drag queens, and spontaneous human combustion? Or has it always happened this way, every night, at Aunty Bob's Quake City Club? (978-1-63555-723-7)

Serenity by Jesse J. Thoma. For Kit Marsden, there are many things in life she cannot change. Serenity is in the acceptance. (978-1-63555-713-8)

Sylver and Gold by Michelle Larkin. Working feverishly to find a killer before he strikes again, Boston Homicide Detective Reid Sylver and rookie cop London Gold are blindsided by their chemistry and developing attraction. (978-1-63555-611-7)

Trade Secrets by Kathleen Knowles. In Silicon Valley, love and business are a volatile mix for clinical lab scientist Tony Leung and venture capitalist Sheila Graham. (978-1-63555-642-1)

Death Overdue by David S. Pederson. Did Heath turn to murder in an alcohol induced haze to solve the problem of his blackmailer, or was it someone else who brought about a death overdue? (978-1-63555-711-4)

Entangled by Melissa Brayden. Becca Crawford is the perfect person to head up the Jade Hotel, if only the captivating owner of the local vineyard would get on board with her plan and stop badmouthing the hotel to everyone in town. (978-1-63555-709-1)

First Do No Harm by Emily Smith. Pierce and Cassidy are about to discover that when it comes to love, sometimes you have to risk it all to have it all. (978-1-63555-699-5)

Kiss Me Every Day by Dena Blake. For Wynn Evans, wishing for a do-over with Carly Jamison was a long shot, actually getting one was a game changer. (978-1-63555-551-6)

Olivia by Genevieve McCluer. In this lesbian Shakespeare adaptation with vampires, Olivia is a centuries old vampire who must fight a strange figure from her past if she wants a chance at happiness. (978-1-63555-701-5)

One Woman's Treasure by Jean Copeland. Daphne's search for discarded antiques and treasures leads to an embarrassing misunderstanding, and ultimately, the opportunity for the romance of a lifetime with Nina. (978-1-63555-652-0)

Silver Ravens by Jane Fletcher. Lori has lost her girlfriend, her home, and her job. Things don't improve when she's kidnapped and taken to fairyland. (978-1-63555-631-5)

Still Not Over You by Jenny Frame, Carsen Taite, Ali Vali. Old flames die hard in these tales of a second chance at love with the ex you're still not over. Stories by award winning authors Jenny Frame, Carsen Taite, and Ali Vali. (978-1-63555-516-5)

Storm Lines by Jessica L. Webb. Devon is a psychologist who likes rules. Marley is a cop who doesn't. They don't always agree, but both fight to protect a girl immersed in a street drug ring. (978-1-63555-626-1)

The Politics of Love by Jen Jensen. Is it possible to love across the political divide in a hostile world? Conservative Shelley Whitmore and liberal Rand Thomas are about to find out. (978-1-63555-693-3)